ACR

THE

SILENT

SEA

Gabrielle Barnby

Printed and bound in Great Britain by Clays Ltd, Elcograf S.p.A

To Cat and Fran
My brilliant sisters

'What we cannot speak about we must pass over in silence.'

– *Wittgenstein*

'Wheesht'

– Orcadians

Charity

My mother was the best nurse I could have had after the accident, practical and caring. Today it is Monday, one year since the
accident, and she has brought me to work among bales of musty
second-hand clothes. I am now thirty-five and once left Orkney
for Oxford Street.

I fumble the hanger and the shirt drops.

I hate her for leaving me here.

'Dinna mind, Esther,' says Bridget, my fellow volunteer. She's
not bad, a kind soul. 'Plenty more hangers. Shall I move them a
peedie closer?'

I shake my head. A cool snap of pain travels down my spine.

– *Time's up.*

The next black bag is cheap and flimsy; a browny-orange
curtain pokes through, plastic hooks still in place. There's a
procedure for pricing curtains: I measure length and width,
then write a pair of figures on a piece of card and gun it into the
fabric with a tag.

A woman comes into the back room and roots around in
the container of baby clothes. She is fat, buttons puckering the
shiny blue cloth of her anorak. No matter how much I stare I
can't tell if she's pregnant.

When the woman has left Bridget says under her breath,
'Ah'll hiv a tidy roond later.'

She delves into a black bag and holds up a sheepskin jacket.

'We can start puttin coats oot noo hid's cowlder,' she says.
'You ken this one's seen better days.'

Now I've forgotten. The pen scratches out the figures, re-
writes measurements. It doesn't feel I'm doing it at all.

– *Who is doing this? Me or you?*

It's been a long time since I was me.

– *Doing badly now. Going downhill.*

I work on the ground floor. It was my mother who arranged it all, arranges everything. She has that sort of energy. I'm losing my way, forgetting how to do things for myself. Sometimes I don't have the motivation to even stare into space.

I get out my phone and show Bridget the screen.

'Go where?' she says.

I add more text. Her forehead creases.

'Let me get these oot the way.'

I move across the strip of worn carpet. She follows, bustling, always bustling is Bridget. I don't mind her.

Today, she is wearing a bright green body warmer she picked out for herself from a bag of last week's donations. She scoops up an armful of winter coats.

'Will you be long?'

I shrug.

One of the coats she's holding is dove grey, soft padded to keep out the breeze. It is my grandmother's. Her garments spread out slowly from the bags my mother leaves. They're freshly laundered, but still I imagine her scent and feel a warm ache around my heart.

I must see that our family cannot look after her. I must see that she needs fewer clothes now she's moved to Stembister House.

It's shocking, though, to see her things amongst everything else, touching the unwanted things.

A fine thin pain slices behind my shoulder blades.

The bright days of spring six months ago were a ruse, my body responding to light like the mindless narcissi, feeling a sense of recovery, but wellness did not come.

My fingers are searching. It's that time of day.

'Do y' need somethin badly? I could go,' says Bridget.

I shake my head, her sympathetic look follows as I go through into the main shop.

A customer is buying knitting needles and a coffee bean grinder. At least the knitting needles will work. No one tests the electrical equipment. If people want something they buy it. If it doesn't work the object finds its way back. I'm sure the coffee grinder has been sold twice already.

The customer has tufty brown hair and silver glasses. She's the same build as my mother, broad-shouldered, rectangular, waistless. Her eyes fix on my face, examining the scars. I want to hold up my wrists like Wonder Woman. Shoot the stare back and knock her flat. Kapow!

– *Can I do that?*

– *Am I doing this? Am I in one place? One piece?*

I wasn't all in one piece last autumn. My jaw was broken and my teeth were knocked loose like peppermints, they rested on my tongue in a pool of salt and iron.

It was impossible for them to soft-soap the damage once they took out the catheter. In the hospital bathroom there was a mirror above the sink; it hung on a sickly green wall next to a red emergency cord. My new face shocked the sound out of me.

The nail varnish line crept up my nails and dated my departure from life. Up, up, up, it went.

They're bitten to the quick today, it makes untying the black plastic bags hard. It's easier to tear through, fleshy fingertips pressed against the grey membrane.

'Hid's good o you to hiv her here,' says the customer.

Bessie or Bettie or Bernie, or whatever her name is that's behind the till, says, 'Kathleen said she needs to gae oot more. An nobody goes through-by unless they're droppin bags.'

– *I am actually still standing here.*

11

The receiver of stories and money, she wears a gold chain and has a small red mouth. Her hair is grey, short and neat, nothing is out of place. Lucky her.

Pins and needles bloom in my feet. Sometimes, it wouldn't surprise me if my toes fell out of my boots at the end of the day.

The stand of knickers, bras and scarves is close to the door to the street. Leopard-skin lives next to purple sateen and Granny's pale blue woollen scarf. A squint hanger is saddled with layers of belts.

The studded leather might seem like it wouldn't sell, but everything does eventually, from basques to baked bean puzzles.

I take hold of the handle. What if it didn't open? The front door has been painted over again and again. Sometimes I think they've been holding me hostage, keeping me in isolation. Because I'm doing badly.

My mother knew I was not well today. She saw how grey my face was, how at breakfast I was already going downhill.

A shiver passes through me.

What if behind the door there's only another door, and then another and another? But of course, there isn't another door. There's only one door.

The scarves flip and wave.

Outside, there's flying water, heavy and grey, you could mistake it for snow drifting the way it moves. Not snow in October, that would be rare even for Orkney.

'Why don't you bide a minute?' says Bessie or Bettie or Bernie. She has a sharp teacher's voice.

I shake my head.

'Hid'll pass over soon enough,' says the woman with the needles and grinder.

Needles, needles, pins and needles. I am forever going downhill these days.

Needles, needles, pins and needles. The bras and pants shimmy in the wind.

I step out.

Instantly, warmth is gone from every layer. Fists push my denim jacket in tight at the navel. Little torpedoes of icy rain swerve down the street to meet me, the pain giant swings a carefree hook.

It's not far along the flagstones to the chemist. A van passes between the snaking buildings. These were once shops for meat and bread and shoe repair, now they are filled with information boards for the housing association and local groups.

Everyone wants mental health to improve.

A tongue of fern grows from the side of a drainpipe. It's in the wrong place and needs pulling out. There's a CD on a windowsill. I read the title. No wonder they threw it out. Perhaps there was a row. It looks like the sort of place where the people would fight, never getting any light and all.

Step, step, step into a triangle of dirty water. Was that me? It's been a long time.

– *Come on.*

She's not here. She left me.

There's only one thing on my mind, pick-up time.

~

'They're no peppermints.'

– *Who said that?*

It was Mother this morning, brushing crumbs from the breakfast table. Tutting and shaking her head at another packet of Nurofen Plus finished.

My father was passing to leave his cup by the sink. He wanted to put a hand on my shoulder. He couldn't do it, though, couldn't touch me because he doesn't want to make anything

13

worse. Out of everyone he is the one who reads my pain best. He's not one for talking either.

'Your skin wis alwis so bonny,' my mother said, then sighed. She's said it more than once.

Granny Ida says I must rub baby oil on the scars. It makes no difference though. Still, I keep loving her.

~

I'm protected from the horizontal rain in the nook of the chemist shop. Maybe the rain will never hit anything, the droplets might end up blown across the Pentland Firth, or never make landfall at all.

Landfall is overrated. Trust me.

– *No, don't trust me.*

My hand moves and uncovers the side of my face. I see the reflection of the chemist's window. The scars form an archipelago across my cheek, numb when touched softly. Pushing down firmly brings a sweet metallic pain where the skin tethers to the tissue below. It's unlucky that I tend towards keloid scarring, tendrils of tissue that grip and grow.

Everything about me looks like it's walked out of a charity shop. There's even the same fusty smell, a discarded sweetness that objects take on when neglected, a mixture of tuna fish and soap.

The dull aches sharpen, moving down the vertebrae to between the tailbone and out to my hips. No gymnastic, elastic, orgasmic nights for me. I can't even put on a seatbelt without breaking into a sweat.

My mother has stopped helping me get in and out of the car. Perhaps she just got bored of it.

Christ, I'm uncharitable.

Yet, look how I've spent the morning, helping at the Peedie Hoose where everything gets a second chance.

I wonder at times if there is anything left to rescue. There's not much left. You want to be my friend? Get something to take away my pain. Otherwise get lost. That's how it is.

– *I've no friends left.*

There's a bride trapped in a photograph frame smiling her head off, she's so happy, so deliriously happy.

I should use facial expressions more. I don't.

– *Remember to smile when you go in.*

It's Susie Gordon. Apple-faced, well coated in foundation and with eye make-up like a porn star. She's done well to get a job behind a counter.

I show her the message on my screen.

– *Hello, I've come for my repeat prescription.*

'That time already, Esther?'

At least it smells better than the crab factory for temporary work.

'At Peedie Hoose the day?'

I glance down at the cough sweets and tins of Vaseline on the counter. Hands in pockets now, one gripping an empty strip of pills, plastic cutting into palms.

– *For pity's sake get on with it.*

The shop fittings weave and glow. I try to stand taller. Click-click.

'Wis that your back? Poor you. I'll get the pharmacist to check this. You can sit doon if you want. She's new.'

She gestures to the seats. I shake my head.

– *Come on, you can move faster than that Susie.*

The polka dot nail files dance while my fingers rub the seams of my jacket. I've tried waiting, tried to believe the pain is bearable and that it's better for my thoughts to clear. Yet my fingers are always impatient and quick. They cannot treasure the capsule for a moment, not even the space of a breath.

– *For Christ's sake, you're sl-o-w Susie.*

There's no pleasure in the anticipation. The need is too raw, like Christmas when you're seven. It hurts.

When you're underwater, desperate to breathe, you can give up and let the water rush in. But I can't put a stop to wanting and I can't break the surface anymore.

– *Hurry.*

Try to think of something else. Anything. Under the glass there are photographic prices. I run my gaze over the numbers and think of photographs.

In my mind's eye I picture the mantelpiece at Skulstad, crammed with frames and smiling faces. If I could ask my mother to take down the ones that show how I used to be, I would. But there's a lot of things you'd say without thinking that are blasphemous written down. A lot of things.

No, not a good thing to think about.

Susie Gordon returns, the fabric on her uniform stretched tight across her chest.

'She's gaan to come an spaek to you.'

I sigh loudly. The noise takes her by surprise.

'I'm sure there's no problem,' she says. 'She's French, you ken. Mr Muir says she's properly qualified an we've been short staffed since Graeme dislocated his knee. You ken, he should retire.'

– *Shut up.*

I pace by the counter, a few steps away and back again.

– *Do you think I'm an addict? Or just dependent? Is that better or just as bad?*

Susie looks past me. 'Can I help you, Mrs Flett?'

Mrs Flett is smiling, pearly teeth in a face of wrinkles, holding out a prescription. She doesn't mean any harm, but right now I hate her for being here.

'A cowld wind the day.'

Her voice rises and falls.

There's someone in the doorway where the drugs are kept. A woman with dark cropped hair. She pauses, glances towards me, then moves out of sight.

I stand shoulder to shoulder with Mrs Flett.

'Just wait a minute, Esther,' says Susie, voice firmer now.

She hands Mrs Flett a paper bag. I glance down, statins and steroid ointment. Nothing worth taking.

I step to the front of the queue. I need something to tide me over. I type a new message.

'No I can't,' says Susie. 'Here she comes.'

The gold badge on the new pharmacist's tunic catches the light—Claudette Petite. She speaks with a pronounced French accent, my name is velvet on her tongue.

'Esther Russell? There is a problem today with your prescription.'

'She disnae spaek,' says Susie. 'Since the accident. They've tried everythin…'

– *Christ, my life story.*

'…went sooth to study and had all these plans for luxury tours comin here.'

'Perhaps I can explain,' says Claudette. 'Can you come and sit down?'

Her face is sleek and foxy.

I move away from the counter towards the shiny red seats in the window alcove. Rain is being hurled along the gully of the street. As you can imagine it isn't a very private place. I think Claudette regrets this.

I show her the screen.

'Yes, I understand,' says Claudette. 'It is a long-term prescription for severe chronic pain. However, there are rules that must be followed.' She holds out a leaflet about prescriptions. 'Your prescription was valid for twenty eight days. You must go to the

17

surgery and request a new prescription. It will be ready in four day's time.'

– *No. You're wrong.*

'I understand you need the medicine. But I cannot give it to you. If keeping track of doses is difficult I can give you a pill box to help your organisation. So this problem does not happen again.'

– *I don't want a f–ing pill box. My mother called the surgery on Friday.*

Then she says more firmly, 'I cannot supply Tramadol even in an emergency.'

A freak ray of sunshine floods the window, the light hits and her irises glow violet-blue. The room pitches and rolls away.

'Are you not feeling well, Esther?'

I wonder if she has a knife. Do Frenchwomen carry knives? They should. It would be a distraction.

– *Who said that?*

My breath is hard to catch.

'It is a two hundred milligram slow release dose?' She speaks more rapidly now, her tone serious and concerned. 'Your doctor must have explained the body builds up tolerance and has side effects. Stopping the medicine suddenly is not recommended. When was your last dose?'

I hold up six fingers.

'Six heures. Should be okay,' she pauses. 'You do not look well. Perhaps you have a cold or something?'

I shake my head then slump back in my seat, chin on my chest. I stare at the irritable bowel information display. It would have been better if I had died on the road.

– *Don't give it to me then. Tastes like shit anyway. I'll buy a bottle of gin. I'll buy two.*

'Can you tell me how you take your medicine?' says Claudette.

– *What?*

'Do you take it with water? Chewing the tablets is dangerous. This dosage into your bloodstream will make you feel very sleepy and sick.'

I lift my gaze, there is sympathy in her eyes.

Claudette begins to speak more slowly.

'You must get a prescription from your doctor, or the accident and emergency doctor.'

Her face is very close. The smell of her perfume seeps around the borderlands of my craving.

– *I'll stop chewing the tablets and I'll cut back on the packets of Nurofen Plus. I promise. Give it to me.*

I see she cares, and that she wants to help, perhaps wants to be my friend.

– *It's my mother's fault—an administrative error.*

'From what I can see,' she says.

– *That's right Claudette, you can give me the pills.*

She places a hand on my cheek and looks into my eyes. It takes a moment before I realise she's checking my pupils. She's just like the rest.

'I advise you to go to your doctor. Also ask for something that will help you sleep.'

– *Do I disgust you? Is that what it is?*

'I will see you soon,' she says, motioning towards the door.

Dr Copik's grace and favour

There's never a bus around when you need one, to jump on or under. The need for medication compels single-mindedness. Since the hospital is closer than the doctor's surgery I choose the hospital.

The streets are hardly impressive, houses rising and falling in stout grey lumps, windows sullen and deep, as if hacked out by a square-ended gouge. There is porridge-grey, slate-grey, rust-smeared-grey and drooping swags of wet-grey where the guttering has failed.

The wind-pounded walls are grimy with mustard-coloured lichen, the spreading disease of stones. A huge hydraulic crane crosses over the roundabout and barely makes it around. The hook jerks against the tether holding it fast, just in time to stop it from smashing into the Salvation Army notice board.

A dull, stupid pain sits in my head, pushing thought to the outer edges. On my phone, fingers move quickly.

– *Mother, mother, mother. If only I could tell you how I feel.*

I read back the message then delete everything.

Claudette, there was something about you, I'm not sure what, but it made me think you understood. Afterwards, when it is swallowed down, the feeling's never as good as I think it will be. But I believe in it more than ever.

– *What was I doing?*

My feet move over the pavement. I'm wearing trainers that were abandoned for years until my mother dug them out and put them on my feet so I could leave hospital. My clothes are all from the back of the wardrobe: black jeans, denim jacket. Nothing is warm enough.

I compose a new message. It must be polite. 'I've run out of Tramadol because my mother abuses her power over me. I may not always follow the rules, but I am in genuine, long-term pain. Please give me a new prescription. Yours, Esther Russell.'

I stop on the curb, tip forward slightly and nearly fall into the side of a passing van. The honk of the horn sends me back onto the pavement.

'Huh.'

Funny that, how exclamations sound normal. Laughter can be the same. Not that I laugh much.

The electrician's van stops.

'Needin a lift, Esther?'

I never thought him worth the time of day at school, dark scruffy hair and blue-white skin. I found fresh blood in the south. I found Simon Sands offering personal travel services to the rich and aimless. We made a deal that was business and pleasure.

I shake my head.

– Get out of my way.

The van pulls away. I cross behind and taste diesel.

On the pavement there's a sequence of dog mess from the recent to the eroded historic. The part of me that avoids dog turds is still working.

In the hospital I screen out the smell of pastry and beef from the kitchen, brace against the snug warmth and walk past the collages with poetic words and heart-warming images.

– Who is it aimed at?

Repeated extensions and make-do-and-mending create a convoluted path to the accident and emergency department. It's a good job I'm not dripping blood.

I reach the nurses' station. Nina Gorse is on duty, kindly efficient.

'Whit like, Esther?'

I type a message.

'The doctor will spaek tae you,' she says. 'Go an tak a seat through-by.'

I hold my phone screen closer to her face.

'He'll be wi you soon as he can.'

I don't smile in return, but I do go and take a seat.

'Through-by' was a phrase that made people look strangely at me, a figure of speech difficult to drop when I shed dialect in London.

There are broken fingers and an elderly ice-packed knee waiting. They're fine. They're going to be fine, go home, get some rest, strap it up, come back tomorrow, give it a week, all that shit.

It's hard to make sense of why I'm here.

– *Why am I here? Why am I here?*

Nina comes through and takes away the broken fingers. The man is wearing white rubber boots and I don't know him. Maybe he's from the west.

– *Nina, Nina, in-between-er. That's what we used to call her.*

Something like that. I wasn't very nice to her at school, and now I can't get enough of her kind, efficient face.

'Doctor's got a peedie minute noo, Esther.'

– *About time.*

She shows me into an examination room. I suppose there's going to be a sort of test.

Doctor Copik moves lightly for a man whose white coat buttons are fighting a losing battle. There is a smile and an eye-twinkle when he looks at me.

'Miss Esther, take a seat on bed will you please. Much improved,' he says, indicating the scars. 'A little colour on the cheeks and no one would pay notice.'

– *That's a big fat lie.*

There is a computer on the counter by the nurses' supplies. He types something, then says, 'A lot has gone under the bridge with you. Never one day sick and then we have you under our walls for a long time. Herniated disks, whiplash. Trouble with back trouble is slow recovery. But will improve with care.'

– *No, it won't. It hasn't.*

'Perhaps you do not believe it,' he says.

It's funny, he speaks like there's a real conversation going on between us.

'Better to not fight with belief. Better to take one day after another. *Our greatest stupidities may be very wise.*'

The eastern European accent becomes heavier when he runs out these little philosophies. I do not mind listening, small talk and big talk are both a thing of the past.

He shines a pen torch into my eyes, presses two fingers against my wrist.

'No. I think you are become atheist. And now also I think you have forgotten how small mistakes can be dangerous.'

As if to confirm this, the muscles in my legs begin twitching rapidly up and down. I shake my head.

'If slow release is taken correctly these symptoms will not be happening,' he says. 'If only correct prescribed medication is being taken.'

He raises his eyebrows.

I type quickly and show him the screen.

'You do not look fine,' he says. 'No you are not fine, Miss Esther. Must feel headache, sick, dizzy.' He pinches the ends of my fingers. 'Tingling in extremities, I think. And your back, if you think about carefully, pain is not gone. Yet this medicine should be more than enough for this type of pain. To be on this dose for a long time is not advised for you. You are under-standing?'

– *I need more.*

'You must make an appointment with Doctor Carnegie and review treatment.'

He wanders over to a calendar on the wall and runs his fingers across the page, then walks back to the computer.

He begins to type, then pauses and says, 'What is a sixteen-year-old boy wanting for his birthday? I have no idea. It is impossible to get right. His mother says, "Send a voucher," But no one really wants voucher.'

– *I just want my pills.*

The printer begins to whirr. He tears off the page, reads over it and signs.

– *Good old Doctor Copik, I knew you'd come through.*

I want to keep him happy. I type a birthday present suggestion and show him the screen.

'Yes, I also want pizza and beer at that age. But I think… what about set of books? A young man should read great books. No or yes?'

I open my mouth and almost speak.

– *You are very clever, Doctor Copik.*

Silence drains back into the room.

'Confusion in body is between withdrawal side effects and feelings of pain. Headache goes away only because your body has what it is accustomed to. Coffee the same. Nobody calls coffee painkiller, but if addicted to caffeine and you miss your morning cup then headache. But then drink coffee again and poof!'

Dr Copik kisses his fingers and blows an imaginary something into the air.

'The headache is gone after your next espresso.'

– *I get it.*

'You need to sign here also.'

The pen barrel rests awkwardly in my fingers as they form a signature. Doctor Copik watches intently.

He strokes his moustache, the most neat and orderly part of his appearance.

'I worry, Esther. I have worries that my son—Stan his name by the way—that he does not think of me. Neither to love or hate. In his life there is no space for thinking of me.'

He lifts his chin, black pearl eyes stare back at me.

Doctor Copik would make a terrific vampire, apart from being too kind. Why does he speak to me like this?

'It is not all I worry about. You and I we know each other some time now, Esther. And you do not convince me. I see you suffer, but I do not understand why you must. Yet, what else can I do to help?'

Doctor Copik leans forward. He takes the piece of paper, letting his broad warm fingers rest for a moment on my hand.

'You are cold.'

– *Don't look at me like that. I cannot bear it.*

'Yes, I know. I know you really suffer,' he says, tutting his tongue against his teeth. 'I will enter an urgent request to Nord-land Practice for a month supply to be ready for tomorrow.'

The dryness in my mouth gives way. I reach out.

'This is for only two doses, today and the next day. Then you must have review appointment with own Doctor Carnegie. I will make appointment now if computer can link,' he says. 'Will be useful if you write down for him how you are feeling.'

– *I can't.*

'We must finish paperwork,' says Doctor Copik. 'Nina, you have form?'

The inside of my head throbs and I hear a constant drone.

'Nina thinks I should go to New York and jump out of a cake box. Ta dah! Stan, here is a big birthday present!'

He lifts his arms up in the air and grins.

'No....I see you think it is a bad idea,' he laughs. 'What can I do? Bloody vouchers again, eh?'

I shake my head.

'You can go and collect dose now.'

A lot of muscles are needed to make a smile. All I can produce is a twitch either side of my lips. Tears well up.

Nina turns away. Doctor Copik pats me on the shoulder.

'You can be better, Esther. But learning to live with pain needs practice—must persevere. Must go to clinics that Doctor Carnegie recommends.'

I nod and for a moment the barriers relax. Doctor Copik turns, someone has his arm, dragging him away. I notice the hospital smells, and memories of the accident crash like a wave back. The muscles around my stomach contract and my body begins to tremble.

It feels real, and I cannot escape. I'm on my back, on the trolley again. I am about to die. I lean on the wall, my lips closed tight, blowing air through my nostrils. There's the stink of bleach, the floor is shifting.

'Shall I call your mother, Esther? To pick you up?' says Nina.

I fight myself back to the present, and try to find something to hook onto, but the sour smells and the corridors lock me in the past. Everything is filled with rushing, bursting noise.

I dig fingernails into my arms, the pain is sharp and fresh, something real. I squeeze tighter. Keep moving.

– *I have to get out.*

~

A tractor rumbles past, pulling a trailer stacked with bales.

– *I'm back.*

The sweat on my clothes cools rapidly as I walk along the road. The physical sensation roots me in the present. I recognise the leaping stag, John Deere. I really couldn't tell in the dark, it was just two lights, high and close. I knew the bend would be tight. I didn't know it had a rotary turner on tow.

Everyone was waiting for me at the launch. It was the coming together of months of preparation, the pitch, the deal, the detailed planning and local knowledge. We were providing luxury, up-market, bespoke tours to the most beautiful and historic of the Scottish islands.

The slipstream of the tractor catches my hair.

– *I'm working hard here. Keeping it all at bay.*

These days I always keep something in my pocket for emergencies.

– *I shouldn't let myself get so bad.*

Nurofen Plus, if I'm honest, I have to be careful taking so many. There is a risk.

There's also a buzz.

If I'm honest.

– *Maybe the Tramadol aren't the problem?*

In my pocket there's a vibration. A message from my mother. I am not where I am supposed to be.

Simon on the train, feeling lucid

Between the hospital and Peedie Hoose Esther slows to a saunter and takes an opioid train ride. The Tramadol pill is designed to slowly release its painkilling, addictive load, but Nurofen Plus is quicker off the blocks.

Without hesitation it makes for her brain, soothing neurones like calamine. Her mind mellows, lucidity flows. The squalls turn playful and malice falls away from the faces of passers-by. She feels they notice her disfigurement less.

The hands of the breeze comb back her dark hair, with its distinctive streak of grey. Light grows in the darkness of her eyes. A high-pitched squeak from a starling on a rooftop brings her to a halt. Its throat feathers bulge in the wind. There's a whistling shriek then a volley of peeping, twittering song.

Esther whistles.

Rain drips from the spouts.

Beneath her feet the sycamore leaves are slippery, like a flock of yellow moths downed by the wind.

Esther points her index finger, raises it to eye level and takes aim at a starling. *Pop-pop. You're dead.*

She'd heard gunshots at dawn. Six o'clock. Pop-pop, pop-pop, over Redland. A tractor had bombed down the road as she crunched up the last pill.

It was getting harder to tell if she slept at all these days.

A man deep in conversation with himself walks past, hands flapping. He's well known around the town. She carries on her way. She knows it is easier to see failure than recognise pain.

Further on there are ruddy-faced men in hunting gear, banter flowing up and down their camouflaged line, happy as kids on a school trip.

Hunting, more specifically shooting, had all been part of the plan. No longer content to migrate over these islands, these green brooches on the ocean, the greylag geese now stay year round for bed and breakfast. They're a nuisance, eating the growing grass tips needed by the ewes. Their flippery feet spoil and blacken the ground.

Bird scares and professional shots try to address the problem. If you purchase the purple-blue burgers in the butcher's shop, do not be surprised when you get home that the packet says goose.

At business school in London, Esther had taken a job with a walking tour company to earn extra money. Ambitious, she'd wanted to make her name in marketing, but at that point hadn't got very far on the streets of London. She'd noticed people were interested in her island home, although there was also a subset whose eyes filled with horror at the thought of the retail deprivation.

After graduation, Esther worked for a spell at Kemp College co-ordinating summer programmes for international students. She made arrangements for fussy, time-poor, cash-rich parents who wanted their teenage children occupied during the vacations.

It was there that she'd met Simon Sands who arranged skiing excursions and city tours. His favourite place was Tignes and the Grande Motte Glacier. He'd taught her how to claim expenses and add commission, and to never do anything for free. She'd told him it was different where she came from and he'd laughed.

The relationship became intimate. Life moved quickly and Orkney was a forgotten crumpled ball of paper. Sure, they'd battled a few things out.

Eventually, not ready for any domestic commitment, an entrepreneurial idea was born. Simon with luxury tourism connections (he never skied down just any slope) and Esther with island contacts, the match made sense—it had been expedient that she keep to herself how poor the weather could be, even in summer.

The mood before the London launch had been high. Esther had secured exclusivity on luxury accommodation and negotiations were coming to a conclusion with a whisky distillery and gin company.

They'd arranged a private function room, caterers had laid out bannocks and smoked salmon, whisky was waiting to christen the first season of *Island Fling – bespoke leisure holidays*.

~

Before they'd left the flat Simon had mentioned a change in his plans. No warning was given. Right there and then, on the overland train from Clapham Junction to Waterloo, it had turned into a fight.

Orange poles the colour of tinned spaghetti linked ceiling to floor and there was a jagged space-invader pattern on the seats. A tired woman with kids around her like shopping bags sat in a diagonal row, the children had nothing to do except fidget and listen to their argument.

'Even in jest,' said Esther, 'I'd never say it.' She worked hard to keep her voice steady, and accent flat. 'You really don't like me.'

Under the carriage light Simon's tanned skin had taken on a green hue. It was muggy and he'd turned up his trousers an extra fold.

'If it were my family of course I'd go,' she'd said, temper rising. 'But that's different.'

It was a white lie.

'But going skiing, with *your* father,' she'd said, 'when you see him *all* the time. Then *not* telling me.'

'Don't call me a liar,' said Simon.

He wouldn't mollify her, or even properly join the fight. He'd turned away to the window and fiddled with his hair, twisting and fanning the fringe with a compulsive movement, never quite satisfied.

'How can you do this to me?' said Esther. 'You promised you'd be there.'

Then she too had stared into the window. She looked through herself as if she wasn't there, past the slim nose and wide set eyes, her grandmother's features, and into the roar of the tunnel.

She muttered bitterly to the suburbs, 'Never, never, never. You said you'd never let me down...' Then she'd turned back with fury. 'Those were your exact fucking words.'

She'd wiped away a tear.

How demanding she was, thought Simon. He wasn't going to compromise just to make her happy. It simply wasn't on offer. If only she wasn't so irrational and prone to overreaction.

His silence had filled Esther with rage. To be so stubborn over something as trivial as cancelling a pleasure trip was absurd. Coldness soaked into her, like a sleet shower.

Simon simply refused to ask his father to rearrange things, he said it was *impossible*.

It wasn't the fact he was missing the Orkney launch that most disappointed Esther, it was that he put his family ahead of her; he needed them, when all the time she managed without.

~

The night of the Orkney launch it was sheeting rain and gusting forty knots. The roads of Redland were slick with water, hidden puddles gathered in the hollows of bends.

It was embarrassing when Esther didn't arrive at Orkney's finest restaurant, overlooking Scapa Flow. The launch was a washout commercially, but the food was a consolation for the guests.

Later, when the extent of her injuries became known, people were more sympathetic.

Mother's waiting

I'm watching the chemist's queue through the window. The new pharmacist is handing a purchase over the counter to my father, to her he's an anonymous man in blue overalls. She asks questions and I watch the pantomime of head shaking and nodding that he must perform to secure my next box of Nurofen Plus. Alabaster skin and wide lips, she's different, conscious of her own allure.

Who? What? How long?

– *Easy does it.*

The door opens and he walks out carrying a small paper bag and a silver box and almost goes straight past me. He's walked past me plenty of times, a habit we developed when I was a teenager out and about in the town.

'You canna mix oil an water,' he'd said once.

He comes and stands next to me and hands me the paper bag. He's also been summoned to meet in the car park.

– *Thanks Dad.*

Quickly, I open the packet and push out one of the pills through the silver foil pouch. I chew, breaking up the pill, wincing in disgust at the taste, fighting against the gag reflex. One of my false teeth presses against a nerve, it is screwed into a cow bone implant that replaced shattered bone.

– *I could kill my mother sometimes.*

My father pulls out a packet of peppermints and offers one. The minty taste does not provide relief.

– *You are not meant to chew these pills.*

Behind the partition separating the shop from the dispensary area I catch a movement. I step sideways to watch. Claudette's fingers scuttle crab-like over the contents of the alphabetically arranged drawers. She's tapping her foot, concentrating on her task. I cup my hands against the glass and watch.

When she notices, she holds a hand to her chest in mock surprise.

It's funny.

– *You see Claudette. I do need them. Come out.*

The chirpy face of Susie Gordon appears through from the shop. Claudette twists around and walks smartly away.

– *Inside, I'm humming now.*

Every object on display is ridiculous. The bride in the photograph frame giving me the come on, the vanity bag decorated with llamas. Why is there a rack of sunglasses? Where's the need? A swimming happy feeling rises. I feel I'm rolling warm on the back seat like a bottle of water in the sun, and smile at the humorous mugs that teach the world how to live: *Always be Awesome* and *Follow your Dreams*.

Laughter rises in my throat. Can't dream if you can't sleep.

'Esther? Yir here?'

There she is, my mother coming towards me, carrier bag at her side.

'Didna you get any message? Where've you been?'

She does this a lot: asks questions. For future reference, I usually shrug in response. She cannot reasonably expect me to reply.

'They said you left at eleven o' clock. Whar've you been? Bridget's snowed under.'

I write her a message. She nods but makes no apology.

'Weel, you'd hiv been fine until tomorrow if you hadn't been taking too many.'

She reaches out and touches my jacket.

– *How can you f–ing forget to order my repeat prescription?*

'Wet? Noo you'll hiv to change. Ah'll get you something to wear fae the back room. Wait here wi yir fither.'

33

When she's out of sight my father pulls out a tobacco pouch and offers me one he rolled earlier. I shake my head. He lights up, cupping the cigarette in the palm of his hand between draws.

We don't talk.

Silence is one of the options few people take with me, but he does silence well—all that practice listening to my mother. He's a Caithness man and some people here find his accent soft and strange; silence is his choice.

Above the gully of the street, white and grey clouds scurry over the crow-stepped gable ends. Another starling, high on a gutter that's sprouting fuchsia, begins to trill and chatter. The smell of cigarette and coal fires waft over us.

Back in Peedie Hoose I imagine the conversation.

'On the scrounge, Kathleen?' says Bessie or Bernie or…

'Esther's soaking weet and cowld.'

'No doot. She'll fit in that.'

My mother will offer money and be refused.

'Put that away, cheust bring hid back the morn.'

The bird's finished singing by the time she returns. I'm handed a navy-blue jumper, called a gansey here. It's ribbed with sewn patches on the shoulders and smells sweet and fusty.

'Ah'm no takin hid back until the morn. Either wear hid or carry hid home. If you've any sense you'll wear hid.'

During the exchange my father has extinguished and stowed his butt and now stands ready, hands in pockets.

– *Somebody's watching me.*

The show's not quite over. I peel off my coat and pull on the second-hand jumper. It is wool and warm. Anyone looking through the chemist window will see scars as my shirt lifts. There's stiffness between my shoulders as I lower my arms. Reflex makes me shrink and protect the damaged parts of my body, but I am moving better, and there is Tramadol on the way.

My father makes brief eye contact; his face momentarily clouds with guilt, then he shambles away towards the alley leading to the car park.

'Seems yir capable of gettin things done when you want,' says my mother. 'Watch yir shoes. Whit a mess a dog has made.'

I walk ahead, minding my feet as we go. More rain is coming.

My father's on track to the red van in the corner, faded evidence of postal service livery across the sides. Driving separately is a thing my parents have always done, a hangover from my father's working days and volunteering for the lifeboat. Nothing my mother says cures him of it. I suspect he has other reasons as well.

'There's a stop I want to makk,' says my mother.

I stop and look at her.

'Whit is hid? Dae you want to say somethin?'

– *It's been a year since I last said something.*

'Hid's an idea Maggie had. Are you sittin front or back?'

I open the passenger door of the small silver car. My heart rate shifts up a gear. The handle is gripped, I lower and lift my legs around. I am careful, my face tenses with pain.

My mother leans across to fasten my seatbelt.

– *I can do it.*

I shake the buckle loose from her grasp and it knocks harshly against her arm.

'Miss Independent noo! Weel, you'd get a demn sight further if you'd tak the drivin seat wance in a blink.'

When I'm ready she reverses backwards angrily.

The van is long gone. It'll be turning up Clay Loan and out of town. We're heading in the same direction, at least to start with. Uphill we're caught behind a mobility scooter for a long stretch before she overtakes. She is slow, but she's the only person I can trust.

– Can I really trust you?

I reach for the radio, twirl it up loud.

'Wheesht, there's nobody worth hearin this time o day.'

She turns it down until the discussion gives way to a folky tune.

'…that was Ruby Love with her new tune…'

'What kind o body calls a daughter Ruby Love?' says my mother.

The second-hand jumper releases scent as it warms, air freshener and the odour of something fried. It's not the sort of gansey that gets grown out of, or someone becomes bored of wearing. There's never a day my father's said, 'Ah just dinna fancy wearin the blue overalls. Ah'm goin to get mesel a set o John Deere like those dapper farmers is wearin.'

No. Either the garment has been banished because someone is sick of seeing someone else wear it day after day, or the owner is beyond needing clothes.

At the top of the brae we leave town. My grip tightens on the door handle and my knees brace against the sway of the vehicle. Adrenaline bumps into the Tramadol and mixes with codeine. Sick, dizzy and drowsy, heartbeat on overdrive.

– Can you stop the car? I want to get out.

'I suppose maybe hid's a performin name,' says my mother.

– Sick, sick, sick. Call the doctor quick, quick, quick.

The land dips, a wide sweep of road. On one side sheep are scattered like broken teeth, thick with fleece and fattening. Bales have appeared overnight in black winter shells.

'Hid's aal right, Esther. I ken you'll enjoy hid once you get the feel fir hid.'

– Feel for what? Where are you taking me?

The car triggers memory, uncorks panic.

The cloud-scattered day disappears, and black night is suddenly all around me. There I am, wearing a tailored dress with a crescent moon silver collar. The speedometer shines green neon.

– Hi Esther, enjoying the drive? Let's talk about this.

In the darkness, a red light flashes, cut by wind turbine blades. Further on, a row of lights indicate a barn where kye are winter captives. Poor, dumb, forgetful animals.

– We're still here in the dark.

The Esther in the driving seat changes into third gear, the car tilts into the bend. Sweet, spicy perfume fills the car. She taps the gearstick with a manicured nail, stochastic and rapid as if she's trying to remember something.

– Esther? We could have a conversation. Maybe it would help if we talked about it.

She takes her hand away from the gearstick and wipes away a tear. My heart is thudding like horses' hooves. I want to tell her that it will hurt a lot more than she thinks. I want her to lift her foot off the accelerator.

But she's not listening.

'Esther?' says my mother. 'You'll hiv a shot won't you?'

Skirled back to the present, my body is braced for impact.

– Why am I wearing a dead man's jumper? Where am I going?

'We've taken just aboot everyone's advice aboot yur voice. Weel hid's no wirkin. You dinna stick tae anythin. Aal tha blowin intae a straw and writin that diary and aal the things the doctor said tae dae. Weel, this is somethin new.'

– For God's sake what are you talking about?

I've had flashbacks before today, but I've never remembered that I was crying.

Passing the place where I was injured triggers more and more memories. Maybe it's a side effect of the medication. Maybe it's because land and sky are returning to the same season and Accident Corner again looks the same.

37

You might think it's a bad thing, and let me tell you it is terrifying, but sometimes it's also a release, to remember the very worst of it.

~

A couple of minutes after the airport there's a scruffy downhill sort of turn that leads away to a cluster of houses once served by my grandmother's shop. This is Redland, where my parents still live with my brother and his family in the converted shop. An old sign still in place at the junction says *Shop*, but nothing is bought and sold anymore, there's just the house, Skulstad.

To a stranger like Simon, Orkney was an empty place. It was ridiculous that such small scraps of land even bothered with names. He didn't stay once the deals were sealed, he had to leave before the launch because he had an urgent skiing holiday booked. To save money I moved from the hotel back to Skulstad.

Fatigue rolls over me, Tramadol and company are in flood tide. The muscles now tense only briefly when the car judders. My head sinks backwards, drowsy and sickly.

Shivers run through the car as it's exposed to a side wind along a straight portion of road. It's sucked towards a cluster of buildings around an irregular courtyard, and shoots through the protected air before being sent shuddering sideways on the other side. My mother wrestles the wheel to keep the right side of the line.

'He's taken ower Pipersquoy, top o Smittler Brae. Past Jimmy Dingwall's owld place. Hid's no far fae where Granny used tae bide wi hir cousin at Brek.'

The words flow like a nonsense poem and roll me to the edge of sleep, my feet dangle and water foams at the cliff base below.

'When wis the last time you saw Granny? She wants to see you. Fits wi me choir practice for you to go an sit wi her a peedie while.'

Sand invades the asphalt on either side. I recognise Dingie-showe, a narrow piece of land that separates Deerness from the rest of the Mainland. The sand dunes creep steadily northwards in league with the sea grass. I camped here years ago; we threw canisters into the bonfire, pop-pop.

The car slows and turns from the main road onto a steep track that rises upwards around the cliffs. Seaweed hangs on a fence half lost to the sea, shiny from its last drenching. The car lurches into a slop of water, sand and mud, then bounces up and out onto compacted ground.

– *This is going to hurt.*

My mother turns and smiles.

'Hid's very good o him tae agree.' She lowers her voice. 'I ken he might be short o cash.'

Away from the land there's a vast wedge of blue sea, the sky holds a mess of clouds heading resolutely west.

The road crowns the brae before ducking downward. In the distance there is a small grey bungalow harled with dark stones. The track splits—one branch to an inland farm, the other to an isolated cottage. Black plastic flaps in the breeze on a barbed wire stock fence; *witches' knickers* Granny calls them.

I could write a message IN CAPITAL LETTERS and demand to know where we are going. But I can't even lift a finger. I go where she takes me.

'We're nearly there noo,' she says. My mother looks at me sideways. 'Yir no gaan tae be difficult?'

– *Did you want the drugs out of my system for this? For what?*

The thought is hard to catch hold of, but when it settles the events of the morning slide together and make sense.

– *Did you want the real Esther Russell? Is that what you want?*

The weekend had been ugly, so bad my father had gone out and broken the lawnmower. There were silent bitter quarrels that had lasted hours. I'd refused to let my brother take down the shelves in Granny's room. I blocked his path and he'd cursed everything about me—short of wishing I was dead.

– *Some things are better not said.*

The car climbs steadily upwards towards the cottage. It looks like a model, picked out in detail by the sharp October sun. The location is totally exposed, fields to the back, and to the front southwest-facing cliffs. Outside, there's a mound of stone chips and a rust-edged Volvo that looks more abandoned than parked.

My mother pulls up behind and stops the car. I start typing.

'No need fir aal that, Esther. Aal you need to ken is that hid's a new idea an yir gaen to gae it a shot.'

I drop the phone on my lap and gesture with my hands.

– *What the hell are we doing here?*

'I dinna hold wi aal Doctor Copik blethers on aboot, and you might think he's a strange body, but mind on he's up on aal the latest ideas.'

– *Doctor Copik? He's not even my doctor.*

A piece of paper is pulled out from her pocket, sections are highlighted in yellow.

'You can read on later, but there's research gaen on in a university he kens aboot doin musical therapy for voice disorders. Hear me oot...'

– *It's not like I can interrupt.*

She opens the paper and starts to read, her accent still rises and falls but she makes an effort to read out the words as they are written.

'...in health and illness there are three component parts: biological, mental and social. Individuals with voice disorders suffer inappropriate tension of muscle groups accompanied by

40

mental and social stress. Targeted exercise can aid adjustment and compensation of impaired function.'

– *So we're at some sort of therapist? A therapist that's short of cash?*

I can be as bad as her sometimes.

'Weel, it happened that Maggie wis at the folk festival an she wis spaekan to wan o the bands who came in the shop, not knowin it wis closed down. This wan fellow was doon on his luck because of an accident wi his bow, cost a tremendous…'

If you're getting a bit lost, don't worry. This is how my mother always explains things. To be honest, I'm finding it hard to concentrate.

My heart's a generator on full whack and there's a bad taste at the back of my throat. Everything is light, limbs empty, like they're fading to nothing. I am gossamer. Even though the car has stopped I feel like I'm still moving.

'…so she mentioned yir problem wi spaekan. Then I wis sayin to Doctor Copik when I met him in the Co-op how blowin though straws and water hadna been helpin you at aal. An this musician body also plays the flute.'

She finishes triumphantly. I still have no idea why.

'No harm bein early.'

She's out into the wind before I have a chance to say anything (joke). Then she's opening my door, and to be honest right now I have the urge to be obedient and go with the flow. We shelter for a moment in the lee of the house by a gas bottle, then she takes my arm and guides me past a patch of earth with wilted potato tops around to the front door.

– *You still haven't told me why I am here.*

Welcome to the crooked moon

With no doorbell to ring my mother knocks briskly. There's no sound from within. A grey veil of rain advances towards the headland, if we're not inside in two minutes we'll be soaked.

I reach for the door handle, my mother restrains my arm and repeats her knock, keeping her eyes averted from the advancing rain. She adopts her stoically waiting at the bakery pose, hands clasped in front of her belly.

Whoever it is we have come to see had better arrive soon.

I have my arms wrapped around my body, hands hidden in long jumper sleeves, I turn away and face the wind. It shoots hair from my face, traces my scars, finds sensation where everything else fails.

There's a scraping sound as the door opens.

My mother leans backwards in satisfaction then stiffens. I turn around and see a half-naked man clutching a small, worn-out towel around his waist.

The smell of citrus reminds me of the chemist. It wafts out of the door and mingles with the salt sea air. He's holding his legs together to stop the flash of flesh at his hip from growing.

– *My mother thought you were expecting us.*

'Sorry, I thought you might be the post.'

'Niver mind. Hid's us to blame bein early,' says my mother.

– *I am not to blame. We should go.*

Water drips from the straggles of the man's hair onto his shoulder, his goatie beard is scattered with wavering droplets.

'Aye. Er…what're you here for?'

The man's nipples have shrunk to tiny pink points, retreating into a forest of hair.

A giggle rises to my lips, it comes out quite naturally. My mother flicks me a sharp glance then says, 'My dowter-in-law Maggie arranged fir you tae meet Esther.'

I meet his gaze briefly, fleetingly conscious of the scars across my face. His eyes are dark and cautious, slowly the corner of his lip rises.

'Esther?'

– *This is ridiculous.*

Not one for superfluous body language, my mother does not tap her foot. She simply waits and then states firmly, 'Fir the flute lesson.'

The man is trying to remember something. I touch her arm and nod towards the car.

'You dinna want us tae leave dae you Mr Macrae?'

'No. Aye. Call me Marcus.'

It's not a full-blown genuine smile, but it's enough for my mother.

A lightheaded, go-with-the-flow feeling is overriding the social horror of the situation. I lift my hand and give Marcus a small wave. His eyes widen.

– *Sorry, that was childish. You can see I'm too old for this.*

'Come in,' says Marcus. 'Excuse the mess. I'm unpacking.'

He shelters behind the door as we bring the cold inside. The hall leads straight through the centre of the house. At the back there's a kitchen, to the right a living room with a conservatory.

'I'll get dressed,' he says. 'Somethin a wee bit more practical,' and disappears into the bedroom.

Maybe he does see the funny side.

The rain hits at forty-five degrees, rattling off the windows. While we wait my mother examines the sitting room, giving the oil heater and the dust-covered grate disapproving stares.

She makes a thorough circuit.

'There's no been anyone livin here since John Harrison passed awey,' she says. 'Canna suit many folk bein oot this way.'

The southerly windows are caked in a thick, greasy layer of salt that filters out the sharp sun that has followed the squall. Outside, the monstrous clouds are crisp and bright.

The contents of an open suitcase overspill by the wall, bundles of clothes that match my dead man's jumper.

There is only one ornament in the room, placed in a nook to the right of the fireplace. It's made of crystal and the shape of a gravestone. Along one edge there's an intricate Celtic knot design and carved in the centre are the words *Marcus Macrae, Best Solo Album. The Crooked Moon. The Northern Alliance Country Music Awards, 2014.*

My mother nods her respect at the ornament, then moves on to tut at the windows.

Nerves settling, headache gone, mood improving, still the room is unsteady. Outside the horizon tilts, the movement catches me off guard and I lower myself into a worn leather chair.

There are newspapers tossed on the floor, empty beer bottles and a used bowl sit on a low table. The comfort of being out of the wind has already worn off and the room feels damp. I envy the freedom of the sparse mess.

My mother stands by the ticking oil heater.

– *Can I go now? I think I need to lie down.*

Marcus comes into the room wearing grey shirt and jeans.

'Right folks, didn't remember the day I'd said. Sorry about that.'

There is much less song in his Highland accent than an Orcadian voice; I can place him as from around Inverness, but it's definition is blurred from travel.

'It's no bother at aal, Mr Macrae. Yir awful kind to let us tak up some o your time.'

'Call me Marcus, but you'll have to remind me…?'

'Kathleen, an this is Esther. She disna spaek. She used tae…'

As she relays my medical history my attention wanders. He nods and glances at the floor. My mother spares nobody.

Birds, ground-ridden all morning, are foraging over the open water, black starbursts of fluttering wings sweep and scatter across the clouds.

Maybe this is John Harrison's jumper. Except the house feels longer abandoned than the sweater—there's a quick turnover of clothes in Peedie Hoose in a town where there's not many options for apparel.

'…since then not a soond.'

'Didn't she laugh,' says Marcus. 'At the door.'

'Sometimes she makks soonds. The doctor tells me that involuntary things is different to spaekin.' She hands him the printed sheets and points to the bottom of the page. 'And co-ordination of muscle groups an posture is aal linked to breathing an articulation…'

'I'm not sure what I can do to help.'

'Maggie kent you'd give Esther lessons. Dinna worry, you'll no do hid fir nothin.'

She casts her eye over the room and points at the heater.

'Should get a fire goin. This one'll cost a fortune, an you'll niver be warm.'

Marcus looks up from the printout and over to me.

'You want to learn?'

I shrug.

'Aye, the thing is I'm waitin for a batch of parcels to come up the road. I didn't get much notice when I left London. The truth is I've no flute to teach you with just now. I don't really play it so much nowadays.'

45

His voice drops and carries a hint of regret. It's all the opportunity I need. I push myself out of the chair and begin walking towards the door. He rises to follow.

'We'll come back when yir ready. Ah'll mak oot a cheque in advance if you dinna mind,' says my mother.

The chequebook slides out from her bag.

'I don't want to take your money for nothing,' says Marcus.

– *Now that was half-hearted.*

'Hoo much shall I makk hid fir?'

He hesitates then says, 'Aye, I can show her something when it arrives.'

My mother signs over three hundred pounds and secures his expertise.

'So, you'll call when the flute comes home,' says my mother.

'Aye. And we'll see how it goes,' he adds.

I feel his gaze on my back as I walk away. I rest my hand on the door frame and pause.

– *It feels real. This is an honest doorway.*

Then I go into the hallway and push down the latch of the front door. A change in pressure cuts through the house as I leave.

My mother is smiling broadly when she catches up outside. I sense we are being watched—something has made Marcus Macrae curious.

'Hid wis more a casual arrangement that Maggie made,' she admits. 'Dinna worry, Esther, he's keen enough fir the money. There wis a flute tucked in a bag o claes at Peedie Hoose a few weeks past. Ah've had hid aal cleaned up, and hid's in the car. I'm no gaen to stop tryin, yir gaan tae spaek again whatever it taks.'

– *Whatever?*

Dead man's flute

Esther is driven away from Marcus Macrae's temporary home and braces herself for the bumpy ride down Smittler Brae. The stones below, wet and glistening, glow like the backs of tiny seals. She's sleepy, it's a fake, sluggish tiredness she knows is not real.

When they are back on the asphalt road, dunes on one side, flat calm on the other, Esther relaxes fully and gives the seat her weight.

The road is pixelating and platinum bright under the squint autumn sun. A stunted sycamore and clump of willow mark the turning to Redland. The leaves shake and curl, browning in the wind's invisible flame.

Esther's drowsy, enjoying the needles of orange light flickering between the grass blades.

Of course Kathleen had planned to order the repeat prescription—at some point. But in Kathleen's opinion a year to recover is long enough. In her experience pain does not last that long.

Kathleen has put the flute on her daughter's knee; its case has the texture of cheap car upholstery. Esther pictures a skeleton hand inside, the knobbly phalanges of the fingers arranged in gentle curves as if in repose on the cherry-red velvet.

There was a school visit to St Magnus Cathedral when Esther was a girl, a tour of blood-washed walls, saintly bones and lists of the dead.

Esther is not dead, but she sleepwalks from car to house. Is it fear of death that keeps her awake? Fear of the nightly death when everyone else lies down to rest in peace. The edge of a sharp shower passes over, a fine mist soaks her face and clothes.

'Ah'm on the lookoot fir a book o tunes,' says Kathleen, turning her key in the lock.

The letterbox has been long taped shut and there is a roll of rags at the bottom of the door for keeping out the draught. Esther slides the flute case onto the kitchen table.

'Won't you even hiv a look at hid?' says Kathleen.

Perhaps the bones would make good soup? Or is that sort of thing in bad taste? Esther's stomach lurches, bringing up the taste of bile and metal. It's a long time since breakfast.

'Dae you want a roll? Soup?'

Esther doesn't know. The relationship between mind and body is tangled since the accident. Tramadol does not help matters, although it always offers to be a friend.

'Could warm some chicken up fae last night?'

Esther whirls around and faces her mother.

Sharp, aggressive movements explode in the gloomy kitchen. The mime is a mute equivalent of a toddler tantrum in the supermarket. Her hands lift and turn, fingers splay to indicate being sick, and then she purses her mouth very small and raises her hands in a corny impression of playing the flute. The invisible instrument is swung down and broken over Esther's knee. She wags her finger to and fro.

Kathleen keeps her hands folded over her belly. It is very hard for her to believe this is her grown-up daughter, the one who lived in London and made all the fancy plans.

Esther turns an imaginary knob, throws her head back and begins to scrub her armpits.

In overalls and stocking feet Andrew enters the room. He goes and stands by the bread rolls on the counter.

Esther remembers she has another Tramadol pill in her pocket and it's enough to bring her temper back down. The sight of her father also helps—she loves and trusts him, yet she cannot be his passenger.

The performance comes to a close.

'Ah'll leave it oot, so you can makk hid yourself,' says Kathleen.

Keeping a steady voice when her heart is racing is something Kathleen has mastered. It is a useful skill, a powerful way to refuse other people victory, and Kathleen is not a loser.

Meanwhile, Esther pats the pocket of her jeans to make sure and heads through the back passageway to the bathroom.

Click-plink goes the pull cord, an eco-friendly light casts a dull glow over the pink suite. Once a shopkeeper always a shopkeeper, Kathleen has replacements lined up behind each bottle.

Esther strips off and lets her clothes fall to the floor.

One of her silver hairs lies across the rills of her dead man's jumper. The smell of the yarn has sunk into her skin but she has left an imprint too, layers of sweat and metabolised by-products. This two-way transference is something Esther does not think about much. She's a one-way sort of girl these days.

Slim and out of condition, her muscles have wasted into an adolescent form. Cover up the scars, dye her hair and make her smile and you would have something close to a magazine cover model.

There was a photoshoot with Simon for the *Island Fling* brochure. They were a picture-perfect couple. He had fair hair and a square jaw, and wore shoes with no socks.

The shower knob is clear plastic, ridged and thirty years out of fashion. It squeaks twice then releases cold water.

'Brrghh,' she shudders.

– *Did I make that sound?*

She steps in and pulls across the opaque white curtain.

Simon showered with her before, but it was not like this, a metal snake over a candy floss bath. Sex would be no good in a shower like this, there is nothing sturdy to lean against.

The spider plant in its string truss would no doubt be upset if there were two people beneath the shower, whatever their position.

Esther places her hands either side of the plastic rose and leans on the wall, head bowed. The posture stretches muscles from the base of her skull to her tail bone. The damaged vertebrae form a line of straggling irregular dunes up her back. The miniature streams are warm and gentle on her skin, the last remaining physical pleasure. Another thing she shares with her grandmother.

The water empties her thoughts down the drain and into a whirlpool.

It's only natural that she should have flashbacks.

~

In her mind's eye, Simon sits sipping gin in a rooftop bar, white teeth perfect, hair flicked to one side. The skyline of the city is marked out with red lights, The Shard thrusts upwards into the nocturne of a dull blue spring night above London. He turns and smiles at someone entering the cocktail bar, his ankles are on display.

'It's coming together with *The Gourmet Society*. They're very excited about offering a Scottish island experience to their members.'

'Are we going on somewhere after this?' asks Esther.

Something doesn't feel quite right.

'I didn't think we were…hold on, there's someone I've got to catch up with.'

He leaves her alone. She waits sipping gin and watching all the people she doesn't know. Sometimes, he throws glances like lifebelts, other times when he isn't watching she lets herself sink.

~

Back in the shower, Esther doesn't feel so good anymore. The water is finding its way into her eyes and nose, through the edges of her lips. She straightens up.

The scrubber is loosening, blossoming into a chaotic bundle, and the foam stinks of fake vanilla. Esther scrubs like she's cleaning an animal, up, down, right, left, front, back, underneath, behind the ears. No pussyfooting around the scars.

No pussyfooting around.

A swirl of soap and hair slips down the drain. Esther is so clean and fresh, she might damn well do something this afternoon. She dismounts the bath and takes a towel from the rail. Jeans are left crumpled on the floor, wetted by footprints.

Up in Esther's bedroom, the flute waits in its peedie coffin case in the centre of her bed. How are you going to deal with this one Esther?

~

Meanwhile, Marcus Macrae has tucked Kathleen's cheque into his wallet and gone outside. The mobile signal sticks long enough for him to make a call.

'The system's telling me they've been delivered,' says Annie Simpson, Customer Services, Clacton.

'Where to?' says Marcus. 'They're not here.'

'Is it Smittler?'

'That's a house, the road's Smittler Brae.'

'Well, I don't know. Do you have the proof of postage or reference number?'

'No,' says Marcus. 'This is Orkney, I thought you couldn't go far wrong.'

Marcus sets out in his car for the house called Smittler down the track. The Volvo is now nearing its final days and moves like a recalcitrant horse.

An old man opens the door, his eyes blink as if unaccustomed to light.

'Hello. I think you've a package of mine,' says Marcus.

A hand goes to the chin, thought is taking place.

'Yars?' says Jimmy Dingwall.

'I don't have a reference number.'

'No.'

'Should have gone up to Pipersquoy,' says Marcus. He points to the squat bungalow at the top of the brae.

'Yars, I ken Pipersquoy.'

There's a shake of the head. It could mean regret, admonishment or acknowledgement. Marcus can't tell.

'Twa-three boxes in the car,' says Jimmy Dingwall.

'Can I get them?'

Jimmy makes a dismissive gesture with one finger and turns back inside. Marcus catches sight of an accordion hanging on the wall.

When he turns to the car he sees a windscreen crammed with everything from insulation rolls to gutter pipe, flower pots to sacks of dog biscuits. Lines of algae mark the edges of the windows and rust flowers around the wheel arches. Marcus tugs open the passenger door, he identifies three boxes with his name and address on the label.

Marcus sees Jimmy watching from the window, glancing occasionally at the sky. He steps back and catches his knuckle hefting the parcels out of the car.

The next shower approaches, a grey-brown heart opening from the west, covering the hills. It drenches Skulstad and then passes on towards Pipersquoy.

With wet socks and a cold face Marcus Macrae carries the boxes into the living room. They were packed by someone who had once loved him, but more recently had ordered Marcus out of her house, and had barely let him kiss his daughter goodbye.

If the flute is there he'll speak to Kathleen about those lessons. He has her money.

He's puzzled about how the daughter can laugh but not speak. She wasn't pitiable like Marcus had thought from the sister-in-law's description, but she was strange. The whole thing was strange. If the flute was there, could he bear to play after so many years? After spending so long building a relationship and earning a living with another instrument, can he still find the breath?

Dried and tinned goods

The mirror doesn't admire my naked body. I pull on cotton pants and vest.

My mother calls, 'Ah'm gaan tae put these on, then go an visit Granny.'

A moment later her head pops around the door. She's hugging the laundry basket to her chest like a child. 'Do you want anything fae the supermarket?'

– *I'm in the middle of getting dressed.*

'Why dinna you come an see Granny? She's on her own most o the afternoon. You niver spare a thowt fir yir Granny noo.'

– *I do think about her.*

Goose pimples rise on my flesh, the warmth of the shower and the memory of Simon (and this was a good one) is eradicated by my mother's presence. She looks me over again and then walks away, leaving the door open.

'Yir far too skinny, that's what she'd say if she saw you noo.'

Off she goes, down the stairs.

'I left the rolls oot…an yir fither's taen apert the lawn mower agein. Will you hang these up when thir done…an there's tatties tae peel fir tea.'

I move across to the Velux window. There's goose shit on the glass, a thick Pollock-like splatter with strands of half-digested grass. It's less romantic than the drifting lines as they collect and cross the sky, yet there is still the same regular spacing in the small explosive splats.

I crane my head and wait to watch the silver car carry my mother away.

~

In the back garden my father is whistling, walking to one of Skulstad's outbuildings. His hand moves to the windowsill, rubs the joint between the glass and the frame, then he goes inside.

Tick-tick-tick.

Seconds stretch when the landscape is empty. Yet, rapid change is taking place, dozens of minutes are lost every day. The wind eases only to draw breath and blow stronger, and unlike in Aesop's fable it will succeed better than the sun. The rosa rugosa patch is moulting, dropping yellow-flooded leaves—although nothing really falls, few things have such vertical movement because of the wind.

Tick-tick-tick.

I purse my lips and blow, mimicking the soft sound of the wind outside, deflating my chest. Another shower is coming, cat-grey, covering the cliffs, brushing across the turbines.

Another-another-another.

Fingers slowly climb up to my face and begin to massage the tethered scars and the tissue beneath, a spidery, sharp yellow pain flourishes as the filaments stretch and yield.

The phone rings.

The impulse to answer stirs. Stupidly, I stride towards the noise and skin a heel on the stairs. Caught unawares by muscle memory I catch the door frame and pivot as perfected in my teens, and swing around into our mink-blue living room.

– *I didn't know I could do that.*

A handset is mounted on the wall, the cord hanging below twisted together like mating snakes.

I pick up and hold the receiver to my ear.

– *Hello.*

'Aye, this is Marcus Macrae.'

– *Marcus? You're kidding. You're actually calling back.*

'Canna have a word with Kathleen?'

– *No, she's out visiting Granny Ida.*

There's silence. Of course he's heard nothing.

'Is there anyone there? I'm tryin to get Kathleen Russell. It's aboot flute lessons.'

– *I'm here. It's Esther on the line. Speak, I am listening.*

Rain starts tatting on the window. There's no reason why I shouldn't hang up.

Then unexpectedly, I cough.

'Is somebody there? Esther?'

– *This is embarrassing. Sorry.*

As the phone travels back to the cradle I hear his fading voice saying, 'The flute's arrived, so I can…'

– *Goodbye, Marcus Macrae.*

Why am I disappointed when he doesn't call back?

There's just the drone of the washing machine, stuck at one pitch until some invisible obstacle is overcome and it begins rolling again.

The well-hugged basket sits empty beside another, full of my nephews' clothes, waiting on the concrete floor of the passageway. Inside the machine, a metal button on my jeans is tapping, trying to get out.

– *Drowning.*

It's possible to see deep inside the mass of clothes as they slosh round; there's white foam like on the beach and a scrap of something silver, floating like a fish scale. It's a piece of foil with a pharmaceutical logo printed on one side and a torn edge.

My heart trips.

– *Sh–t!*

I bang the glass.

I run my fingers over the tiny oddments and things rescued from the wash, the toothbrush for cleaning the taps, the lost zipper from father's second-best overalls, a big five pence piece, a pine cone…

No Tramadol.

I check, rearrange the caps and laundry paraphernalia that my mother keeps with the Brasso and Dettol. Nothing.

No Tramadol.

I press and hold the cancel button, a small padlock symbol appears, but the machine keeps turning. I kneel, head against the plastic rim of the door. The position is agony.

I open my mouth and silently scream. The essence of the sound passes up and out of the top of my head, scorching through my face and skull.

The back of my throat burns and I gag, bringing up belly air. It makes my eyes water and

swish-swish-swish the phone does not ring and

swish-swish-swish I must go upstairs and dress and

swish-swish-swish I come back down again and the phone does not ring and the Tramadol steel drum band plays mezzo forte.

Swish-swish-swish.

It's going, going, gone.

The sounds are a hallucination, but company of a sort.

De-de-de-de-dah-de-dah-dah-dah.

In the kitchen I help myself to eight Nurofen Plus then re-trieve potatoes from the large paper sack in the larder.

– *I must remember to say thank you.*

At five o' clock my father comes inside, exuding the quiet satisfaction of having created a long task that will call him from the house in the morning. It was only the wheel that needed fixing, some piece had rusted through. It flew off and rolled down to the dyke, a mini drama. Something to take apart is just what he needs.

He makes two cups of tea. I lie on the mink-blue sofa and we watch a gameshow whose title sums up so much about life. We smile at incorrect answers. I can tell he dislikes the man with the bow tie as much as I do by the way he looks over his tea.

I should sit more upright, practise using abdominal muscles to build core strength. But there is no comfortable position, and for a moment Nurofen Plus makes everything okay.

– *Thanks Dad. You're a great personal shopper.*

At five twenty-nine, just as the programme is reaching its epic climax my mother returns, dragging shopping like a fresh kill over the threshold.

'Whit a wind oot there noo.'

She takes one look at us, tightens her lips then goes through to the kitchen. She'll see tatties ready and through-by the washing hung up.

I checked the drum with a torch, searched every crease.

My father and I stay watching the television, even though the news appals us both. All his life spent driving, delivering and fixing office equipment. Now his compass points back to dismantled machines in his workshop.

Eventually, he takes up his cup, gathers mine and pushes the biscuit wrappings into his pocket.

– *Yes, you'd better go and change. There's the smell of onions and pork.*

For a moment my eyes close. I used to try not to sleep during the day thinking naps caused insomnia, but I've given all that up.

The brief blackout ends and my mother calls me to eat a plate of sausage, mash and glistening gravy.

'What a yawn. Still no sleepin weel?' says my mother. 'Did you hiv a rest this afternoon? You ken yir Granny's on less medication than you and she's comin on ninety.'

My father gestures towards the salt.

'There wis a visitor at Stembister Hoose the day, speaking aboot family history. Gey interestin, but they've no attention fir it after lunch. Mercy, hid's kept warm in there. Granny wis right bossy tae the other folk. Canna bear their fidgetin an wanderin aboot when somebody is spaekan. I told her you would come next time Esther.'

The skins of the pink, salty, sweet meat from the local butcher are thicker than the supermarket's, but swallowing is not the problem. The specialist said there's nothing wrong with my throat, it's the entire autonomic nervous system. Try saying that quickly.

'The mower's taken apart,' says my father. 'Need a few spares the morn.'

'We're at Peedie Hoose in the morn. Hiv tae keep on top o hid this week, don't we Esther?'

Halloween dressing up clothes and monster masks are being collected in preparation for a new window display. I've added a ceramic pumpkin, orange tinsel and a white screaming mask. There's a bunch of plastic vampire teeth (unused) from last year's supermarket stock.

 – *Marcus Macrae telephoned to say the flute has been delivered. I think he wanted to arrange my first lesson, but our conversation was cut short (didn't really get started actually). How did you ever think of such a humiliating plan? He's won awards, practically an icon, and I'm…I'm…*

At this point conversation falters and changes direction.

– By the way, thank you for doing my washing.

'Maggie says the internet's awful slow. They're gettin a booster box or some such thing, so wur phones work better.'

'Where's that?' says my father.

'I dinna ken where they're puttin hid. They're getting ready fir when the renovations is done.'

My brother Findlay eats his tea next door in the old shop with Maggie and their two boys. At thirty-five it is I who must stack the plates.

Maggie has big plans for maximising the space.

It's years now since the Post Office counter closed, but only eighteen months since my mother closed the shop. The last of the canned goods are still being eaten. Nobody likes tinned prunes.

There's no door in the passage between Skulstad and the old shop and a moment later there's the sound of running feet and yelping boys in the corridor. My mother smiles and eyes the doorway, my father looks at his watch.

Beneath thatches of red hair the boys have rosy cheeks and bright blue eyes. George, the elder, is growing a nose like an owl's beak and shows signs of taking after my father. The younger boy, Erland, is still undefined.

As they skid around the cramped space something chemical cascades and I start to sweat. I hold my breath and brace my arms to steady the plates.

Erland kicks the kitchen cupboards and heaves himself up to the biscuit barrel.

'Granny, Granny, Ah'm starvin.'

He beams impudently.

'No chance, you've just had yir dinner,' says my mother.

– Hard luck beuy.

My father relieves me of my burden so I may leave. George becomes solemn when I pat his head and walk past. I head upstairs and unfold my laptop.

– Gotta keep in touch with the world.

There's an email from Simon's friend in *Highland Leisure and Game* about the last opportunity to be included in their brochure for next summer. The tone of the message is enthusiastic and friendly, and cuts like east wind.

I type, '*Island Fling* will not be happening. Not ever. By the way, could you ask Simon if the chalet maid had a boy or a girl?'

– Send?

Oh, Claudette

The room was a tidily packed-away childhood when I came. A double bed, an easy chair, a desk and knee-high set of drawers, a wardrobe and full-length mirror, everything a girl needs. Like forest succession new clutter grew. On first arrival a Scandinavian bag and expensive clothes, then afterwards a muddle of medicine boxes and the smell of hospital clean. The recovery layer was next: magazines and leaflets from the British Voice Society, and exotic glass devices that look designed for making coffee.

The designer bag has been pushed into storage space through a little white door. It holds the clothes of a London life and stands shiny and stiff next to a pile of pornography magazines circa the millennium that belonged to Findlay. I suppose they still do. Perhaps I'll give them back. Of course I'd choose my moment carefully.

The computer makes minutes tick-tick-tick nice and quick. They slide as I wander the labyrinth of online forums. Pain, insomnia and voice loss are common, there is nothing life-threatening about them, but you know how people like to complain.

The online pharmacy offers fifty tablets of two hundred milligram slow-release Tramadol tablets for ninety-nine pounds and forty-nine pence plus consultation fee and post and packaging. They can also help with erectile dysfunction, hair loss and cystitis.

It's the natural next step.

I look up from the screen for a moment and double check the walls. Sometimes there are spiders, their legs dancing and scribbling on the walls; at night the lines vibrate then coil and uncoil with the buzz of stranded flies. All the flies want is a way out.

There are voices downstairs.

Real voices.

'She's up in her room,' my mother will be saying, and they will all exchange looks.

My search term blinks across the rectangular Pandora's Box. I press enter.

Although much of it is several years old, it surprises me how much there is to be found on Marcus Macrae. The photographs capture energy totally missing in the man. Well, he had only just got up.

The cursor hovers above a video of him playing, but the bedroom door swings open. It's Maggie.

'Won't you come doon? The boys are here.'

I shut the laptop quickly so she cannot see.

'Kathleen says you met Marcus. Whit dae you think?'

– *It's a ridiculous idea, I have no idea who he is.*

I shrug.

'Gae it a chance. He's no a bad hand. Doctor Copik thinks hid might be wirth a shot.'

– *Very much an ideas person, aren't you?*

'Findlay's tearin oot shelves in the back. Why don't you drop by when the boys are in bed?'

– *I've some magazines you could have if you're short of entertainment. I'm afraid they are pornographic.*

The computer makes a low bleep.

'Tryin tae work?' says Maggie. She produces a sympathetic sigh. 'Shall I leave you tae it? Is that what you want?'

I nod and turn away.

Perhaps this is why I don't get many visitors any more.

~

When she's gone I watch Marcus Macrae in concert. There's hours of footage, none of him playing flute, all fiddle. His eyes fix on the strings like a bird of prey on its quarry, sweat spins away as the bow flies up and down. One set after another, giving everything he's got. He finishes empty and satisfied. When I saw him at Pipersquoy, he just looked empty.

Eventually, the rooms below quieten. It is time for the hours in the slow lane. The screen is no longer effective at distracting me from the drugs wearing off.

'Get some rest,' says my mother on her way to bed.

My father's in the background, they go to their room through whose thin walls they can hear Findlay and Maggie fighting and making love, making life.

– *Thanks again for doing my washing.*

~

I lie in bed fully clothed, wrapped in blankets. The skylight is a picture of stars, the Milky Way floating like froth on a sea of black. My feet feel as if they are above my head, tipping me

back, and my arms extend away stretching infinitesimally thin.
A body filled with painful memories, damaged nerves that
cannot forget, cannot move on.

Remembering the lost pill brings tears to my eyes.

I'm floating away.

– *Help me. Please help me. There's nothing here.*

The seconds drag their feet like prisoners of war.

– *Just old books and dirty clothes. Nobody wants them. You
can't sell something if no one wants it.*

Tick. Tock. Tick.

– *You're scaring me.*

As my eyes adjust, details gradually become visible, the
world becomes real again. Tick.

– *I'm in the void.*

Tock.

My teeth chatter, click-click, a string of pearls dropped into
a pocket. Shivers pass from head to toe, goose pimples follow
in a wave. I sit up and press my forehead on my knees, sweating
heavily. My heart is quick-quick-slow and even breathing re-
quires concentration. I rise drunkenly, then with jelly elbows lift
and sip a glass of water.

A black low passes through my body, snaking along every
vein. Nothing knows how to work any more.

The pain grows and settles deep in my head.

– *I will go insane if I stay on the bed any longer.*

I get up and make my way downstairs to the kitchen. My
knees are wobbly, my breath short and shallow. I fumble the
packets from the medicine cupboard. My stomach clenches and
I stumble to a chair.

Every limb is heavy, lead-weighted, ligaments useless,
twanging like overburdened suspension wires. I lay my arms
on the table and my head flops, pain throbs and bursts through
the crown of my head, heat that flushes through my body. Sweat

pushes into my clothes, I stare zombie-like at the tablecloth, feel the trickles at the back of my neck. I work out where being sick would make least mess.

Would anyone come down to help me or would I have to tidy it up myself?

The memory of Simon sipping gin and a crying red-faced baby floats up in the dark.

– *Where is that baby from?*

My clothes are soaked, my cheek creased where my cannon-ball heavy head has lain, hair wet at the roots.

There is a packet of pills on the oilcloth. Everything has to be done with exaggerated slowness. Sleep-deprived commands connect poorly to actions. I empty the foil pouches and line up the remaining eight Nurofen Plus, then take a glass from the cupboard. Don't worry, for me this is not a big dose, and they can be bought over the counter.

– *Thanks Dad.*

In the hour before dawn the crisis passes. The sweats do not return.

With the breaking light and the sound of squabbling geese lucidity arrives. The air is dead calm, the land unmolested by urges of high and low pressure. There is the pop-pop of a bird scare.

It's the time when I am most likely to fall sleep, but I am sitting at the table.

Doctor Carnegie is retiring, after a diver died under his care in the recompression tank in Stromness. My case will be passed to somebody else. I'm sure they have better things to do than deal with my intractability.

– *It will be easier for everyone if they prescribed just a little more.*

'Ah'll makk some tea,' says a voice by the door.

'Huh?'

My father averts his eyes and fills the kettle, I pack away the boxes and discard the empty pill packet.

'Didna mean to shock you,' he says.

– *It's okay Dad. It's to tide me over. There was a mistake with my repeat prescription.*

Confronting my mother is unlikely to be of any benefit. She has control.

~

I'm ready, fresh clothes and hair tied back.

– *Let's go Mither. I've somewhere to go.*

'Ah'll just pick up that bag o things by the coats,' she says to me from the open door.

Dack-dack.

Two shots, not a bird scare this time, a gun. A greylag is falling. The 'V' wing broken.

Dack-dack.

I'm seated and strapped in the car before my mother is even ready. It takes the wind out of her sails.

– *What are you looking at me like that for? Come on, start the car.*

She does and we move. The need is keen and the pain re-turning.

Our neighbour's hens stutter and panic as we pass, one black, one grey, one red. No foxes to worry about, but the stoats have come.

Air stirs and gulls rise from a freshly sprayed field. Soon we near Accident Corner. My mother takes the turn slow enough for me to pick out the exact place. The scar across the bank healed over during the summer, covered by chickweed, rye grass and red clover. My accident was their chance for life.

I can't stop my heart racing or limbs trembling.

– *I want to get out. Stop the car. I can't breathe.*

'Ah've picked up yir flute.' she says.

– *My what? You did what? I want to get out.*

'In case Mr Macrae calls my mobile.'

– *Jesus. Help me.*

There's nothing else I can say. My head falls backwards onto the seat rest.

When we reach Peedie Hoose I take refuge in the back room. As soon as my mother goes into the shop I write a message and show Bridget.

– *I really need to go this time.*

Bridget nods.

'Will you be long? Your mither wis searching fir you?'

– *As long as it takes.*

The side door goes into the alleyway and avoids my mother, broody as a hen over the till. There's a line of wheelie bins, seeking safety in numbers and sheltering from the wind. I outwit the sprawling recycling boxes, not bad for someone with a herniated disk or two.

I try out a smile in the chemist window and walk inside.

– *I'm not drug seeking, if that's what you think Susie Gordon.*

Before my turn she sells athlete's foot treatment, blackcurrant pastilles and *Nice 'n Easy* hair dye.

Susie Gordon looks me over, trying to think of something nice to say.

'Back agin.'

I hold up my phone.

'New? I'll ask the pharmacist. You ken her from yesterday.'

I stare at the *Relax and take me away* bubble bath display. The shop's boiling but I've got to keep control, sweating doesn't look good. I exhale slowly and unbutton my jacket.

– *Keep calm.*

Claudette is wearing a mini-skirt and high-neck brown sweater.

'Esther? Esther Russell? I would like to discuss your prescription.'

The lining of her skirt rustles as she walks to the red chairs.

'Repeat prescription.'

Nod.

She looks me straight in the eye, sizing me up, and I must admit I am doing the same with her.

'You are not taking any other medication?'

Nod.

'There will be a small wait. Usually this will take four days for paperwork. Doctor Copik has requested express service, so I have nearly ready.'

An exhalation of relief escapes my lips.

Claudette places a box of tissues next to me, her hand rests gently on my shoulder. I shelter my face. When I am this close to the next dose my impatience becomes a flame, seeking oxygen to stay alive.

Perhaps she feels guilty after refusing yesterday, but for some reason I sense she wants to help me.

Road tripping

A glass of water is provided from backstage somewhere. Claudette watches me swallow the first capsule from the packet.

'Follow the instructions, taking medicine at the regular intervals is important.'

– *Can I go now?*

Claudette looks back to Susie Gordon, pink and shining and presenting a bilious-looking man with a prescription.

She sighs, then seals my paper bag with a sticker.

'Be careful,' she says. 'I must work.'

Outside, the grey walls are watermarked around window-sills. A metal hook is sunk deep beneath my shoulder blades, but it's going to get better soon. It is, not I am.

Back in Peedie Hoose there's buckets full of children's shoes to be sorted out and a set of white curtains with red cherries to be measured. There's a packet of incontinence pads, which I add to other oddments on the back table.

My mother has come through and is trying to figure out how to assemble a new scarf hanger that's already got the better of Bridget.

'She doesna look so weel the day,' says Bridget.

'No. I dare say she slept badly.'

'Hid'll be the medication.' She pauses, then says, 'You'll hiv to tell her aboot that call.'

'Marcus Macrae is ready to give you lessons noo,' says my mother.

– F–king hell

'Whit kinda buddy is he?' asks Bridget.

'Plays highland folk fiddle, so Maggie says. She watched him at Catcher's an says he's quite guid. He wis spaekan aboot being classically trained on the flute. You ken, he has an award on John Harrison's shelf at Pipersquoy.'

'So, yir learnin fiddle?' says Bridget.

'No,' says my mother. 'Why would she want to learn fiddle? It's flute, so she can learn tae breathe and get spaekan.'

My mother abandons the scarf hanger and pulls out a pair of baby pink high heel shoes from under the table and holds them up.

'Size four.'

– What could I possibly want with those?

'They'd be fine fir a night oot,' says Bridget, smiling.

My mother puts them in the bag and tidies away my prescription. By the end of the day they'll appear in my room, along with the rest of the things she's picked out, planning my recovery one second-hand item at a time.

'Dinna worry Bridget, I won't leave until Rognvald shows up.'

I go and stand opposite Bridget at the sorting table. Together, we select a sack from the wall of black bags, and begin the routine of pulling out clothes and setting them on hangers that wait on a shower rail hooped to the wall.

'So, he's gaan tae teach you the flute.'

– I don't know. Why would anyone try?

Bridget smiles kindly, then holds up a pair of small corduroy dungarees. 'Aren't they bonny? Shall we say a pund?'

By eleven o'clock the pain is middling. I mime biting into a sausage roll to Bridget and slip away.

My reflection is walking more upright.

Sausage roll bought, I take a walk. A heavy shower has just passed through and the air is fresh and clean. I head down an alley to the chemist's carpark where there is a wall with a seat. The baby-pink salty meat is good.

My mother's car is close by, flute case visible on the parcel shelf. Directly in front of me there's a red two-seater with a fold-down roof, faux zebra-skin seats and a silver luggage rack. The next car is the same model as the one I was hauled out of like a dead fish; I never blacked out.

The smell of solvent wafts over the pastry and pork. I turn and see Claudette in smoker's pose by one of the back entrances. She comes over, pushing out a plume of vapour from the side of her mouth.

'Hi.'

It's remarkable the way sunlight splinters into shards of violet in her eyes.

'I see you working at Peedie Hoose, going in, coming out.'

The words Peedie Hoose roll awkwardly from her lips. Her French accent is southern, that much I can tell.

She dusts something off her skirt, silence falls. At least she doesn't ask questions.

'Susie Gordon told me your accident. It's a long time to recover.'

– *I'm not recovered.*

Claudette's eyes skim across the body of the sporty car. She takes another inhalation and releases a cloud of vapour.

'This,' she says, 'is chemically more addictive than cigarettes, less negative for health, but really no one knows much yet. Addiction is big business. They are unpopular in France.'

There's a moment of eye contact, she sighs and softens her pose.

I want to go somewhere, do something and not go back to Peedie Hoose and jars of buttons and porcelain figures of dancing dogs.

The screen smears with grease as I type.

– *Now, I want to go.*

She indicates the red two-seater after reading the message.

'This is mine.'

I type again.

– *She must eat. Mustn't she?*

'For an hour. I must get my keys and coat.'

Another message.

– *I gotta have something to blow.*

'Yes, but…why do you need it?'

I do not respond, but scrunch up my empty paper bag. She shrugs, then tucks away her vaporizer.

– *Let's go and see Marcus Macrae. I'm curious.*

70

Blow

When Esther enters Peedie Hoose her mother is busy packing a bulky smoothie maker, with the tag line '*As Seen on TV*', into a plastic bag. A woman with '*Nice'n Easy*' coloured hair nods in satisfaction, lips puckering in anticipation. More likely, the contraption will never be used.

Esther walks through, slips the car keys from her mother's handbag and then goes out the side door.

Over the last nine months she's been referred to the pain clinic and speech and language team, but no one can make her attend. She stayed sitting in the car, while her mother ranted. Today, it is her decision.

She takes the flute and transfers it to Claudette's passenger seat, then returns the keys without her mother noticing.

For Esther, getting into a car driven by anyone apart from her mother is an occasion worth noting.

For Claudette, well, it is difficult to say what it means to her yet.

The drugs steady Esther's nerves, her surroundings have the sharpness and flatness of a sleepless night. The pain with its cause is still there, she just doesn't feel it.

After lowering herself in, Esther sits with only moderate discomfort.

'You will have to give me the directions,' says Claudette. 'I cannot return late.'

Esther nods.

Claudette's legs are elegant in opaque black lycra, her calves clothed in leather boots. Good legs—Esther and Claudette have that in common.

Inside, the smart wooden dashboard is undermined by the faint smell of burnt clutch. The small plastic rear window is torn and taped, and the car is damp.

Esther shivers and grips the miniature flute coffin on her knee when the engine starts.

She does not know what will happen. She doesn't know anything about Claudette, except that being with her brings relief. She fears dying a little less.

She braces herself at the junction onto the main road, impact could come from any direction. Her heart starts to race, her head pound. But it doesn't come.

They turn and follow a plumbing van. Esther taps the dashboard and points up Clay Loan, towards Gallows Ha' where the witches were burned.

'I live over there,' says Claudette, gesturing towards a cul-de-sac on the hill. 'I must move because there is no proper heating and the bathroom grows mould. It is very unhealthy. I can afford a better flat. I do not need to live with other people.'

Esther gives directions at the top of the loan.

'I cannot play any instrument,' says Claudette. 'For me the effort to play takes away the pleasure. I like the music here, island music. It is very best live.'

Esther wrinkles her nose. She's not into the folk music scene, although it was very much part of her *Island Fling* holiday plans, part of the 'authentic experience' of coming to the isles.

'I have been to The Catcher for many evenings. It is lively.'

The evenings have made an impression on the usually unromantic Claudette. When she remembers them she taps her foot, and her body warms.

'I go alone,' she says as if this was important.

The car heads east out of town over the brae.

Above, the sky is gentle, washed out from the last downpour. Geese organise in lines and cross to the open water.

The airport turning passes. At Accident Corner Esther is transported back in time. It is dark, orange lights spin and she flies, cut loose from the road, gravity and velocity brawling for control of her body. Then she's back again. Covered in sweat, trying to find something real to cling on to.

'A pain clinic can help you,' says Claudette. 'So will Valium, to help you sleep.'

This isn't what Esther wants to hear. If she's honest, she enjoys the aural hallucinations that come and go with the Tramadol, an angelic, metallic chorus. She doesn't notice the mood swings so much, but she knows she's not who she used to be.

There have been plenty of clinics.

The jaw, fractured upper and splintered lower, had her referred to a maxillofacial team. They enjoyed the challenge of her face. In fact, there was a degree of pride afterwards. An ambitious junior had even put forward that Esther's case be submitted to the *Clinical Journal of Facial Reconstruction* for the innovative use of bovine tissue and tooth implantation. Senior colleagues, conceited though they were, sensed that Esther's consent would not be forthcoming.

There was never a decent celebrity-sweat-patch-diet-binge-love-triangle-secret-heartache magazine in the waiting room. Balloons with slogans warning of mouth cancer were cheerfully given to children who attended the clinic.

They were brimming with hubris that lot.

The mechanical defects of the throat and mouth are on the whole less cryptic than the psychology of post traumatic stress disorder, vocal paralysis and selective mutism. The relationship between the Maxillofacial Clinic and the Holistic Voice Clinic could best be described as mutually 'unsupportive' in their approach to Esther's silence.

The therapy sessions in the hospital were crammed with people of her granny's age, people with strokes, progressive illnesses, head injuries. They had watched her spit and swallow, made notes and listed specific goals. Esther often left before the sessions were over.

Really, they'd need a time machine to properly understand why Esther doesn't speak. She has frozen the meaning of events, locked her perspective.

~

The sun, a diffuse pearl behind disintegrating cloud, silvers the scar of road. Before long sand encroaches on either side. Esther indicates the track they must take.

'I've been all the way,' says Claudette indicating ahead on the main road. 'To somewhere called The Gloop. The water flows in and out making noise. At the visitor centre there were rats swimming in the puddles. I don't like rats. Does anyone like rats?' Claudette stops gesturing with her hands and changes gear. 'It is bumpy. Sorry.'

Arms and legs braced, Esther is trying to stay safe.

~

Marcus Macrae has had a quiet morning, spent mostly getting cold and wet on the hillside while trying to find a phone signal to contact his record label. Sodden-footed he returned to the house, took off his trainers and contemplated the dead man's wellington boots that stood in the hall. He's found a pair of rubberised trousers in the wardrobe.

Marcus Macrae's windows look over to Copinsay, its holms and its horse. The chief landmark is the lighthouse, a lantern held aloft by a white column whose structure comes and goes like a mirage. The island is flat-topped with sloping sides, the curve of land running down to the North Sea distorted by a gun emplacement.

All this and not a single tune comes to his mind.

There is an old tub of Vaseline inside the flute case. While waiting for Esther and her mother, he greases the joints and slides the instrument together. He forms his lips into an embouchure and begins to play, the muscle memory is deep and strong. Rondo Alla Turca springs from the instrument, and Marcus remembers his mother nodding along to every note. He played it over and over again for her, and then the night after he'd graduated there had been a terrible accident. He had laid the instrument down because she was not there to listen any more.

The gates of grief open.

He feels a sharp need to see his little girl, but he's got to begin over, banished because of choices he's been making for a long time. He'd lost his temper, but really it had been all about grief.

~

Close by, there's no escape for Esther. The bumps jolt, pop-pop-pop through her pelvis up her spine.

'I think if I slow the wheels will become stuck,' says Claudette. 'The ground is very wet.'

She drives differently from Esther's mother, she has more attack.

When they finally stop next to the pile of stone chips Esther is panting. Claudette takes out the keys and puts them in her pocket, then places a hand on Esther's shoulder. She gently swipes away a lock of stray hair from her new friend's face.

'Sorry.'

Slowly, Esther recovers. She sends a text to her mother explaining where she is and raises the phone for Claudette to read.

'I did not know Marcus played flute,' says Claudette.

As they reach the front door a muffled trill comes from inside. Esther knocks and they wait.

'This will be interesting,' says Claudette.

A man needs a maid

As we wait, I see that my reflection looks younger today, hair in a ponytail, clothes better fitting. Nothing compared to Claudette—she has an unconcerned, bored elegance that is unheard of here.

The door opens. Marcus smiles and holds up a silver instrument.

'Just reminding myself how to play.'

His voice tails off, stops.

'Claudette?'

She glances down at the flattened cigarette butts on the doorstep.

– *You know each other?*

'Have you been there long?'

'No,' says Claudette.

'You're friends?' says Marcus looking between us.

'Esther asked for a lift,' says Claudette. 'Can we go inside? It is cold.'

'Good. Aye, why not,' he says and steps back.

– *Why are you nervous?*

When we're inside I notice the award on the mantlepiece has been removed. Claudette walks through the clutter and takes up a lookout position at the window. The dim room smells of burnt dust.

'Aye. It's a fantastic view,' says Marcus. 'On a clear day you can see all the way over the Pentland Firth to mainland Scotland.'

Claudette doesn't reply or turn, but jingles the keys inside her pocket. It seems an insolent way to behave. I may not be a die-hard fan of Marcus Macrae, but he has done something to have an award on show.

Then I get it.

– *Exactly how long ago did you sleep with him, Claudette?*

Marcus drags his attention away from where Claudette sits to where I am waiting.

'May I take a look?'

I notice there's a tear across his knuckle as I hand him the flute case, a barbed wire wound for a city dweller.

'I didn't know you were living here,' she says. Claudette reaches into her pocket for her vaporiser and then replaces it; clearly she would prefer a cigarette. 'You said you were going back home to Inverness.'

'I was,' he says. 'Then I was in London and aye, well I'm figuring out some new tunes and here isn't bad.'

'And music lessons?' she says.

He looks over to me.

'Aye. She's not had a good time. From what her mother says they've tried everything.'

– *Don't believe the old witch.*

Marcus walks over to the window. They stand together, Claudette looking out, Marcus head down and thoughtful. He has a strong presence, charisma, yet there is something uneasy and dark about his demeanour.

– *Are you both thinking about sex? Are we all?*

The window suddenly stops being interesting to Claudette. She moves into the centre of the room and stands detached.

'I thought she wouldn't drive with anyone else,' says Marcus.

'I met Esther in the shop,' says Claudette, turning in my direction. 'She asked me.'

It's there again, the sympathy between us. I want to smile.

'You have no good chairs for her,' she says.

– *There's not much good here at all. If you can drag yourself away I would like to leave. This is a mistake.*

She walks towards the kitchen. Marcus does nothing to prevent her leaving. We are alone.

'Aye, how are you today, Esther? Feelin like a wee lesson?'

– *Questions, questions, questions.*

I answer him as I would my mother, with a shrug. Some people are simply afraid of statements and silence.

'Where did you get this from? Have you had a try? I think your mother's idea is that strengthening breathing muscles will help your voice…To be honest, I didn't catch on to everything she was after and there's no way I'm a music therapist… Flute's not even something I play much any more.'

He closes the case and returns the flute, the black surface is warm from his hands.

– *It doesn't matter. Keep the money, let the lessons drop.*

'I've seen stress affect performers before, loss of confidence to play or even go near the stage, aye. Like it was suddenly life and death if they didn't get it right.'

– *Claudette will come back.*

A mouse scuttles in the fireplace and the sound disappears into the dark. His brow furrows.

'They worry they'll forget what to do.'

Claudette is back in the room. The frog of a bow is gripped between her finger and thumb. The horsehair forms a curve imitating the shape of a treble clef, and the white tip swings free.

There is a change in Marcus's posture, shoulders curving inwards, limbs stiffly held. The expression in his eyes becomes guarded.

'What happened?' she says.

'You went in the bedroom?' he says.

'To get a better chair. The case was open.'

'It broke,' says Marcus.

There is a fleeting expression of pain across his face but he's very quick to regain control, head tilting casually to one side as if it were unimportant. A strained smile stretches his lips.

– *You're lying.*

The tension in the room rises.

'I've a spare,' he says.

I sense the physical effort being used to keep his voice level—I can tell he hates the spare. Not because of its inferior quality, but because it's an understudy to the one he loved.

'Anyway, Esther's here for flute.'

– *Am I?*

'You can get it fixed,' says Claudette, eyes still fast on Marcus's face.

I'm not sure what she wants from him.

'No,' he says. 'It's not important. Anyway I'm here to write.'

There's a quick knock on the front door, it's pushed open and a box lands on the mat. A waft of soft wet air comes into the room.

Marcus looks puzzled and leaves us to find out what has arrived.

'He is heart-broken,' she says, examining the heel of the bow more carefully. 'He loves this bow.' She weighs it in her hand and reads the small inscription then touches the horsehair, it sticks to her fingertips, a bemused smile rises on her lips.

'I had no idea he even played flute. But it does not surprise me.' She raises an eyebrow and adds, 'If you know what I mean.'

She points the bow at me, swinging it as she speaks.

'Yes, I remember now….there was this very boring woman who would not stop talking to him after a concert.'

There is a photograph of Maggie on my phone. I type, 'Sister-in-law, Maggie' and show her. She nods.

It is Erland's birthday, he has a pirate cake covered in black icing. Maggie and Findlay are standing either side, George is at the table, glaring at his brother. Claudette nods.

When Marcus returns he's tearing open a parcel. He riffles impatiently through the contents.

There is that guarded look again. He throws himself down into a rattan chair holding the box on his knee. It is full of cards, pink and purple, glittery with the social norms of a young girl's birthday dreams.

Marcus looks at the hearth, staring into and through the stone.

'I need to go back to work,' says Claudette.

She takes away the bow and returns it to the bedroom.

'She's an unforgiving sort of woman,' he says.

– *Claudette's not so bad. I've a bit of a crush on her to be honest because she's a pharmacist. Smart, beautiful, excellent access to narcotics…*

Marcus is not in joking mood.

'She's some stubborn. Being protective she'll say.'

– *I see. No, I don't see.*

I realise that I am cradling the flute in my arms like a baby. The glossy wallpaper stripes glimmer, their pewter colour echoing the light over the sea.

Vertebrae click and shift as I pull up through my spine. He turns, puzzled for a moment then his expression softens.

Claudette is back in the room.

'Ready?' she says. 'Unless you want to stay.'

I shake my head slowly and stand.

'You're here for a lesson,' says Marcus.

– *I don't think you want to give me a lesson.*

'Whose are the cards?' asks Claudette.

The tone of her voice indicates she already knows the answer, but she wants him to tell her.

There's a pause.

'My daughter's,' he says. 'They're from Helen. Ach. She doesn't mean it. She's just mad. She's a right to be.'

– *Helen?*

'His wife,' says Claudette.

'I'd end up sending two or three sometimes,' he says. 'I was going places, touring, recording, couldn't say no.' His chest falls heavily. 'Turned out to be a shite father.'

He raises a foot and shoves the table. It slides briefly, scraping the floor and the cards tumble to the floor.

An uneasy silence returns. It is broken by the ping of hail flying into the chimney. Claudette and I exchange a look and move towards the door.

Outside, hail streaks, hits hard then pops up from the ground before coming to rest.

'Merde,' says Claudette.

The hail needles my neck and steals between collar and skin. Claudette follows me into the squall and hustles towards the car, but Marcus is coming out behind us.

His voice is gruff, 'Come tomorrow,' he calls. 'Try to get a sound. I've taken the money. I'm going to give the lessons.'

The side mirror is all sky as Claudette reverses towards the precipitous edge of the cliff. It does not seem to bother her at all. A black-backed gull, wings two metres wide, is being buffeted overhead towards the house. She turns the wheel sharply and presses the accelerator.

The back window buckles then swells in the wind; somewhere coins slide and rattle as the wheels bump over the rough ground.

When we reach the main road she says, 'I have to hurry.'

– *Left! Left! We drive on the left! Jesus!*

My stomach heaves.

Claudette crosses back over the white line and settles into a racing pose, one hand over the wheel, her eyes narrowed.

'Don't worry.'

Country road, country home

Fence posts skitter past, leaning askew where cattle have grazed the verge in the summer.

'He can have a bad temper,' Claudette says, she is excited, eyes bright. 'He is emotional. You will see the way he plays, magnifique.'

The escape is over.

I can't face returning the same way with Claudette behind the wheel. I type with one hand while the other holds tight.

'Okay,' she says. 'Give me directions again.'

At the turning for Skulstad hens scurry into half-flight as Claudette swings into the driveway and noses the red bonnet into the tattered crocosmia.

'Remember,' she says, 'ask your doctor for Valium. You need sleep.'

She picks up the flute case from the footwell and passes it to me.

– *Will I see you again?*

'Bonne chance.'

Then she is away, and I walk stiff-legged towards the house and shop. My father's whistle carries on the breeze. I purse my lips, curl my tongue inside my mouth and try to copy the refrain.

'No bad at aal,' says my father, coming around the house.

He puts his arm around me and kisses the side of my head.

While the kettle is boiling he opens the flute case and scrutinises the pieces. He checks his hands for dirt, then picks up the larger middle section and begins to construct the instrument.

'I've no idea whit to do next,' he says, and hands it to me.

I pretend to play it like a trumpet and make him smile. God, it's good to see him smile.

'Go on, gae it a blow.'

I hold the instrument sideways, turn the hole towards my mouth and blow gently downwards.

There's no noise.

– *Must be broken.*

'Harder than it looks,' he says.

The effort of blowing makes my throat ache; after a sip of coffee I try again. This time I pucker my lips outward like a duck's bill.

'It'll tak some gettin used to.'

– *I'm not sure Marcus Macrae is a born teacher.*

'Well, I had better get on, Maggie wants new shelvin. Your brother's got fine plans for the shop, but it'd be a sight easier if he tried to become a better hand. I ken he's gotta do somethin new, working fir the council is takkin him nowhere.'

He makes instant coffee in a chipped mug for taking outside. Coffee made with fresh beans and pressurised steam shocks my father, his whistling goes awry. He looks over at me.

'Your time'll come, lass.'

He'd take my scars onto his own face if he could, he'd lay me out and put me together again if he could.

– *Sorry Dad. I'm not a lawnmower.*

~

The house hollows when he goes. There is stillness, no commotion from Maggie's renovations. It's a strong vocation of hers, taking apart our family history. You'd think it'd keep her off my back. Wasn't that kind of her to speak to Marcus Macrae and mention me the night he went home with Claudette.

An empty house doesn't do me good. I start thinking about the next Tramadol. The new prescription is in a bag at Peedie Hoose. A whole month's supply and I can't get my hands on it, I have to wait.

I take to the sofa and close my eyes. There are minutes I don't remember, but it's not quite the same as sleep. A red-faced baby is staring at me again. It hangs around terribly.

– *Simon?*

Don't f–king grin at me like that. It was meant to be a skiing holiday with your father, that was *the point*, not some f–king procreative jaunt. Did you have an intuition I was not an attractive long-term prospect?

I kick the table and the baby goes flying into the fire.

My eyes are peeled back and I'm holding my breath, body held rigid.

Tick. Tock.

– *How long I have been staring at the blank television?*

Tick.

Cars are arriving outside, doors open and shut, feet trample inside, I hear my mother and my nephew's familiar voices. A bubbling rush of sound and voices, reaching out and infecting the silence.

'Ah've been oot aal day and she's no done a thing. And such a visit wi Granny. Ah'm plain wabbit this evening.'

'Gae it back, Erland. George made it at school,' says Maggie.

'He's broken the head off,' says George, tearfully .

'Hid's aal right, Granddad'll fix hid,' says my mother. 'What's hid meant to be?'

'A brushin teeth robot.'

There doesn't seem any reason to move until I remember my mother has the prescription, then I move like birthday guests have arrived.

'Esther? Were you sleepin?' says Maggie.

I bend and hug Erland, mime toothbrushing and point to his model. He looks at me suspiciously.

The room becomes quieter, I'm a dampener. I pick up the flute from where it lies next to the pile of peelings.

'Can you play yet?' asks George.

I shake my head and hand it to him. He blows hard and makes a shrill peep.

– Better than I can do.

Maggie takes it off him and starts pulling it apart, matching the pieces into the imprints of the case.

'Whit an efternoon. Granny wis aal a rambling on aboot this an that efter a visitor buddy came by tae ask her aboot memories of whit it wis like efter the war. Kept gettin up fae her chair an wanderin aboot. Ah've no idea whit's botherin her. She wouldna hardly eat anythin. No even a teacake, and she'll alwis hiv a teacake. I think if you opened her up there'd be nothin but Tunnocks inside.

'She wis spaekan about your grandpa an aafil lot yesterday, tellin when the shop made tea fir the soldiers when she wis a lass, on an on about those awful tin cups.' Then she turns and beams at Maggie. 'She did love tae see the peedie boys, though. It wis guid of you to bring them after school.'

'Do we *hiv* to see Granny?' asks George, politely removing his finger from his nose.

'No wan *has* to see Granny,' says my mother. 'But hoo'd you like tae be so owld an left aal alone aal the time?'

– Yeah, yeah, we get the guilt trip.

'How wis your lesson?' calls my mother after me as I leave the kitchen. I search the coats for treasure.

I don't answer.

My gaze travels down the passageway to Granny's back room, caught in the last glow of the sun. It was kitchen and sitting room in one, where she'd cook and sew and sit in the evenings after Grandpa George died.

As a child the back room had been my favourite place to go. There was a tiny circular window in the range that glowed orange day and night. You could open the firebox door or lift the metal plate to load coal from the top. The chimney flue gave heat to the room where my mother and her sister Elspeth slept, and that Findlay and I later shared.

Grandpa George was older than Granny, he'd come to Orkney to man one of the searchlight stations watching over Scapa Flow during the war.

Granny had moved between the shop, the back room and Grandpa George. We'd hear them laughing and being sharp with each other, as did the customers, but no one ever got red-cheeked about it.

The best time to be in the back room was when the waxy light from the east made everything glow, then it looked less old and less dirty. The stove smoked awfully some days and coal dust got everywhere.

I have come to the doorway.

The light is softening after the hard, bright day. The cups that were on the shelf above the stove have left pale patches on the wall behind. The high units where dried goods were kept are off their brackets, dirty-blue paint on one side, raw wood where they were fixed to the wall for half a century.

The room is being demolished, but it still has the feeling of being Granny's back room where bannocks and pancakes were cooked on a griddle and wool was turned from thread to gansey, cloth to breeks.

There'd be a scolding if she found me fiddling with anything. She'd call, 'Kathleen, Esther's in here meddlin again.'

I loved to trace my finger along the embroidered roses on the cloth that covered the sewing machine. It had more silky attraction than any of my toys, despite the risk of my foot being crushed beneath the treadle.

One day, Granny found me holding papers I'd found in one of the sewing machine's peedie drawers. Granny Ida never cursed, coming from the kirk side of the family, but there was the blackest curse in her eyes when she caught me.

She'd taken me by the arm. 'You'll get a skelpin this time,' she'd said. 'Always pokin aboot whar yir no wanted. Get oot! An no greetin to yir fither.'

She'd hit me along the back of the legs, put me outside and closed the door. I'd bitten back my tears and stood where she left me. Through a crack in the door I'd watched her folding up the pieces of thin blue paper then she'd hooked open the lid of the range, the orange light reflected on her face, and she'd dropped the letters inside.

At the time, I could only read well enough to know the letters were from Granny's cousin Winnie who'd moved to Canada after the war. Granny rarely spoke about these foreign relatives, yet I knew there must be something special about these people who lived halfway around the world because they could make her cry.

Not long afterwards Grandpa George died.

Turning my back on the evening light I return to the coats, unhook my mother's bag and retrieve my prescription. The printed label says, 'To be swallowed with water ONCE daily.'

It was about a month before I came back for the launch of *Island Fling* that Maggie and Findlay suggested Granny would be happier in Stembister House. It would let them get on more efficiently with their renovations.

My mother had agreed.

Midnight feast

I come down when I am called, everyone is eating together.

– Don't worry, the Tramadol is safe.

'So,' says Maggie. 'How did the flute lesson go, Esther? You ken he's classically trained. Studied at the conservatoire in Edinburgh before he made a name in folk.'

– I don't want to talk about it.

'Aye, we saw him at Catcher's,' says Findlay, forking grey meat into his mouth.

He picks something fallen from off Erland's lap and puts it back on his son's plate. Erland licks a finger and cleans his trousers.

'Who d'you get a lift wi?' says my mother.

My father stops eating and looks at me.

– What? Aren't I allowed to trust someone?

'You'll be drivin yirself next,' says Findlay.

He winks at me.

– Don't Goddamn wink at me.

I lay down my knife and fork, too loud to be ignored. My father reaches out and covers my hand with his.

– What? What's that for? Why do I need that?

There's a lag before I realise that the woman sitting in my place, being me and eating my food, is crying. Chest shaking, lungs filled with sickly pork-laden air.

'Are you hurt yoursel, Auntie Essie?' says Erland.

– *Yes. I did. I think I hurt myself.*

My mother passes me a tissue. Usually I would leave the room, but my father puts pressure on my hand to stay.

'She still has a sore back,' says Maggie. She tells the boys, so they will not think it was Findlay's wink that caused the trouble. 'She's gaan tae learn flute so her voice will come back.'

– *It's not a bloody lost dog.*

A warm flush of shame blooms on my cheeks.

~

They eat while I sip water, it feels as if someone else raises the glass to my lips. But that's fine, that's Tramadol.

Outside, the sky is sliding, lit with streaks of green, grey and bronze. The day length is changing rapidly. We've had our turn, it's time to move on, the heavenly bells are ringing in the dark.

– *They're back. I can hear them again.*

'Who gave you a lift?' says my mother.

The sound is bright and vibrant, colours of bronze and gold resonate inside of my head.

'Who gave you a lift?'

I think I'm being addressed.

– *Ssh now, be quiet angels.*

'Hmm?'

Everyone has stopped eating, a stunned look on their faces. They lean forward expectantly. It is very quiet as I write 'The new pharmacist.'

Their faces fall. I don't know how, but I've disappointed them all.

The dishes are cleared, Maggie removes the boys and my father speaks to Findlay about shelves. I watch my brother faking interest in the details and the decisions to be made—he just wants it done for him.

Before Findlay leaves my mother says to him, 'Pop in to see Granny when yir in the toon. Hid would do her guid tae see more folk she kens.'

'I dinna hiv time,' he says. 'Esther can go.'

Findlay looks at me.

– *Don't you dare wink.*

He winks, then walks away to look over the muckle mess they've made of the shop that used to be neat as a pin. Granny's room'll soon be gone.

I dry the dishes with my father.

'What kind o buddy is she?' he asks, gesturing back at my phone.

I write, 'French,' then add, 'I need to see Doctor Carnegie.'

'For whit?' he says.

I type 'Sleeping pills.'

The tea towel slows in his hand, he presses harder and more methodically over the dinner plate.

~

When we're finished my mother takes the scraps for the hens.

I go to the medicine cupboard. On the bottom shelf there are Granny's china cups from her wedding day, a set of four with a faded blue-and-white Dutch scene. Above there are stacks of small boxes and old ice cream tubs filled with pills.

I remove a sheet of Nurofen Plus and conceal it in my trouser pocket then turn around and show the empty box to my father. He shifts his weight from one foot to the other.

I rub my back and wince.

'I ken. But I canno hiv Susie Gordon thinkan wur whole family is seek wi pains.'

– *Why the resistance today?*

'Ask me the morn,' he says, and takes the box.

He stands by the cupboard and waits for me to leave.

Upstairs, my mother has left me the pink shoes. I toss the Nurofen and Tramadol onto the stack of travel magazines as if I could hardly care less.

– *It's a relief to know you are here.*

Nearby the laptop glows, there are messages waiting: Re: *Island Fling* enquiry, Re: Orcadian Food and Drink Fair, Re: Inclusion in Tourism Orkney Brochure, Re: Russian girls near you right now, Re: Car insurance premium renewal, Re: We're getting married.

The last one is from Simon.

I close the laptop, breathe back the tears and for a moment feel a flicker of motivation to do some stretches the physiotherapist demonstrated.

A deep ache runs through the muscles, and the act of simply leaning sideways and reaching down my thigh brings hot, tight pain.

– *It wasn't easy to give up. But I did.*

Even all stitched back together, a mended doll is never the same.

I must not start playing solitaire on the computer. It's too early. Red on black, jack on queen on king. It's a long night.

There's a knock at the door.

'I brought yir flute,' says my mother. 'So you can hiv a practice.'

– *I'm not going back.*

'He's been on the telephone agin, apologising for the raffle he wis in today. An says tae pass on he's lookin forward to seein you the morn.'

She lays the case on the table.

'Ah'm off oot tae choir.' There's a pause then she adds, 'You need tae get weel agin Esther. We need tae get on.'

The poor electric light makes her hair look darker and emphases the sturdy rectangle of her face. There's something she wants to say but she can't.

'You found them,' she says at last, nodding at the prescription and the strips of Nurofen. The words my mother really wants to say still don't come. At last she says, 'They're bonny,' and nods at the shoes.

After her footsteps fade I go and sit on the top of the stairs. There's a picture of Granny Ida propped by a sea anemone shell.

Findlay found the shell on the second barrier beach, he's good at finding things. Neat rows of white spots running up and down the sphere, a navel-shaped hole in its crown, the orange and pink faded now.

– I have lost my voice. It doesn't belong any more.

Granny looks at the camera confidently, her gaze sweeping the horizon beyond. She's wearing an open collar shirt with a mannish V-neck jumper, hands in her pockets, hair lifting on the breeze. No one in the family doubted she loved her man better than anything else.

Simon has a family now and is to be married. The child will not be French because the chalet girl was actually from Bedford. Occasionally, I can see the funny side of things.

My father comes to the foot of the stairs.

'Bit late to be sittin on the stairs. Get you a cocoa?'

The pain makes me flinch as he helps me to my feet, I throw him a beseeching look.

'Ask me the morn,' he says again. 'Ah'll get you some more.'

Off he goes to bed. The dull afternoon has left nothing but lethargy. A tide without the energy to turn. Old sweat sits on my skin.

~

The shower is on. It's my routine. The thing I do. The thing I can do. The pleasure I can have.

I tug the curtain across then fix the controls for heat and cold.

My knees bend, my mouth opens and I gag on the spray. I close my eyes and in my mind's eye see a body wrapped in shrouds floating down to the ocean floor, then body after body, into the great dark silence. Sleep seems seconds away.

The bathroom suite is gummy pink and laughing, because this is the wrong place to sleep.

– *No you cannot do it here.*

Shaky legs walk me upstairs to my room. As I put on pyjamas the belief that I will sleep abandons me. I lie flat and stare. I stare and stare, and feel I'm falling, and then come the hateful feelings of wanting the baby gone and the woman burned because sometimes I want to keep Simon. Bury him and keep him.

– *Time's up.*

The foil bursts and releases a capsule, the lark ascending rings in my ears. Half black, half military blue, it's the first in the line with six Nurofen Plus to follow. I can't face the shitty taste, and this time the capsule goes down without being split. Then the rest.

~

My mother and father sleep in the room where Grandpa George died. Erland and George sleep in bunk beds in the room in which my mother and her sister Elspeth used to sleep. Rooms layered by time, like cliffs full of shells waiting to be scraped free by the ocean.

Granny stays at Stembister House. At Skulstad, Grandpa George kept a spray of silk roses high up on a shelf to remind

93

her of summer. Year round the wind keeps company through the night.

The Nurofen take effect, a feeling of calmness settles and I sit up and answer emails.

'Congratulations,' is the title of the first reply, the second begins 'In due course,' and the next, 'Apologies for the long delay.' I'm on a roll. 'Please renew my policy for another year.'

When dawn comes I'm playing solitaire, and none of the emails have been sent.

Red on black, jack on queen on king.

There has been no sleep. I did not dream of flying or burning.

Outside on the estuary, two white swans cruise across the water. Three large goslings flit between them, scooting their bodies forward to keep pace with their extended necks.

The water and sky are empty and flat. I think I may be beginning to lose my mind. There is so little to hold on to that's real. Gradually, the light comes and the grey separates into sea and sky. Their identity returns.

I open the flute case and begin to assemble the instrument. The buttons are cushioned and give quiet clicks as they return to position. I support the weight on my palms, fingers open.

Only breath.

I hold it to my lips. When no one is watching and no one is listening there is no tightness, no pain. The problem is the breath. There's no strength in it. I lower the instrument, abashed. I think of Marcus and feel a subtle physical energy. It passes through, away and gone.

The landscape looks totally empty, but in the mid-distance a movement reveals small dark birds, their wings kissing the water as they turn and rise.

~

Outside there is a cock-a-doodle-doo.
– *Time's up.*
The night was real. Wasn't it?
There's always one smart alec.

Grandpa George was from Portsmouth

Quietly, Esther leaves her room.

In the summer, when visitors come to the island, there's hardly any darkness at all. Tractors burr all night long in their happy pursuits, Orkney voles are delivered to doorsteps by domestic cats and house martins comb the air for insects, all drunk on an endless chase. The days blend and Esther's insomnia had felt less overpowering because at least there was light.

The change in seasons bring back the memory of darkness.

The replication of the day when the accident happened is extraordinary. The temperature, wind direction, even the dying back of the giant daisies are the same at the moment. The closed-off stump of the petrol pump is the same, the reeking tank beneath ground is an echoing place where the way out is sealed—there is nothing it can ever be except empty. Not even a buzzing fly wanting to escape.

Esther is standing balanced on a chair, she feels like she is floating, body and mind disconnected.

Her nerves are so accustomed to pumping out messages of pain they don't know how to stop, they are oblivious to healing.

Pain is their job, their purpose to curtail movement and protect the body.

Esther regrets not putting the light on so she can read the active ingredients on the various medicine boxes. She regrets not asking her father to pick up more Nurofen Plus. Although Susie resists the transaction, she still sells the pills to everyone in Esther's family. No one has told her to stop.

There is a thump in the room above and Erland starts to cry. Esther takes warning and climbs down. She needs sleep.

~

In another house, Claudette is rising. She curses her flatmate for using her bathroom products, curses the black mould in the shower and then curses in earnest the coffee and her memory of better coffee. She curses her homesickness for a dull provincial town—a town so caught up in its own personal dramas that she feels it will have forgotten her completely already.

A tanker, silver and shiny, grinds past her window on its way to collect milk from the farms; it will be bottled or made into cheese. Claudette cannot fathom the difference between one block of yellow cheddar cheese and another. And why, she thinks, are some of them orange?

~

Up at Pipersquoy, overlooking the sea, Marcus Macrae sleeps on, his body clock derailed by years of performance even when the gigs have dried up. Torn-out pages from a note-book lie crumpled in the grate by a fish-and-chips carton. The mice are getting used to Marcus being around and are gaining weight. In the night he dreams of his daughter riding a unicorn and wakes remembering the time he carried her piggyback by the River Ness to feed the ducks. He cannot write a single song.

~

Elsewhere, the keypad of Stembister House is on the blink again and Susie Gordon's mother Helga has to enter her code number three times before the lock clicks back and she can get to work on the morning tea tray. The kitchen is only just recovering from the scrubbing inflicted on it the evening before. The last thing Stembister House needs is norovirus going around like it did last year.

Granny Ida couldn't visit Esther in hospital. She was lucky to pull through herself. It would have been wrong either of them dying yet.

Today, Ida also wakes early and sits in her chair by the window and reads a week-old newspaper. She thinks it's awful hot in Karachi for the time of year, then begins the crossword puzzle. The song of a blackbird comes through the open window and her pen pauses. She misses the whaups and herring gulls, and lately even the geese that fly over Redland. She wonders if anyone is listening to the dawn cries of the birds over Skulstad.

She remembers holding a sleeping baby at dawn, the relaxed weight of the warm body, and the denseness of sleep measured against the lightness of breath. After six weeks there was a smile. Every joy gave a reminder of loss. Motherhood had complicated emotions for Ida, it was easier if she held back.

Ida wonders if her daughter will come and visit.

It bodes to be a bright fine day, a day to see the island at its best.

~

Not much later, Kathleen is bustling about the kitchen, fetching a pair of rolls to give to Maggie for the boys, setting Andrew's boiler suit folded and tutting at a drinks can caught in the guttery mud where the daisies are dying back.

The kitchen sink sways then drops forward as Esther tries to fill a glass of water. Everything slips one way and then the other. She steadies herself, hip against the counter and takes her Tramadol. Months of sleeplessness are catching up with her, the headaches, disorientation and stupidity merge with the effects of pain and pain relief. She wonders how many Tramadol it's going to take to feel better and why the cupboards were empty of their usual bounty.

The floor ripples beneath her feet, advancing in a wave that'll knock her down.

– *Claudette thinks Valium is worth a try.*

Esther holds up her phone. She is dressed, hair tied back.

– *I'm losing track. I need something new.*

'I dinna ken why you want tae see Doctor Carnegie? You've got your pills.'

– *But I'm losing track. There used to be days and nights. Claudette says Valium.*

Close your eyes and go to sleep.

It's not difficult.

It's impossible.

Esther pours out a bowl of her nephews' super-sweet-coated cereal. At least it's something.

In between mouthfuls of toast and eggs Andrew watches Esther closely. He knows what she wants. He listened in the night, he heard the faint sound of the flute, long and low like wind through gates. Try harder lass, he thinks. Don't go taking more demned pills.

Kathleen has the phone.

'Aye, it's Kathleen. Ah'd like an appointment fir Esther the day….I ken….a long time…weel, whit can you dae? Don't spaek… Ah'm ower tae Stembister Hoose….then Esther has her lesson…Aye, cheerio.'

She hangs up and goes to the dishes.

Andrew is saying a silent prayer. He doesn't see the scars on his daughter's face or the white streak in her hair anymore, he just knows she suffers. It was all too much for her, he thinks. That fella Simon was no good and whatever he did or whatever went on between them he should be mightily ashamed of never coming to visit her since. A poor way to behave. She's not to blame for finding it difficult. If only she could be easier on herself.

There's famous folk who've fallen in with pills for years. It is often their undoing.

'Ah'm gaan tae put a rod in wi Willie,' he says.

'Whit aboot the work for Maggie?' says Kathleen.

'It'll bide. Aal the bruck wants shiftin oot o Granny's room afore I can do anything.'

He leaves the boiler suit, it's waders today.

'We'll see Granny first,' says Kathleen to the dishes on the drainer.

Esther is fighting to keep her breakfast down. The table is trying to tip everything onto her lap. Sitting is hard—walking is worse. Walking in her shoes does not have a waiting list.

The flute is taken from her room and placed on the parcel shelf.

When they've left, Maggie goes to the back room with a crowbar. She's wondering if she can be bothered up-cycling anything after all. She's not in that sort of mood.

A clear band of sky stretches east to west, the sun hidden behind a strip of lavender-tinted cloud. There's softness in the air, close to stillness, a pause between breaths.

When they are over Redland burn Esther clears her throat. Kathleen turns sharply because the sound is so similar to when someone prepares to speak. She cannot hide the flash of hope that passes over her face, after a whole year it's still there, deep underneath the duty.

But they carry on in silence, and the trauma bears down on Esther afresh as they repass the site of the accident. She is still breathing hard when they arrive at Stembister House, Assisted Living Facility.

~

There are all sorts of silences, a great many stay in Stembister House: there's the silence of not hearing, deafness that cuts off the mind from stimulation and numbs the brain; there's the silence of boredom and waiting without knowing what's being waited for; there's the silence of day-dozing and medicated night-sleeping; there's the silence of remembering and wanting to go back.

Esther has become a connoisseur of silence.

She compares the silence of tea trolley wheels as it stops outside a very elderly person's room to the silence of a child's bicycle as it waits in the garage for its next ride—she can hear the subtle contours of quietness.

There are days when Ida Young speaks as little as her grand-daughter Esther Russell, yet nobody is rushing to give her flute lessons and get her talking. Marcus Macrae has not been paid to get this old granny making more noise.

Ida finishes her crossword and wonders if her daughter will come to see her today. She wishes she could get her window open a peedie bit wider. The smell of coal smoke reminds her of the back room and the cloth with embroidered roses draped over the sewing machine. They had a big iron kettle on the stove for filling smaller pots to make tea. She helped her mother serve it to the soldiers. George had been a searchlight operator, years older than she was, and handsome as the devil.

Her reminiscences are interrupted.

'Whit like the day, Mum? Esther's come by to see you,' says Kathleen.

Trolley wheels move closer, encroaching on the silence of the room.

'Would you like some tea?' says Helga, holding up a pot.

Her hands are reddened from early morning scouring. Kathleen declines for all and the trolley bustles away.

Esther takes the visitors' seat. She holds out her hand and touches the side of Ida's face. The skin is vellum soft. Ida's eyes are clear and untroubled by the wateriness that afflicts many of her peers, her cheeks rose pink. Today, her hair is gathered at the nape of her neck. George took joy in finding this area had particular sensitivity.

– I'm sorry for not coming.

The smell of coal smoke catches in Esther's nose; they smile, each remembering the stove.

'Is me dowter comin the day?' says Ida to Esther. 'She promised she'd come back.' She tuts at Kathleen fidgeting with her bedside arrangements, then says to Esther, 'Yir hair's gettin awful long.'

They sit together holding hands, while Kathleen fusses and turns the peace lily plant to get an even amount of light. The faded flowers on the lily are shedding their pollen.

'She wouldna cheust no come,' says Ida. 'I wis gaan tae spaek tae her aboot her fither. Hoo he'd stop fir tea on the way into toon with the other servicemen. She'd want to ken aboot that.'

Keep close watch

Holding Granny's hand I don't think about the lack of pills or the over-taking of pills.

'Hid wis the pictures an dances fir some, could hiv been dancin every night, but me and George just used tae walk. Mind, I wis too young to be takkin aroond. Cousin Winnie wis always ahead o me,' says Granny.

'She wis owlder,' says my mother, satisfied with her dead-heading.

'Aye,' says Granny. 'I wis young fir aal that. But sometimes you canna help whit you'll dae.'

She pats my hand.

Silence comes into the room, a thoughtful seeking into the past silence. My mother doesn't want it here.

'Will I get you a new paper?' she says.

'If there's wan,' says Granny. 'You ken most of hid disna mean much tae me noo. I don't ken the folk. How's the shop gaan on, Kathleen?'

– *Maggie's wrecking it. They've got no idea what they're doing. Dad's having to make half the things they need and he'd rather be fishing with his pal Willie.*

'They're pickin awey,' says my mother.

'Canno picter hid any different. Still mind the midwife comin when you and Elspeth were born. Mind on, she wis more bothered aboot tidyin the place than lookin efter the bairns. Wore on me nerves efter a while. George niver minded a cowld tea or things a peedie bit raffly. George didna mind, no really.'

– *I love hearing you talk.*

'The stations had tae build their own huts, the wind had them doon more than wance before they got them to stand up. Hid wis a cowld winter and they had no boots to begin wi.'

My mother sighs and starts seeking out more things to tidy. It takes effort to concentrate. The story is familiar, yet there are always new details.

'Winnie wis always one fir dances. She had a skirt to the knee and blouses with a peedie collar.'

Granny reaches up to the neck of her shirt and lifts the primrose yellow fabric against the crepe of her neck.

Helga pokes her head around the corner of the door.

'Sure you didna want tea?'

'Mum's a bit confused the day,' says my mother.

– Granny is actually here, you know.

'Yir no bad are you Ida? Ah'll be gettin you in fir lunch in a peedie while.'

– It's not even eleven o'clock.

She flaps her fingers up and down on my hand, it's all the frustration she can muster.

'Ah'm no wantin tae be trouble fir anywan,' says Granny.

– We have to go. I've an appointment.

I kiss Granny's cheek, breathe in the tea rose from her hair and skin.

– She doesn't belong here Mum. She belongs at home. You're letting Findlay and Maggie tear her world to pieces.

'It's no bother, Esther,' says Granny. 'My dowter will be comin after you've gaan.'

'Cheerio Mither, hiv a nice efternoon.'

My mother kisses my grandmother with a stoical smile, the same one she wears for choir practice. It's like a faithful coat. She doesn't have much variety.

Vertigo hits as we head down the corridor, my body can be too tall, too high from the ground. I have to pause and breathe by the activities noticeboard. It's covered with photographs of Stembister residents on a summer outing. A woman in a wheelchair stares into the sea as if it was as familiar as her own hand.

My mother takes my arm, stoical smile buttoned and ready to go.

– *Thank you.*

The corridor remains level on our way to the outer door. I lean my head against the glass and focus on a tiny speck of dirt while my mother wrangles with the keypad. I cling to the dirt quite happily, could've stayed all day, but we have to move on.

It's a short journey through town, past the construction site and new roundabout—there are about half a dozen on the island so this is indeed something for the council to be delighted with. There are no traffic lights here yet. No abrupt stop and go. Nothing like that.

In a line of low grey bungalows, a yellow rose is flowering against a sheltered wall, defying the wind, heedless of the declining year.

~

The surgery waiting room has a sign informing patients that over seven hundred minutes of appointments were missed last month. They have the same '*Coughing-for-three-weeks*' poster that they have in the chemist.

My mother opens a copy of the local magazine and points to a broad-shouldered man with an auburn beard, leaning on a tractor.

'I didna ken Melvyn had wan of those. Did you?'

He's a second cousin on the Slater side. We'd meet sometimes in Shopping Week. Melvyn could hold drink like a tanker holds oil and with the slightest excuse would jump, shouting like a lunatic, into Stromness harbour.

– *Do you mean the tractor or the beard?*

Things start shifting about again, holes appear through walls and when I look down my legs are too long. The window frames glow pink against the grey outside.

'Esther?' says a male voice.

– *You're kidding.*

'Whit like Doctor Copik?' says my mother.

Doctor Copik must be sick of my sweaty, pale face, but he smiles. When I'm balanced I wave my mother away and edge down the maroon corridor, like a dog following its master.

Nothing is said until he has guided me into a chair and the door of his consultation room is closed. Today, a mauve lambswool jumper confines his round body, topped with shirt collar and bow tie.

'If you are wondering,' he says, reaching forward and taking my pulse, 'I decide to be totally selfish.'

– *What are you talking about?*

The hand moves to my neck and presses gently, then an ear thermometer is taken up from the desk.

'I buy flights,' he says.

– *Flights?*

The measurement receives a satisfactory nod.

'For Stan, for his birthday, no expenses spared. He will come.'

– *I'm not going anywhere.*

He takes my hands and gestures for me to stand, then gently adjusts my posture.

'Double appointment next time,' he says. 'Today, we do what we can do. Now, sit. Be comfortable.'

His expression is open and attentive, even his moustache is eager and ready to listen.

I show him the pre-typed message on my phone.

– *I can't sleep. Is this all a dream?*

He nods.

'Temporary insomnia common, is in seventy-five percent of women.'

The tight angry feeling of not being taken seriously squeezes my throat. Tears come and I have to cover my face.

'But this is more,' says Doctor Copik more softly. 'This has been for a long time. Yes? The bad guy really is pain. I want to begin a new programme for you, Miss Esther.'

– *All I want is sleep. I don't want a new f–king programme.*

'I see all your prescriptions,' he says. He glances briefly in my direction, then continues, 'Gradual need to up dose is not from increase in pain. Body is not always friend.'

– *Please Doc, you gotta give me something more.*

'Today, I will give one week of Zopiclone. Take only half tablet before bed. Can start with even quarter. This is also medicine body gets used to quickly. Body does not know if it is in pain or no pain. It is a frog slowly boiling up in pan of water.'

– *What?*

'Body does not know the risk,' he says brightly. Then blows on his closed fist and opens it like a magician. 'Then boiled frog.'

The printer whirrs.

'Take exercise, eat, do normal things. Make appointment for one week time, double appointment.'

He pauses and twirls the end of his moustache.

'Maybe it is waste of money and he will not come. We will see. His mother will be furious.'

This makes him smile.

– *You're too generous.*

'Here is leaflet on pain clinic. Here is leaflet on voice loss. Doctor Carnegie will have already given, but I give again.'

He waits, easy in his chair, for me to take the pamphlets from the desk. I do not pick them up, instead I type a message.

– *I have a flute lesson.*

'Good. I think this will be important for you. I play the piccolo,' he laughs. 'No…no…is joke. I am better suited to French horn.'

Doctor Copik mimics playing, he smiles when I smile.

The prescription sheet is in my hand. When I emerge my mother is in conversation with the receptionist. She falls quiet as I approach and exchanges a look of forbearance with Agnes behind the desk.

'Looks like hid's another wan to try. We'll gae roond an pick this up.'

~

In the chemist, there's no one else waiting to be served.

'Whit like again Esther? This'll be a minute,' says Susie.

– *Go on, I'll have some Nurofen Plus as well. Treating myself.*

Hurriedly, she passes over a box from behind the counter. I pay in cash, stow the pills away then hold up my phone.

'I'll get her for you.'

When Claudette arrives I have a message ready. She reads then checks her watch.

'I have an hour. I will see you in the car park.'

I take my prescription package. In the car park I open the rear door of my mother's car and remove the flute from the parcel shelf.

My mother leans over so she can see my face, her lips in a solemn, straight line. The wind is out of her sails.

'Whit are you daen?'

I toss the new prescription onto the seat.

– *I will look forward to taking those at bedtime.*

I give her a dismissive wave and swing the door shut.

– *Go on. Get out of here.*

A hurt frown flashes before she hides it behind indifference.

We can't go on like this; she can't be included in everything and she's not the one who needs to see Marcus Macrae. Surely, she's got to understand this has to stop at some point. After everything she has done I still need more.

The silver car trundles away broadcasting disappointment. Slowly, I turn and walk over to the red two-seater.

Eyes wide open

Solitary moments are the best times. I quickly pop Nurofen from their foil: one, two, three, four, five...

They're swallowed down before Claudette arrives. She's in brown suede boots, wool coat and bright red lips. I make sure the Nurofen are tucked away out of sight.

She kisses me on both cheeks.

'Doctor Copik gave you Zopiclone,' she says, smiling.

She gets to know people inside out very quickly. Perhaps that's what I like about her, there's no need to explain. I just lower myself into her car.

Claudette nips out in front of a quarry truck and into the flow of lunchtime traffic. It would be a lie to say I am not frightened. My stomach feels full of stones.

On the square of grass at the top of Clay Loan a man is throwing a ball to his mongrel. It's an open patch of ground on which houses have not been built, even though they would have had fine views. Anywhere else would've been built on, but this is the place they burnt witches. The injustice has been acknowledged with a new stone. It is I, and people like me, who now haunt the community.

Claudette slides a vaporizer from her pocket and steers with one hand. The scent of aniseed drifts from the wisps of small grey clouds.

'I found out,' she says, 'more information about the bow, it was made by W. H. Hill.' She struggles with the sounds outside her native range.

'He and his son were bow makers extraordinaire. The sticks are Pernambuco, gold-tipped and the frog they call it, is ebony mounted in gold. They are prized. And expensive. One thousand pounds...more.'

Occasionally, both hands come off the wheel as she gestures.

Transfixed, I hardly move as we hurtle along, dazzled by her confidence. The car is swallowed in the glare of sun on road.

'They are strong,' says Claudette. 'And damage can be repaired. But it will be very expensive and only possible by an expert.'

She pauses, frowns at the road. We're about to pass where I nearly died and the cycle of panic begins. I have to come this way all the time—there simply isn't another road.

I smell aniseed when I return to the present, an olfactory hallucination that accompanies me like the smell of antiseptic leaving hospital. Claudette has a hand on my knee.

'Steady,' she says. 'Be steady.'

No one sees terror or insomnia or pain. People see scars, and the funny thing is they don't hurt a bit.

In the first few weeks after the accident, it was telling how visitors suppressed their instinct to make eye-contact.

For weeks, my father's gaze searched the hospital room corners rather than look at my face for more than a few seconds. He doesn't have my mother's stoicism. After all, making sure I would live was the priority. Then it was being able to walk. Only after that was my appearance important.

Claudette takes the turn up Smittler Brae to Pipersquoy. Nearby, an older track passes close to the shore then disappears over the lip of the dunes; large smooth stones run into the sand and finally give way to the frothing sea.

Claudette pulls up next to the Volvo. She tucks away her vaporizer and checks her reflection in the rear-view mirror, her fine, pale skin is hardly like a Frenchwoman's at all. I notice she has two freckles beneath her left ear that look like healed puncture wounds.

'You will be okay,' she says.

She waits patiently without offering help, then we walk together. Marcus Macrae is waiting in the open doorway. There is a smile this time, and clothing. Yet, he cannot disguise the effort it takes to be welcoming.

'Esther, good to see you. And Claudette, again.'

'Well, she doesn't drive,' says Claudette with a wry smile. 'Can we come in?'

The room smells of fish and chips and the grate in the fire is filled with scrunched-up balls of paper. In the corner there is a stack of freshly opened cardboard boxes.

'Not quite home yet,' says Marcus. He smiles and gathers up orange peel from the coffee table then looks for somewhere to put it.

She walks over to the boxes, peers inside and pulls out a stovetop espresso maker.

'I will make coffee,' she says.

'Aye,' says Marcus. 'Let's make a start.'

I press the silver catches on my flute case and begin to assemble the instrument as best I know how.

– *I think this is all a mistake.*

'No.'

He reaches over and stills my hands.

'We'll use the head joint on its own to start with. It's lighter.'

He opens his case. There is a slight pause and then he gently removes the most slender piece. It has a single raised hole that looks out like an eye.

'You can get a note without all the rest. Hold it up under your lip. And let your lips loose, kind of flopping down.'

I watch and imitate. The metal is cold and quickly becomes wet from the condensation of my breath.

'Lower. Aye, and blow softly, downwards. Watch.'

There is a faint echo from my flute. He demonstrates again, and produces a sharp smooth sound.

'Try again, pull up your head, er…pretend strings are attached here and running straight through your spine.'

– I don't have a straight spine.

'Try blowing harder, drop your shoulders. Watch me again.'

Air circulates through the six-inch-long silver tube.

His eyes focus on mine, his concentration relaxed and easy as he plays.

'Copy me.'

– I'm trying.

He leans forward and twists the mouthpiece slightly. I blow again. This time vibrations move through the tube. I try to open my chest and blow harder. The sound does not come.

My lips flounder, the muscles unused to receiving and obeying commands. They tremble and fidget, fighting against the tickling sensation of the vibrations.

'Blow,' he says.

– I'm blowing.

He leans forward to adjust the mouthpiece again; his scent carries, warm and musky.

– No shower today?

With that thought there is a moment of relaxation and my natural breath flows.

'Good. You're getting a note. Watch again.'

There is a clink of cups and Claudette mutters in the kitchen, '….pas une tasse propre… fainéant…'

Marcus stands and indicates without speaking that I should do the same.

– *I am not deaf.*

He goes ahead and I follow to the entrance hall. Light bends around the oval-edged mirror into a line of neon and orange rainbow. He indicates a position in front of the mirror where I should stand.

– *I just adore my reflection.*

We make eye contact in the mirror.

'This was how I was taught,' he says.

His chin is level with my eyeline, and for a moment I see a faint expression of uncertainty.

'Copy me,' he says. 'Relax. Stand tall.'

His lips purse forwards and downwards. I rearrange my position, pulling up, working against the instinct of my muscles to contract and protect. I grow an inch taller.

Marcus's gaze is intent on the contact my lower lip makes with the mouthpiece.

'Aye, that's it and if you can, not too tense here and this slightly up.'

He corrects the tilt of the mouthpiece, touches my elbow.

I catch his eye again in the mirror. Our bodies still for a moment and I find a natural breath. Then I lower my eyes and blow softly. I feel his fingers rest on my neck just where a necklace would sit, they move ever so slightly as if adjusting the position of a gold chain.

The note reverberates back through my body, tickling along my arms, running into my chest and then down my thighs towards my toes. His hand moves away. We make eye contact again in the mirror and we are two quite different people now, defences down.

Claudette walks into the hall, bringing two cups of coffee.

'I had to wash up,' she says.

– *I made my first note.*

Her gaze runs over Marcus and then me. Her expression shifts and softens, the muscles in her face yield and there is a small smile.

'I see you are making progress,' she says. She looks at us both, then turns and takes away the drinks.

Marcus leaves the mirror first. I lower the headpiece, and take a moment to rebalance. Gradually, the winded feeling eases, leaving me with the sensation of someone having looked right through me.

Ensemble

Away from the mirror I cannot repeat the performance. No matter how much I twist and reposition the mouthpiece the note will not come again.

'Have coffee,' says Claudette. 'Rest. Marcus play something for us.'

She leans back like a bored actress, legs crossed and coffee cup poised.

'On the flute?'

'Your bow is broken.'

His eyebrows knit together.

'I've another,' says Marcus.

It isn't the same—like a face with scars, still a face, still able to do the same things technically, yet it's not how it should be.

– *Don't worry. You're not the only one who took things for granted.*

Claudette makes a tutting noise on the roof of her mouth.

The same fingers that touched my neck find their place on flute buttons. Marcus lowers his eyes and stills his breath. A dimple appears on each cheek when he inhales. He glances up as if checking for someone else in the room. Then he starts to play.

The fingers dance over the silver instrument, but the music rises lilting and sweet. His right knee bobs in time with the beat, a tremor running though his whole body.

The sound is slow, vibrant and restless, and like no flute playing I have heard before.

His gaze is downcast, only occasionally does he look up as if searching for someone. He looks totally alone, trapped in some way. Perhaps it's the codeine making me see things that aren't there.

Claudette listens without showing any emotional involvement, nonchalantly lifting her coffee as a slow counterbalance to the tune.

The energy of the music compels my attention, running over and through me like water, sinuous and unpredictable. When Marcus stops the silence in the room has been transformed. It is rich and pregnant with grief.

Marcus swings the flute down and holds it vertically between his knees, head bowed, face in repose. It takes only a second for his breath to settle.

Claudette is watching him intently, her wrist bent supporting her head.

A brief silence falls.

Marcus taps the mouthpiece of the flute against his forehead. He doesn't speak.

'Dubussy? It is good, but...I prefer your violin,' she says.

– *You can be such a bitch, Claudette.*

He begins taking the instrument apart and arranges it on the black velvet of his case. There are greasy patches where the tubes have been rubbed with Vaseline so they slide together. When Marcus has packed away he stares into the grate.

'I need to go anyway,' says Claudette. 'Are you coming?'

Only when we are both nearing the door does Marcus move.

The mirror bounces sunlight around the entrance space. I glance into it so I can observe Marcus and catch his gaze running over my hair, neck and shoulders. We make eye contact and he abruptly looks away.

Unaware, Claudette frees the latch and lets in a gust of sea-tossed air. The breeze binds us together with cold.

'Practise,' he says as I leave. 'Try to hold the note steady.'

I nod.

– *That was astonishing.*

Claudette crunches across the stones and we climb into the small, fast, red car that cuts through the wind. There's absolutely no reason to linger.

– *Goodbye Marcus.*

Claudette must go back to work.

~

We leave the cliffs and Pipersquoy behind.

In the car, Claudette passes on what she has discovered whilst in the house.

'The second bow is very inferior,' she says. 'I was in the bedroom and there was a letter from a specialist repairer, Thomas Montcrieff. He has given a price for the bow to be

115

mended. Over two thousand pounds for shaft, tip and horsehair with correct materials. He will not guarantee the work at all.'

– *He hates the second bow.*

'He hates the second bow,' says Claudette.

The air is dry today, tractors bailing the fields to the north where Redland meets the sea. I hold up my phone, Claudette nods. She will take me home. She shifts down a gear then pulls out to overtake a tractor pulling a trailer full of grain. I flinch as it scatters onto the windscreen.

The morning shadows have shrunk away under the autumn sun. It's a brilliant sky that will leave cheeks rosy and tight, the fields are giving up their harvest as the combines work and the trailers carry away the barley.

There is a moment of equilibrium. Perhaps it's just the right amount of codeine, or perhaps the flute will save me.

The red car is quickly away from Skulstad, crushing the grains that trail along the roadside beneath its wheels.

With the flute case hugged tight to my chest I head towards the house. Findlay and Maggie still haven't removed the old posters announcing events at the Community Hall. The blind hangs crooked where the sweet jars used to sit.

Granny and Grandpa George used to go to Euchre evenings until he had his stroke. Afterwards, she hardly went out in case he needed her.

The air is green and sweet and I take a moment to look around and scan the wide sky above Willie's barn. The pain is at bay, I have Zopiclone and the hope of rest.

~

Inside it is darker, deader than outside. Particles of dust float softly through the hall and I draw them into my lungs. As I enter the kitchen, I see two paper bags both with the pharmacy logo, both open at the top.

– What?

The packet which held the Zopiclone is empty, and the Tramadol box is on its side, flaps open, nothing inside. Twenty-eight pills to be taken ONCE daily, gone.

Water has been splashed over the sides of the sink. When I step forward I see one of the blue and black Tramadol capsules trapped beneath the metal spider of the plug hole.

A sharp pain cuts across my throat.

– Maggie?

There's no one in the living room.

– Mum!

There's no one in the back corridor.

– Dad!

Then I hear children's voices outside, I throw open the back door and stride robotically towards George and Erland.

– Where are my pills? What have you done?

I grab each boy by the arm and pull them inside.

'Your haddin too tight,' says Erland, squirming to get away.

'Cheust show us whit you want,' says George. 'I'll get it.'

I propel them into the kitchen and point at the empty bags, the box, the bottle.

They stare dumbly. Still holding Erland's arm I grab everything from the counter and point for George to go through to the back.

'Hiv you lost them?' says George, rubbing his arm. His face reddening, tears welling.

'Let go, you're hurtin,' says Erland.

– Jesus! If you've taken them, you're going to need your stomachs pumped. I'll have to call an ambulance. How am I going to tell them?

Maggie is staring at where the sewing machine used to be, no doubt planning more vandalism. All around there is chaos, the room is torn apart. I push Erland forward and hold up the prescription bag then mime swallowing pills.

Maggie is quickly on her knees, down to their level. She speaks slowly.

'Boys, you ken you must never tak any medicine yourselves.' Both nod. 'Aunt Esther's medicine is muckle strong. You'll get a gey sore puggy.'

I know there will be bruises on the boys.

'Did you take any of these pills?' she says.

They shake their heads. I show her the empty boxes again. She turns back to the boys. George is all dark, swimming eyes and seriousness.

'Hiv you been playin wi them? Makin potions? We cheust need to ken. You'll no be in trouble.'

Erland's lip starts to wobble, his knees push down against each other as he sinks.

George starts to croak, 'Hid's no us. It wis Granddad.'

Flighting

'Show me,' says Maggie.

I swing Erland around, and he squirms free to his mother. We pass into the sunless back corridor. The painted concrete leads like a bloody path from the shop half of the building to the main house. The laundry cupboard is open, cleaning fluids that should be tidied away stand on the drainer by the sink. There is a thin acidic smell.

Through the window, strips of blue and bright green water and land are hard and fresh under the empty sky.

George points at the bathroom door. It's a solidly built affair made of thick planks with broad supporting diagonals. There's the sound of water flushing.

Maggie tries the handle.

'Is there someone in there?'

Silence. Then more flushing water and a faint scratching sound, movement behind the door. The boys' eyes are saucers, fixed on their mother. They shy away from looking at me and stay out of reach.

The door cannot be forced. There is a window outside that can be spied through and we go and peer into the narrow pane. An upward draught of wind catches in the nook of the building and sends my hair flying upwards.

Findlay's friends used to press their faces against the glass when I was in the shower. Sometimes, Findlay did it just on his own. Closing the blind is always important, you must remember it is possible to see through net.

I shield the light from either side with my hands so I can see past my reflection.

Three feet away inside, my father is working, applying the same thoroughness used to dismantle the lawnmower to emptying the foil pouches. There is a pile of capsules on the top of the toilet cistern. He sweeps them into his palm and tosses them into the bowl and presses the flush. He watches them disappear and then begins the next sheet.

– *What are you doing? Jesus! For Chrissake stop!*

I pound the glass, raging like an ancient queen powerless to deliver her kin from a death sentence.

'Who's there? Andrew?' says Maggie.

The boys sidestep, their eyes wary.

'Told you it wis Granddad,' says George.

119

'You hurt my arm,' says Erland, pettishly.

He starts to roll up his sleeve to show the marks to his mother, but she is not interested.

'Go and play,' says Maggie. 'Go.'

The sinews in my throat tighten. There's only one packet left.

Knock-knock-knock on the glass, I skin my knuckles.

The shadow in the bathroom moves and blurs, my knees turn to water.

– Somebody stop him.

Breath leaves my body and is barred from return, my head drops and I lean for support on the glass. The sound of foil tensing, snapping and tearing plays in my head.

'Why's he doing hid?' says Maggie.

There's nothing kind about her voice, just curious. She turns and looks towards the boys, thinking about the bruises she'll find.

I press my face against the window.

The last Tramadol pill.

– I can do nothing.

Scoop, flush.

Then from a faded overall pocket he pulls out two flat silver boxes. There's a pause.

He looks across at the window towards me. His workman-like expression wavers for a moment, my arms push hard on the glass.

The strips of pills are emptied and piled together, a white cairn on pink porcelain.

Scoop, flush.

– Bastard.

The second packet. Most murders are by family remembers, remember that.

– Bastard. Bastard.

Straight away I'm thinking about getting some replacements.

Maggie folds her arms against the chill, her body cooling after the effort of wrecking Granny's room.

'Everyone has thir limits,' she says matter of factly.

I go back inside and wait outside the bathroom door because he has to come out, and I hold onto the desperate hope of a U-bend, up-to-the-elbow-in-shit rescue.

The bolt scrapes, the door swings open and his determined silence bulges towards me.

– *That's my medicine. Mine. It belongs to me. I need it. I have pain. Every day. Non-stop. You have no idea what it's like to live like this. I don't sleep, I think my body has forgotten how. There's no time off. I can't get away from any of it.*

Tears roll down my face.

– *Do you understand? You f–king moron. They were mine.*

I can't breathe.

'Hid wis too many,' he says quietly. 'There wis a programme on the radio sayin aboot painkillers. An I mind on thinkin whit you're takin, an noo I ken that hid wis too many.'

– *It's my choice. My choice. Why d'you buy them all this time if you thought it was too many?*

'Then your mither cam back wi more that you got from the doctor. Pills not even allowed in some countries.' His voice hardens. 'Hid's too many. You'll do withoot.'

Splinters of anger condense and focus into a tight point of rage. It must have release and I must get away from him.

I stalk through the dim corridor back to Granny's room.

A crowbar is waiting. It feels exquisite as it swings up, the weight over my shoulder and then down hard on the counter. The top cracks. Vibrations rip up my arm into my shoulder then cut jagged down my spine.

Swing. Crack.

Into the wood, the place where she stood. Where she made bannocks and dusted shortbread with caster sugar.

Swing. Breathe. Swing. Crack.

She's so small now, left in Stembister. She nearly died too.

Swing. Breathe. Swing. Crack.

The patina of wear and human grease, cracking and cleaving, revealing the rude, white wood. I jam the crowbar down and heave, the wood tears upwards, sweat breaks over my back, tears roll on my face.

You gave Granny away and flushed my pills down the toilet.

Swing.

The needle-sharp hate, the nerves and the pain.

Swing.

Maggie and my father at the door.

Swing.

The sounds explode.

Open mouthed, they watch as if I'm stark naked. Because I am someone who does not move, who does not speak, who does not matter.

– Go on, stare.

I see them through strands of matted hair.

– See. Hear.

Breath flows in, angry and powerful, filling every part of me. It rises, up between my legs, through my belly and chest and then pours out through my mouth in a wall of sound.

– I cannot control the noise.

~

They cry and they plead, but there is no stopping me. Walls are slashed and raked, the counter scourged, the cold tap crimped over and its top sent flying free. The plastic pegs for drying cloths are so brittle they explode on contact.

There *will* be total desecration, no rescue for the room or the pills or for Granny. No rescue for me.

~

Eventually, I move into the shadows. My blood changes. The relief from violence begins to wane and the crowbar drops from my hand. I sink downwards, back against the wall.

My father stands sentinel in the corridor and the boys gawp as they are ushered past.

In the corner of the room, in the dark where the sewing machine stood, I see Granny Ida lying there bleeding. I don't know who I am anymore. I think I have become a monster, but I will stay by her side.

~

Light from the corridor cuts into the back room. It had acquired peace at sunset, it had become less desolate.

'Whit you daein in the dark?'

My mother has found my father.

The crowbar lies an inch from my leg, pins and needles pinch and flare in the numb flesh. The tangle of cupboards and panelling and torn down shelves make it look like a storm has ripped open the house. It is a sick and broken place that I do not want to see.

The light goes on, a bare bulb that glows white-green. My mother doesn't see Granny bleeding next to me. She doesn't understand the safety of the dark.

'Whit hiv you been daein? Whit's happened with yir fither?'

– *I'm not talking.*

'Fir the love o God, whit's wrong wi you girl?'

The voice isn't kind, isn't gentle.

A plastic wire rack still stands untouched in the corner of the room.

– *How did I miss that?*

I used to stack the birthday cards, I loved the cars, tractors, flowers and teddy bears. I used to spin it round and round, and often thought it was all the way round when really it wasn't quite there. There were strips of paper saying *Birthday* or *Get Well Soon* to indicate what sort of person you were buying for.

– *What sort of person are you buying for?*

My mother is asking questions.

From the corner I crawl forward then rise and stand, balancing on dead legs, reaching towards the stand. I push the plastic covered wire and it turns, smooth and light without the weight of cards. There is a soft squeak.

I like the way everything moves at once. There's no front or back, no getting back to the start or seeing something new, because everything is empty and I can see straight through.

The questions have stopped.

A hand is under my arm, guiding me away. My father is gone, Granny has vanished. My mother bathes my face with a warm cloth, she takes away my dust-covered clothes and leads me upstairs.

~

When finally I am left alone, the weight of loneliness is crushing. Every thought is bleak. There is no subtlety, no refinement of feeling, every action and every contact, every memory passes through a sharp black lens.

The silent minutes grow and I'm transported to an underpass streaked with traffic. I see a young woman stepping out into the road. It is me, face flat, cheeks soft, eyes dead ahead, staring through the blur of cars. Her face beautiful.

Her face beautiful.

Her face beautiful.

Dreaming man

The combines strip one field and then the next. It's the sort of night when Andrew Russell would like to go for a night walk then take a dram. He'll not go tonight though. He'll stay in the house and watch television with Kathleen. That's his life.

He can't undo what he has done, what he has washed away.

~

Meanwhile, Helga Gordon has finished her shift at Stembister House. There will be a hot dinner waiting for her at home. The horizon is blushing red to the west and twinkling with the coming stars.

The last visitor to Stembister House has signed out her name, Veronica Harvey. Although she is rarely called Veronica. She's usually Ronnie, but her father sometimes called her Alice, her middle name.

Veronica had hated it when the president of the country next door had the same name as her. That had been in the nineteen-eighties when she was in full swing, still swinging pretty well now for someone drawing a pension half a dozen years. There's never a dull moment with Ronnie around.

Being in the isles suits her well. She's noticed the stars, glimmering like fairground lights, tullimentan—that's what they call it here. They used the word to describe the anti-aircraft ammunition popping over Scapa Flow when all the guns were roaring, thousands of rounds spent in a matter of hours defending the precious fleet. She's read that Scapa Flow was better defended than London.

She has learnt a lot about the war and how it affected the islands and she's discovered that the scallops are a match for those in Vancouver Island, where she used to go on holiday as a child.

The familiarity that comes naturally to Ronnie does not come naturally to all. For James Pirie, who's been working behind the desk at the hotel this week, it's been a challenge to serve someone who seems so personally interested in him.

'I'll take a table in the restaurant tonight, James,' says Ronnie.

She smiles warmly, then takes out emerald-framed glasses and reads the menu on the counter. Her lipstick is bright, her teeth neat and white. It's one of the benefits of being brought up in a country that cares greatly about the colour and arrangement of teeth. Her father's teeth had been like old sails come adrift.

The glasses come down, her cheek rests on her hand.

'I had an eyebrow piercing once,' she says, noticing the inflammation on James's brow. 'Look carefully, you'll see the scar,' she leans forward to show him. 'It had to come out in the end. A doctor saw me in the street, stopped dead and said straight out, "That comes out today." You're meant to leave them for so many weeks, so I had just left it in, I thought the swelling was normal. But when he said that, well, out it came.'

James Pirie moves his fingers away from the ring in his eyebrow.

'I need to take some notes up to my room, will nine be too late?'

'No bother,' he says.

Ronnie casts another concerned look, then smiles and leaves.

Later, after sweet scallops and tender local beef, she retires to the comfort of the guest lounge with a dram, something recommended by the bartender. She has plenty to digest.

~

Later still, Marcus Macrae stands on the pile of stone chips outside Pipersquoy. Above his head a satellite crosses the band of the Milky Way. It's not helping with his earthly communications.

The wave of stars, caught together in mysterious beauty, fails to draw his eye from three short bars in the corner of his phone. They disappear one by one during his conversation with Steve at BlackHouse Media.

The call does not go well for Marcus. Steve is in a restaurant, heavy with background music and conversation.

'Yeah, since you're away and it's one of those things of being on the spot, you know Dougie's got big exposure after winning at Country Music. He's got that sound at the moment, it'll lift a tribute album to something new. Make it popular too.'

'What do you mean 'sound'?' says Marcus.

'And he's totally professional, gets the tracks down and knows what he's going to do technically right from the start. Did you know he's vegan?'

'Vegan?'

'Yeah, the scene's different now, a few years and it'll change again. Right now it's downloads and social media, making people feel connected even if they never go to a gig. It's totally understandable that it's not for everyone.'

'I'll come down.'

If anyone should play on Hendry Rolland's tribute album it should be Marcus—the bow Katie had broken belonged to the great man himself.

'How's the writing going? New album would kick start things. Something fresh, but referencing what you've already done, but you know—bringing it forward. Yeah. What? No you're breaking up.'

'Let's meet. When's the recording for Hendry's album?' says Marcus.

The line goes dead.

BlackHouse rides an award winner long and hard, squeezes out every drop, every guest appearance, every collaboration possible.

It's already happened for Marcus Macrae. Now, it's Dougie's turn. BlackHouse own his back catalogue and next album too. Only when it's written and produced will he be free, no agent or label to represent him. This need creates the perfect conditions for a severe creative mental block. The broken bow is simply the final touch. The way the bow balanced in his hand had made it part of him, directly connecting him to the music.

An ordinary listener wouldn't hear the difference with the 'other' bow, the sound would appear the same, but for Marcus the magic is gone, playing has become hard labour. The music is coerced. A sort of shame he cannot name fills him when he plays.

It's not simply about the way he treated his daughter, he should never have lost his temper, but it's linked to something else—an uneasiness about being authentic, about participation and desire.

If Marcus lifted his head and saw the tullimentan, the twinkling stars on petrol silk sky, maybe it might bring back a memory of the way Hendry Rolland used to play. The way he drew silken notes that spun into breaking storms. He'd remember Hendry's half-smile and little nod, the changes when you needed them, when you were ready for them to come.

Nothing makes Marcus look up.

Out to sea the Copinsay lighthouse signals, indifferent to anyone watching. Marcus does not want to become a lighthouse, he hasn't the strength. He scrolls through the pictures of Hendry Rolland's broken bow that he sent to Thomas Moncrieff and remembers a gig in Dublin where he got drunk and played badly, rather than going to his mentor's funeral.

When he'd returned and was on the way back to Inverness, Marcus had gone to see Hendry's widow and apologised for not being there.

'Hendry never planned,' she'd said.

They were in the den, the music room that ran the length of the house. She'd laughed, exasperated.

'What am I going to dae with all this? The boys dinna play. One's signed for Ross County, the other'll never touch a fiddle again noo.'

She'd handed him the bow.

'It's too much,' said Marcus.

He'd held the slim cylinder tightly, immediately impatient to try out the bow.

'He'd two nearly the same so it'd not matter if one broke.' She gestured to the wall. 'It should go back in a case. But I can't take it down.'

Her voice trailed off.

A Cooper Signature Violin, the belly rubbed to a shine, hung on the wall as if waiting for Hendry to hold it again, to raise it up and play.

'So many years of hearin that sound, and then it's no there anymore. Plenty of things make me think of him, but here when it's quiet like this—it all feels so empty.'

She'd looked around, as if searching for something.

'You'll put it to good use,' she'd said eventually.

'Aye,' he'd said.

She'd touched the bow case lightly, then had gone to make them a cuppa.

Marcus Macrae had stayed a while in the den. He'd looked over the awards, the pictures of Hendry with the best players of his generation, under purple, pink and orange stage lights. He'd died of a brain tumour. It'd all happened in a matter of weeks and Marcus had not gone to see him once. The thought of using the bow made his stomach flip. But he knew he would.

The bow had burned like a coin in his pocket in the back of the car. Helen had never had money, all her life, and it showed whenever she held expensive things. When she held the bow he'd told her how much it was worth and her eyes had glowed with glee.

It wasn't long afterwards that he began winning awards. She was persuaded to become Mrs Macrae, and then despite precautions became the mother of Katie Macrae.

He'd played with the bow on *Welcome to the Crooked Moon*. He'd pictured Hendry and borrowed his spirit.

Marcus Macrae slips down the pile of stone chips and walks along the clifftop searching for a signal. There's a cold breath from the shore where the sea idly rolls the kelp and stones.

When he finally finds a bar of signal he pushes Helen's number.

'Aye, Helen it's me,' he says when she picks up.

'I'm going to bed.'

She sounds sharp, and not in the least drowsy.

'Wait. It'll not take long.'

'Some of us have tae get up in the morning.'

The breeze ushers Marcus along the cliff path. He turns and looks down into the bay, a long, pale crescent strewn with boulders.

'How's Katie?' he says.

'Asleep.'

Helen has learned to give him no quarter, to blank the charm, to be deaf to the music.

'Yourself?' says Marcus.

'What is it you want, Marcus? I sent all your stuff on. There's nothin o yours here anymore.'

'What aboot Katie?'

'I told you, I'm gettin ready for me bed,' says Helen, her voice harder and emphatically less tired than before.

Marcus works a pebble free and kicks it towards the fence posts and the edge of the cliff.

'I'd a call from Steve about playing on a tribute album for Hendry. It'd earn something, everyone's heard of Hendry. It's ten years since he passed, and the songs deserve to be heard.'

'Steve actually called you?' says Helen.

She knows how to keep Marcus in his place. She's learned to cut through the bullshit.

'Aye. We were just on the line. It's a shame I can't be involved,' he says. 'Then it cut out. I'm having to walk about ootside to get anythin.'

'That's the isles for you,' she says. There's a short silence. 'So why aren't you goin? That's what you want me to ask.'

'It's the bow,' he says. 'The other's nothin compared to it.'

'Didn't it cost five hundred pounds? To most people that's not nothin.'

There's a loose post by his hand. Marcus rocks it to and fro, the wires ringing as they stretch and recoil. He thinks what the hell.

'I've money coming in from private lessons, booked for a wedding gig over in Westray, sooner I get the thing mended the better. I just can't write anything new until it's fixed. Can't play on the album.'

'Why d'you need a bow to write?'

'It'd only be a loan for a short stretch. Five hundred would go a good way, more if you can.'

'You're bloody havin me on,' says Helen.

'It's always ups and downs, you know that.'

'You've the bloody, barefaced cheek to be askin me for money.'

'I'd repay soon as I can. I'll set something up that's regular for Katie. That's what you want.'

'She is *your* daughter,' says Helen.

'I want to look after yous both.'

'No you don't. And I don't need you to look after me. You're bloody bollocks askin for money,' says Helen. 'I'm goin to hang up.'

'Don't Helen. Think of it as an investment.'

'You're on another bloody planet. You're lucky I don't tell her you're knocked doon and died.' Her accent becomes heavier, the pitch and tone becoming more extreme and the rhythm running like a railway train. 'She is four bloody years old and she broke the bow by bloody accident because it was left lying around.'

'Calm doon.'

'You left a hulkin bruise on her that lasted over a week. She never fell. You pushed her away. Didn't I bloody see you through the patio doors. You are a liar, Marcus Macrae.'

'I didn't mean to do it.'

'Well you did. And you're not bloody forgiven and you're not gettin any of my money again.'

'I still want to see her,' says Marcus.

The line goes dead.

He taps the phone against his head, tempted to hurl it over the edge.

'Forget I ever asked,' he says. 'Shite. Shite. Shite. Shite. Shite.'

He repeats the word over and over as he walks back to the house.

The flute is assembled on the table. It's been years since he really played, not since he studied for his last examination at university. Not since his mother died. He turns his back and goes into the bedroom and picks up his fiddle and the secondary bow. He begins with a polka, sliding into a reel, the start

132

of a set he's played on tour many times, but it's not right. He throws the bow away and plays pizzicato holding the fiddle like a guitar, perched on the edge of the bed.

Eventually, he lays it down and strides into the kitchen. He gives the dirty coffee pot a cursory glance then makes coffee from ancient granules that taste of gravy and scorched timber. He thinks about Claudette; was she another misjudgement? He thinks of Esther and wonders what might happen.

Marcus Macrae takes up his biro and his notepad, determined to write new songs, but all he can picture is a small, strawberry-blond girl with fair lashes concentrating on balancing Hendry's bow on its point. Sometimes things that seem strong can simply snap.

Take me to the river

Someone had been upstairs in her room. They'd typed 'Zopiclone abuse' into the search window on my laptop. The results weren't good.

– My father was looking for trouble. And he found it.

A giant black snake has appeared overnight along the length of the field to the back of Skulstad, the bales bound in black plastic where football was once played in the war. I heard the baler working through the night. I hear the farmers clock in and out.

I *used* to think it was magic, but I was just a girl then. I'd never even left the island and I didn't want to because the world offered me nothing.

Everything flipped when I went to secondary school. I joined in and swore friends for life and all that shit, but there was only restlessness to leave.

A light comes on in Maggie and Findlay's bedroom. My mother is at the sink filling the kettle for tea.

She hasn't seen that I am sitting in the driving seat yet.

A curlew flies over, 'Whaup…whaup.' Its curved beak ploughs a furrow in the air.

The low, hollow sound of kye protesting in the byre reverberates from Willie's farm. The sound drifts for miles if the air is calm. It's a fine, clear night, lines of clouds arriving slowly in the dog hours, glowing in the moonlight.

At three o'clock in the morning I'd emptied the bathroom bin onto the floor and checked packaging thoroughly for stowaways. I'd examined the kitchen plughole. I'd eyed the plastic U-bend and brought a wrench, part of me knowing they were already dissolved. Perhaps I could drink the water?

– *No!*

My parents had forestalled me. They'd even taken away the antihistamine and sea-sickness pills. At three in the morning I found nothing except vapour rub in the medicine cupboard. The remaining twenty-four tablets are gone from my jacket pocket.

The hand down the toilet is a low point.

The layers of junk have been ploughed into my room, but my father is a thorough man and there is nothing but empty boxes.

– *I used to be thorough. Well, I did my very best.*

Now I'm sitting in the driver's seat for the first time in a year, dry mouthed, fingers tapping the steering wheel, heart pounding pound-skip-pound, feeling light.

I am behind the wheel of my mother's car. The thought of driving makes me nauseous. The blossoming clouds are lowering, they can't help the memories they bring. I'm transported back to a year ago when heavy rain came from the southwest and the water stood in lines on the saturated fields. Combines sat waiting for the wind to come and blow the barley dry. The last lilies at the top of Clay Loan had been flowering—flowers planted in the ashes of witches last longest.

It wasn't a day of good news. Granny was sick with the Norovirus in Stembister, Simon was not answering his phone.

The argument with my mother started as I dressed for the launch. It had been coming for a long time. It condensed a great many things in my mind. Afterwards I had wanted comfort. I'd called Simon while I was driving and finally got through. Nothing I said did any good, his mind was made up, it was over. I'd been wrong when I thought in the end he would stay. I said my last words to him. They were not poetic.

'How can you fucking do this to me?'

~

My father is coming, in blue overalls. He pulls the door open and passes me a handkerchief to dry my tears. It smells of oil.

'Stop playin in the car. Yir showin the boys a bad example,' he says.

I'm numb from the cold because I'm only half dressed, but all the same I'm sweating hard. He looks at me more softly, then says, 'The doctor can't see you until later.' He lowers his voice and mutters, 'By then you might hiv broken the back o it.'

His face flushes purple.

I can't believe he used that phrase.

– *What happened to your smile, Dad? Did Mother take it? Did she find out what you were buying for me? Do you think I'm a fake? Dad?*

After I'm taken out of the car there's a period when nothing much makes any sense. I'm shut in the bathroom for a spell, then made to get into proper clothes. My hair is tied back from my face when I am sick.

'It wis too much fir her,' says my father.

I'm given a glass of water and toast. I tip the plate on the floor and there is a smash. None of it feels real.

My mother's pasted on a stoical face.

Granny is gone and there's screams and pleading, and then my father is angry and shouting and there's scalding water, and the steel brackets for holding up shelves cut into my hands when I grab hold and the plasterboard is kicked through where the range used to be and he drags me away.

The telephone rings and my mother leaves us.

Despite the chaos, she still strips out her Orcadian accent and we hear her say in her good voice, 'No bother at all. Suits just fine.'

It's called chanting, when the music of place is torn out of speech, that process of bettering and losing ourselves.

My father puts me in the car. He leans over and clips the seatbelt then places something black and hard on my lap; he lifts my hands and rests them on top to keep it steady.

– *I'm not a child.*

'You'll go in wi her,' he says.

'Aye,' says my mother.

'She'll be through the worst soon,' he says.

He bends and kisses me.

'The distraction will do you guid.'

– *Please don't send me away. I'll be good.*

There's Maggie watching up at the window of Grandpa George's room, and my father's wearing my mother's stoical expression as he steps away.

– *She must have a spare.*

She slaps away my hands when I try to grab the wheel. I curse her and try to unbuckle my belt and leave the vehicle, but there is a terrible lightness in my body, a restless, irresistible lightness as if I could float away and disappear if nothing held me down. I'm eager to be strapped in, but then I remember the prescription is in the car and start searching the pockets and I forget that it isn't yesterday. It's today. There was a night. There must have been, there just wasn't sleep.

Stubble gleams brightly in the dull morning.

–*I'm going where you take me again.*

My mother drives.

We're over the isthmus and going up the track. She slaps my hands again as I try to push the wheel towards the cliff edge and the sea. She's delivering me to Marcus.

This time when she parks by the pile of gravel chips she keeps her seatbelt fastened. I'm not sure what she is ashamed of most, the me that she sees or the me other people see.

– *I'm doing badly. I see the devil.*

'Hiv a guid lesson,' she says, as if nothing has happened. She hears what she wants to hear.

She takes out her phone from a 'nearly new' Peedie Hoose handbag. 'Ah'm gaan tae call to find oot hoo Granny is. She wisna hersel yesterday.'

– *Did you not see what happened in the back room? Didn't you see her lying on the floor?*

In silence, I tell myself to get out of the car, focus on the handle, then the window and the spiderweb in the wing mirror. I feel like I'm inside another woman who for some reason is struggling not to slip on the guttery slime of the concrete path.

– *Push it away. What's the point of saying anything at all?*

I know the door is solid, yet feel nothing when my knuckles hit. My hands reach up and push. There is the squeak of hinges and the door opens.

There are muddy shoes, dark from soaking up water next to bone-dry wellingtons. The oval mirror reflects my face, my eyes so bright their gaze pierces the glass.

The room is different, a chair has been brought through with a firm seat and straight back. The energy has changed. There is a holdall on the floor and a violin case leaning against the wall. Car keys and wallet wait on the table.

'I'll take the boat and drive down to Inverness, then get a flight,' he says, 'and join the session tomorrow.'

– *What?*

He moves quickly here and there, a flush on his cheeks from being outside. But there's something else too—excitement? Desperation? Like my nephews waiting for a friend to arrive or like watching a prescription dropped into its paper bag.

– *What is it? What is it about you?*

'So I thought you should come before I go.'

– *Going?*

Marcus looks downwards. He grips the sides of the chair for a moment, struggling with what to do next. When he looks up the brightness in his eyes is aimed straight towards me. An impulse I'm not quick enough to repress reaches out and runs between us. I had all but forgotten the sensation of desire—it's been so long.

– *I'm a mess inside.*

A sane person does not behave like I do, last night I could have killed someone. Marcus keeps his gaze steady.

'There's a chance of some work and I'll be away for a few days.' He speaks slowly, communicating more than the meaning of the words he says. 'I did something wrong and I need to see about it. Before I do anything else.'

I nod.

He turns away now and won't look at me.

'I can give you something to practise.'

I step forward and raise my eyes to his.

'You can't talk,' he says. 'Not even a word?'

– *What should I say?*

His jaw muscles are tight. We are pulled together by an invisible dark thread.

Without quite touching he passes a hand over my hair. I catch his scent and it cuts through the confusion and pain and holds my attention, then the feeling changes and becomes something sharp and strong.

He removes the flute case from my hands and slides it onto the coffee table then reaches out, his fingers brush gently beneath my ribs. I picture Claudette lounging across the rattan chair watching us.

I slap his hands away, then step forward and grasp his shirt with both hands and pull him towards me. I deliberately turn my head so he sees the scars. Then I release and push him away. His eyes darken.

– *You want this?*

In the bedroom, I briefly try to hold onto my clothes and then willingly, hurriedly give way.

Our foreheads press together, there is shame and fear. We are in the same desolate place. Yet we are breathing and holding, and searching. Together we find a way to give and receive.

Until finally there's stillness.

I release hold of his hair and his face tilts back, our foreheads separate and we see into each other's eyes. The hold on my wrists loosens. He does not kiss me, he simply holds my gaze. A gull calls overhead.

In the half-light, awash with sensations that blind my body to its cravings, silent tears roll. There's often salt in your drink when you're a woman.

– *I think it's relief.*

He holds me tightly. He does not apologise.

– *Or perhaps it's grief.*

I feel sleep coming, racing like a spring tide, the world dropping away.

Then there's a new sound. A small series of shuffles followed by a regular crunch-crunch, and the sound of someone muttering under their breath.

The arms that held me release and our bodies disunite.

– *Shit. My mother's coming.*

My mime to get the message across is effective. He grabs a towel from the end of the bed and is quickly to his feet.

'Tell her I was in the shower again,' he says. 'And you were waiting for me.'

There is a knock at the front door. I get to my feet and push him aside, hurriedly cross the carpet and lock him out of the bathroom.

Marcus whispers urgently for me to hurry. It takes half a minute to wipe myself down and pull on my underclothes, then I allow him inside the bathroom.

'I don't suppose she'd be very understanding,' he says, cracking a half-smile.

I shake my head and snatch up my jeans. I'm fastening the zip when I realise Marcus has stopped in the doorway and is watching me, his eyes examining the scars on my back. There's a change in his expression, a softening around the eyes.

– *Do you already regret?*

There's another knock at the front door.

Marcus shuts himself in the bathroom and I shrug on my jumper, flatten my hair and go to let my mother into the house. She'll hardly notice the added dishevelment of my appearance.

She stands in the hall, arms crossed.

'Could you no hear me? Whit are you daen in there? I couldna hear any flu'e playin. I'd hiv thowt you'd be weel underway.'

I gesture towards the bedroom. The sound of the shower is audible through the door.

'Agin? Hid's no professional. He wis the one that called to arrange.'

– *Who would have thought.*

She sniffs the air wafting through from the bedroom. I close the door and direct her into the sitting room.

I hold up the coffee pot and she shakes her head, but follows me into the kitchen. I knock out the spent grounds and begin to make a fresh pot, spilling the coffee. Claudette was more at home with the whole process.

My mother is examining the kitchen, mouth pursed, unimpressed by the backstage of Marcus Macrae's life, the whisky bottle at half mast.

– *If you think this is bad…*

I keep my gaze on the tarnished aluminium pot, so she cannot see my smile as the pressure builds and the coffee begins to bubble and spout.

That softening in his gaze, it means something.

'…disna look like he's settlin to stay.'

You always challenge my thoughts

When Marcus comes through he apologises for not being ready, his cheeks flushed. We begin the lesson directly. Under Marcus's guidance my fingers find their position on the body of the flute. The buttons warm quickly under my touch.

After another demonstration of how to shape my lips I produce a swooshing sound of air running through a pipe.

'Try again. Take your breath from down here.' His hand is soft, flat on my belly. 'And slowly release. Aye, let your lips… come forwards….and roll the mouthpiece back a fraction.'

This time there is a low whistle. He smiles.

'And your face, relax the muscles…no…not so much.'

There's another demonstration, he performs a trill that runs from high to low.

'Left foot forward and turning a little.'

There is a gentle pressure on my back to correct my position. He pulls away quickly.

'Sorry,' he says.

– *It didn't hurt.*

My mother watches more closely now, her interest piqued because I didn't flinch or show any sign of pain when he touched me. So different to her.

'Whit boat dae you take?' she says. 'We'd better no overstay. I hiv tae visit me mither.'

He shows me one more time. His gaze snags on my bare wrists as I lift the instrument. I sense his returning desire.

– *Steady.*

'Relax, turn this a fraction and…'

This time there is a sound, like the echo of water and wind, rolling inside a cave.

'Ah'd better gae you Esther's mobile number. So we're no turnin up unexpected,' says my mother.

I glance over to the violin case and wonder why he ever abandoned the flute. My concentration, hanging on by a thread, fails.

– *My time's up.*

142

A tremor is returning to my fingers, pins and needles rise like freezing water up my shins. The instruments are packed away and the lesson is over.

While my mother goes ahead Marcus and I hold each other's gaze for a moment in the mirror. There's frankness this time. No regret. But I am going to be driven away and he is going over the Pentland Firth.

Island life isn't for everyone and you, Marcus Macrae, are free to leave.

~

Once down from the cliffs we get stuck behind a slurry spreader. Its backside is covered in splatter, a brown dribble leaking from the rear pipe.

Either side, the ditches are a tangle of cow parsley and yellowing rosa rugosa with bright red hips. A breeze is shivering the hogweed stems and their umbrellas of seeds. Focusing on the details in the passing landscape can help control my fear of being driven.

– *Not always.*

The effect of being with Marcus is fading, the cravings return defiant. My body is a needy thing. I curse my father. Yesterday could have been a good day, it didn't have to end like that.

My mother fades in and out, 'Helga's run off her feet wae staff shortages. There's wan on maternity leave an wan wi the flu. Disna change the number of owld folk who need gettin up in the morning.'

As we round a corner the slurry tank is caught by a gust of wind and slews sideways.

'Granny wis wantin to gae oot yesterday,' she goes on. 'Started lookin fir her shoes an coat. Said she had a right tae gae oot if she wanted tae gae oot an said she hid an important person tae visit.'

143

– I don't think we knew what we were doing. We just did it.

'Muckle great wagon,' she says and turns off early to avoid Clay Loan.

It's after eleven when we stop in the car park of Stembister House. The engine quietens, there's a snap as the keys are pulled out.

The shaking in my arms and legs is back good and proper, making it hard to move. Weakness sweeps through my knees and my thoughts don't stick, swelling and popping, abandoning me. Small claws scratch away inside my skin.

I'm leaning on the concrete wall while my mother's fingers interrogate the keypad, scampering here and there on the metallic buttons over and over again, until finally there is a sharp click.

– Press, press, press. Until you get it right.

A trolley of plates with metal lids is being pushed by Agnes Bain. She has the frame of a bird and is older than many residents.

'They're through-by in the dining room,' she calls, slackening her pace momentarily.

'Mither's no daen so weel,' says my mother.

'Least she kens whit day hid is,' says Agnes.

She gives me an old-fashioned, top-to-toe looking over.

'No improvin isn't she? Whit a shame.'

She shakes her head and moves on, my mother following the trolley.

I delve into my pockets, searching.

– I could have sworn.

My mother stops and tuts.

– You've taken everything.

I lean heavily on a table already burdened with a huge pumpkin with a face drawn on in marker pen. I control the urge to wreck the whole f–king Halloween display.

144

'You canna stop there,' says my mother.

She takes my arm and leads me though the fire doors. The cooking smells fade, instead there are human smells masked by floral air freshener. I don't mind this so much, I'm rife with human smells. She leaves me at the door to Granny's room and heads back to the dining room to find her mother.

There is an ensuite and I shut myself inside. The walls are green and the suite is white and the room is lined with hand-rails at every possible height. I take a pee and tidy up more of what Marcus Macrae left behind.

It's been months since I menstruated, this is not a fertile body, not like the chalet girl.

– *Ooh là là.*

The bed is made, ready any time of day because you don't know how early night will come or how late morning will be because of the staff shortages.

– *They're doing their best.*

I push off my trainers and curl up on my side. My teeth won't stay still, so I let them run on and listen to the clattery noise like beads rolling. I stare sideways out of the window and scheme.

I could search the other inmates' rooms while their occupants are at lunch. There's got to be plenty of sedatives in a place like this. Granny's not on any medication except iron supplements. Her only other occasional need is prune juice. I suppose I could do with some of that as well.

~

The rose-scented warmth of the room works as a time machine. It takes me back to being curled up on Granny's knee when the shop closed on Wednesday afternoons. She'd let me sit with her if Grandpa George was sleeping. I'd clung onto her skirts to keep her downstairs and away from him whenever I could. But there were times when it'd make me feel warm inside that you could love anyone like that. And it made me proud that at least I came second in her affection—honoured in fact.

My eyes close.

There's peat smoke and pancakes frying on the griddle, sour cream and rhubarb jam. Granny's telling a poem. Poems and bible verses were her stock of stories, her schooling hadn't been regular towards the end, disrupted like so many things by the war. Before the war was over, Grandpa George had been sent away because the radar came and Granny had gone back to school.

Her voice was strong and low, and she could sing on and on without ever tiring.

We are reaping sings the farmer,
We are reaping golden grain,
We are reaping for the garner,
and to keep the groaning wain.
We are reaping, reaping, reaping,
We are reaping golden grain,
We are reaping clicker-icker-icker-icker,
We are reaping golden grain.

The lines were sprinkled with words I'd not understand. She had a habit of cutting dialect out of politeness to Grandpa George. He was an Englishman and didn't know the meaning of Orkney words. She tried to speak more like him to make him feel at home. She's slipped more to dialect since he died and she was moved to Stembister House.

The memories pull away, cold steals over me and I pull the covers tight over my ant-infested skin.

– Everything is falling.

Dark shapes loom close, becoming colossal cities of blackness that slide away then mass together until everything is blocked out. A void spreads over me and there is nothing to cling to and the heavens split open, and the angels are silently falling.

~

'I didna say I wis unweel. Helga canno help busybodyin aroon. Never could, even as a bairn,' says Granny.

'But who's the buddy comin tae see you? That's whit I want tae ken,' says my mother.

The conversation trickles into my consciousness. I picture gulls mobbing an old woman throwing Tramadol onto the water at the Peedie Sea.

Eyes open a crack; I can see my mother turning the peace lily.

'She told me aboot the waddeen on Westray,' says Granny, angrily. 'Ah'm I no part o the family noo?'

She goes to her chair by the window with slow, angry steps. I feel her gaze run over my body.

'An yin lass is no gettin any better. Aal this fuss aboot her spaekin. Disna matter if she disna spaek. Hid matters if she's happy. An plain as yir face, she's no happy.'

My mother clears her throat to answer, but says nothing I want to hear.

'She's no weel the day,' says Granny. 'Poor lass.'

I slide out my phone and type I NEED TO SEE A DOCTOR.

Granny leans over and reads.

'Aye. When are you takin her to the doctor?' she says to my mother.

I type again. THEY FLUSHED MY MEDICINE DOWN THE TOILET.

'Mercy, whit were you thinkin Kathleen?'

'She wis takin too many. Andrew couldna stand it.'

The phone slips from my fingers to the floor. A black look is passing from Granny to my mother, who's picking the phone from the floor and pretending not to notice her own mother.

'You've a message,' says my mother. 'Marcus Macrae.'

I pull myself up on the bed, snatch the phone from her hands then get shakily to my feet.

'Canno be aboot anythin important,' says my mother, eyebrows up.

I read quickly, '*No regrets. See you when I get back. M.*' I tuck the phone away. There's a second message, sent straightaway afterwards. '*Pls.*'

'You ken, he's givin her the flute lessons.'

Granny responds by looking out of the window and tapping her fingers on the arm of her chair. She wants us to go now.

– She's entitled to privacy too. And she might not want her f– king plant pot turned all the time.

Lightheaded from moving quickly, I lean on the bed. Granny waves my mother away then stands to kiss me. She takes my hands in hers, squeezes affectionately and looks me in the eye.

Despite everything, I can't help smiling back at her. I have an intuition she would understand about Marcus. About passion.

'Come past soon,' she says.

My mother takes my arm and guides me like an old woman along the corridor.

The keypad is totally unresponsive now. Short of patience I push on the outer door and find it isn't locked at all and walk out ahead. As I step into the swish of wind and rain it occurs to me that I know nothing about a family wedding either.

The dragon

When I was the woman driving in the dark I didn't think about pedals and gears, control was as natural as breathing.

Today, defining natural is more complicated.

– *Thanks Codeine.*

Houses join and break, cliffs with window eyes and door mouths. I'm brought to the medical practice where performance brings pills—well, it always has done before.

The pots of lobelia and fist-sized geraniums by the door have been burned up by the wind, the luminous blue fading, the red velvet petals crinkling, wet and dark. I lean and gather the strength not to faint.

As she waits, my mother is tapping her toe with impatience.

– *Don't worry. They'll see me, I'm a regular.*

Waiting rooms have a lot of information, little fact lifebelts to keep people afloat. Did you know: *ninety per cent of coughs and colds cannot be treated with antibiotics; you could be the only person who stands between her and another emotional bruising; and the Nordcare Sexual Health Clinic will be running Saturday morning 10.30 -11.30.*

There's one notice that bothers me.

It says in plain typeface, 'Repeat prescriptions cannot be picked up on the same day. The pharmacist can issue emergency supplies.'

– *They are all liars.*

What was it my father flushed down the toilet? Has he got my pills hidden at home somewhere? Did he steal them? Did he take them?

– *What do you do all day in the workshop, Dad?*

My mother is reading *Woman's Own*, smiling at a mac 'n cheese recipe.

– *Why do that to me?*

I get the sensation of being under observation and I realise my name has been called. Doctor Copik is waiting.

I pinch away *Woman's Own* and push my mother's elbow.

– *You have to confess.*

When we are in the examination room Doctor Copik prissily rearranges the chairs and makes sure we are comfortable before he sits down, his eyebrows rising to small peaks.

Of course it's my mother who speaks first.

'She's been takkin twa-three Nurofen every morn and night on top o that Tramadol. An when my husband fund oot you'd given her more pills it went doon badly. The deil took had o him. Doon the pan they went.'

Her tone is as if she is returning faulty goods to the electric shop. Doctor Copik nods.

'They're aal flushed doon the toilet. So we're come here to git some more.

One of Doctor Copik's eyebrows raises slightly higher. He places his fingers together tip to tip.

'Let me show you picture of Stan,' he says. 'Has funny hair and is very slim, but is not bad looking I think.'

In the photograph there is a young man dressed in black. He has almond-shaped brown eyes, full and slightly feminine lips, and a long bleach-blond fringe swept to one side.

Doctor Copik turns the photograph back to himself. A small indulgent frown creases his brows.

'I send flight tickets,' he says. 'I have a big fight with his mother on the telephone.'

At this he smiles broadly, then props the photograph back up against a bottle of hand sanitiser.

'To take too much or stop medication is both dangerous,' he says. 'Please, write what you have taken in the last twenty-four hours for me Miss Esther.' He passes me paper and pen. 'You may go now,' he says to my mother.

When the penny drops that she's being asked to leave, she looks like she's swallowed an egg. To make it clear Doctor Copik stands and opens the door for her, she leaves as if bungee cords attach her to the wipe-clean chair.

'And try to keep devil out of husband.'

– *Thank you, Doctor.*

I reach forward and take up the pencil and scrawl '0' on the paper. The room starts to dance and heat surges up to my face, I flop forward, arms on the desk, head heavy as hell.

Fingers press on my wrist.

'Danger of stopping absolutely. Feeling flu symptoms, confusion, joint pains these are coming now. Pulse is racing. '

– *Why aren't you being kind anymore?*

He points at the zero on the notepad.

'Nothing is very small,' he says.

He waits, black eyes serious.

I shuffle the pen into my fingers, summon the energy to write, 'Nurofen Plus, 11.00.'

'Was yesterday?'

I nod.

'Was how many?'

I hold up eight fingers, then my stomach heaves. There's no vomit and I roll back up into the seat. My neck feels so thin and my head so heavy that it feels in danger of rolling to the floor.

Doctor Copik is leafing through a book. He runs his finger down a page.

'Father did not like Zopiclone?' he says. 'Has bad reputation, but can be very helpful for you. Small doses. You were on sensible medication,' he sighs. 'Codeine is the worst addiction, and

151

ibuprofen gives you bad stomach, bad for heart. And I tell you before, is important to eat more.'

The room swings and all I want to do is lie flat. I have a vision of my limbs moulded on a bed of warm wax. The wrinkled paper on the couch is not as inviting as Granny's bed, and even with the help of the giant steps I would never make it.

My hands slip and dangle.

Doctor Copik leans forward, his voice softens.

'This is worst time. Body missing codeine, can be very bad. I can give Valium to help with withdrawal and anxiety. I think we need make new pain management plans. I *can* give Tramadol again and you can taper from codeine more slowly. But is hard keeping to the regime for you.'

– *I am not a tapering sort of person.*

He twists the wedding band on his finger.

'I will refer you to the community mental health team.'

He says this seriously, but without enthusiasm.

'They have also addiction team, but you are not in mood to hear new plans. And suffering, I do not like—unless is my wife. You see I make a joke,' he pauses, 'But is not right time.'

The printer starts to whirr.

– *I'm going.*

– *Really, so soon?*

– *This is new.*

– *Two voices.*

Who wouldn't do all they could to be pain free? Even for a few moments, so they could rest, anything just to stop drowning.

– *When will they realise nothing works?*

'If we were in big town with many clinics we could find something better, but you have good home. Explain to your mother these pills are for symptoms of codeine withdrawal. Tell father they are for only one week. Also I will see you tomorrow. Make appointment.'

I shake my head when he offers me the prescription.

The mob in my head goes silent, their swimming eyes willing me to run back down the old path. They have no sense of delayed gratification. It seems only a matter of time before they are left in charge.

'This is worst time,' he says.

– *I'm losing the battle doctor.*

Tears run down my cheeks.

And I wish, at that moment, for another dose of Marcus Macrae. Not romance. God, not that. The other. And I remember how it was with my wrists held tight, and I want it again—to be held like an audience, cupped in the palm of his hand.

The thought has strength.

I lever myself out of the sour imprint on the chair. Doctor Copik reaches out and gives me his hand.

– *I showed someone my scars.*

'Take this,' he says. 'Have on standby. Please.'

Sweat breaks over my shoulders as he steadies my arm. The folded piece of paper slips into my back pocket.

– *Can you at least tell me if the pain is real?*

He doesn't answer.

We walk through the blood-pink corridor to where my mother nods approvingly into her magazine. Disappointed, she nonetheless takes my arm and passes a few words with Doctor Copik. The receptionist sighs heavily as we pass her screen.

– *Go to hell.*

Outside, I feel malice seep from everywhere, from the dying roses, and the chimney-pot-perched, recalcitrant gulls.

The engine of the car is switched off.

'Whit are you bein treated for noo?'

– I really can't explain.

'Hand me that prescription an Ah'll get hid. Ah've got to gae in the Peedie Hoose fir an oor. Bridget has got an appointment in the optician and Leslie canna help because he's shifting kye. You can wait in the back a spell.'

– No, I cannot wait in the back with those sacks and that smell, and seeing Granny's clothes mixed in with all those other clothes, the dead people's and the unwanted people's clothes. I cannot.

I'm shut in the car. A shiny sarcophagus, a tomb for babies and dogs when the sun shines. We're spared from that in Orkney.

Curled up, knees to chest, I hold myself ball tight while the rain pitters and patters, and clicker-icker-icker and pitter-pat-ter-patter

and clicker-icker and pitter-patter

and the groaning wain.

There's a muffled voice and a clink. Fingers press against my neck. The hair over my face is moved aside.

A woman with a French accent speaks.

'She will come with me now. You see how close I am. This is my car.'

My knees are eased down and swung out of the car, my arm placed over someone's shoulder. The asphalt is dotted with chewing gum.

'She is not heavy,' says the woman. It is Claudette.

– Help me.

There is a readjustment, my feet must try to take steps.

'I didna ken you wur freends,' says my mother.

'I will watch over her this afternoon,' says Claudette. 'If you please open the door.'

Gravity sucks me down and they place me into the low red vehicle.

– Are you kidnapping me? Why do you want me? Throw me away.

This drive I do not see at all.

My head lolls on the seat belt strap, eyes closed and I'm falling, falling all the way, sliding to the bottom of a great ship that's rocked by wave after wave, and I'm surrounded by the calls of whales begging for mercy. They're so close, the barrier between us so thin. It would be better to join them than to keep listening to the dreadful echoes of their calls. I feel myself suffocating in the deep, hot spaces of their bodies.

'It's okay,' says Claudette. 'Ssh. We are nearly there.'

There's a monstrous groan, the bull whale has been punctured by dozens of harpoons, the sea is frothing red and the desperation to live has turned into the desperation to die. The bounty is driven from the sea onto a Westray beach. The sea is silent.

'Sssh.'

– There is no ransom.

Lying in Skulstad

There are blanks. Yet they pass so quickly that I'm robbed of their moments of emptiness. A man is there and helps me upstairs, there are pauses and silence. There is strong emotion and hard breathing.

Claudette speaks, 'Thank you Andrew. Yes, please bring some soup for Esther. I am not hungry.'

'Aye,' he says.

Footsteps, a pause, and then the warmth of a hand.

When I open my eyes I recognise the spots of lichen surrounding the Velux window. There is still splatter across the glass. Claudette reaches up and pushes the bar to release the window.

– No, I'm cold.

I curl up tighter and pull at my coat. Claudette slips my mobile phone out of my pocket, but she does not get me a blanket.

'You have another message from Marcus Macrae,' she says. 'Shall I read it?'

I nod.

'Back on Friday. Text if you want a lesson. Can do Sat am. Okay?? Marcus.'

The smell of apple and cinnamon and glue fills the air. When I turn my head Claudette is in a cloud of vapour, her thumb tapping out a message on my phone.

– What are you doing?

Not in a fit state. I am not in a fit state to fight.

She blows out thoughtfully, brightness in her eyes, then slides the phone onto the desk. Now she comes over and folds the duvet around me like a nest.

'You don't want to be worried about him today,' she says. 'He may know how to satisfy a woman—but what else does he know?' She folds her arms. 'The woman in Inverness, his wife, he does not, did not treat her well. Or his little girl. Yes, he has a daughter. He loves her of course.'

She's peering through the rectangular slit of the window. The view crosses the old shop forecourt, over Willie's barn and to the fields beyond. She goes onto tiptoe and presses forward to see more.

– Don't fall. It's easy to lose your step.

'I can see Hoy,' she says. 'So this must be facing north, no I lose track. In my town there is simply a river. You cross from one side of the bridge to the other. Here water is everywhere.

'"*Everyone Welcome*" that's what the sign says for my town in France. But it is not true. They need to forget about me,' she says. 'They live, but they have no life. Eh? My parents already are asking if I will be home for Christmas. How can I go home?'

– *What was that you just said?*

She turns her head and says, 'I need to see a map of the island.'

A moment later she steps back and closes the window then begins to rearrange the room, bringing the easy chair next to the bed, unplugging the laptop and moving the lamp nearer. She gathers the garments scattered around the room and creates a mound of clothes that reminds me of Maeshowe.

When my father comes up she asks for cardboard boxes.

While I take small spoonfuls of soup she clears photographs and piles of leaflets and magazines from the desk and shelves. Beneath every layer she finds empty silver boxes, their contents fledged weeks ago.

Tendrils of leek tangle and slide in my throat. I gag on the softness. This isn't what my body wants.

'Be careful…slow.'

She comes towards me, wipes my chin.

– *What the hell are you doing? Get off me. Get off me.*

When my father returns she gives him the first filled box and requests a cup of hot water with sliced lemon. She also asks for a basin of soapy water and cloths.

– *A blanket bath?*

She ignores me and keeps working, going through every drawer, every pocket. Soon only one photograph is left on the wall. It is of me at my final year at university. There is something bright and garish about the young woman, she has an air

157

of Susie Gordon. Claudette picks it up and examines the image more closely.

'This does not look like you,' she says and walks back over to the desk. 'And you are much too old for, what do you call them? Snow globes?'

She drops both into a box, smiles at its fullness and then comes over.

She loosens the duvet around my shoulders, then runs a hand through my hair.

'I have standby Valium,' she says. 'If this is too much.'

She stands up.

'Now, your clothes. This is essential.'

Each garment is held up and examined before being discarded. As Claudette works she talks. Her soft accent rolls words together like waves that meet in the corner of a bay.

'My mother's house should be a museum. She has so many old things, antiques—"brocante" we say. Everyone in the family gives their old things to her. "Oh," they say, "Antoinette will love this, she must have it when we move," or "You always love old things, and that sideboard must have a place, it is a hundred years old." They are brought in like the stray cats our neighbour Madame Crébor feeds across the street. At least the cats catch mice. Eh? My bedroom is full of lives people want to forget.'

She holds up a mauve shift dress that I once wore for a wedding. There hadn't been much chemistry between the bride and groom, although plenty was floating about elsewhere. I think he died in a diving accident while I was in London. My mother said the funeral was well attended.

'This is a crime,' said Claudette.

She holds the reproduction sateen against herself, shivers in revulsion, then drops the dress, hanger and all onto the floor.

~

I remember Marcus. Blood rushes to my cheeks and I pull the covers and hide my head. Not because of embarrassment at the memory of what happened, but because I feel overwhelmed that he might think of me.

– *Don't think of me like that. Think of me well.*

'If you do not help, don't blame me,' says Claudette.

More hangers rattle to the floor.

The floor creaks as she steps to and fro and when I next raise my head the back of the wardrobe gapes back at me.

Claudette is tossing things out of drawers, muttering under her breath.

– *Stop! Go away and leave me alone. I've had enough now.*

She doesn't hear me, so I reach out, grab, aim and throw.

The cup hits the edge of the drawers and rebounds onto the side of her cheek. There's a cry of pain and then French curses fill the air. I'm crying too. Shaking.

– *You didn't stop.*

She scoops a discarded shirt from the floor.

– *You're too much.*

There's a purple swelling on her cheekbone, a narrow bloom of violet where the edge hit.

– *It's my life on the floor. You're throwing it away and it doesn't mean anything to you. You're packing my life into the sacks and boxes like they get at Peedie Hoose, where the clothes of the dead mix with the living and the simply worn out. And no one will even remember that I've worn that. No one will think, 'Oh, that was Esther's. She used to look bonny in that.'*

There are footsteps on the stairs. The door opens. My father does a competent job of covering his surprise at the mark on Claudette's face.

'Do y' want a hand?' he says.

'Thank you,' says Claudette. 'Some frozen peas. And black rubbish bags.'

He starts to come over to the bed then flounders. Much as he hates it, the invisible wall is still there.

'Ah'll bring some tea,' he says.

'Coffee,' says Claudette.

'Aye.'

When he's gone she comes over and sits on the bed. She raises her legs and leans back on the wall by my side. The injury is superficial, yet may result in a black-eyed pharmacist for a week.

'Sssh,' she says, and brushes the hair from my forehead. 'I still have a beautiful nose.'

She smiles and traces a finger along the spine of her long, straight nose, then does the same on mine. Few people would comment on the beauty of something so aquiline. I see the joke.

She speaks again, her voice intimate, her accent more pronounced.

'The men here,' she says, 'They are so similar to your father. They are mysterious. Truly, I cannot believe that they ever speak more than a few words at a time. It's like the landscape, so few trees. Everything is beneath, but how do you know what is there? And if you cannot talk to someone, how can they know what you feel? I mean what can you say to these men? And if there is confusion, that's it, you're finished.'

I lean against her, flinching as my vertebrae shuffle. She continues, 'Yet, when I walk past the pubs I want to go in and speak. But can you imagine?'

She pauses. Silence settles like a crow in the corner of the room. The question rests.

There is the pop-pop-pop of shooting over the water, geese rise from the fields of Redwall.

~

On the desk my phone buzzes.

– Marcus?

'So,' says Claudette. 'You had him.'

I nod, tears come to my eyes.

'With your mother waiting outside?'

She lowers her chin, looks at me sideways then starts to giggle. It is a high, sweet sound like a girl's, not at all what I expected. The side of my lips begins to twitch.

'I am glad,' she says.

The empty surfaces shine. There is febrile rioting inside my head, an echo of the past, and abruptly I have the urge to tip out the carefully packed boxes and search for survivors. All Tramadol must be saved.

When my father returns Claudette is restraining me.

– The problem is my lack of strength.

Seeing him enter I slump onto the bed.

Claudette is presented with a mug of coffee resembling a muddy puddle, an undissolved granule still swirling on the surface. Tea is passed into my hands, they tingle so badly that I can't tell if the cup is scorching or freezing.

'I will stay tonight,' she tells him.

'Kathleen'll be home soon.'

'I booked another flute lesson for your daughter,' she says.

– You did what?

'Careful. You are spilling your tea,' she says to me. 'Marcus, he will help her. One way or another.'

– I could kill you.

'Aye,' says my father. 'Kathleen believes in it. She's tryin everythin.'

'And your daughter is enjoying herself.'

He smiles uncertainly then retreats to the door.

'Thank you for the coffee. It is very nice.'

Doon the shute

The whine and drag of the wind has been playing on Kathleen's nerves at Peedie Hoose. Not proper hard wind, just middling, bringing light showers but no downpour, enough to colour the earth, sea and sky a darker shade.

Plenty of money goes through the till and the bags of donated clothes multiply like rats in the back room. Kathleen thinks her daughter should be here, not be at home alone with that French pharmacist. Why is she so interested when Esther never gives anyone cause to be?

'Friendly kinda buddy, that American,' says Bridget, interrupting her thoughts.

She's taken off her coat and is ready to take over.

'Canadian,' says Kathleen, absently. 'Pulled oot near enough every scarf. Said hid wis cowlder here than she'd imagined.'

'Not many can carry off that pink,' says Bridget.

Kathleen doesn't reply to this.

'Ah'll make a cuppa?' says Bridget, sensing she's said something wrong, but not knowing what.

There's two people in the shop, part of a cruise ship crew that's docked for the day. They're passing comments in Filipino and working their way through the curtains. They make careful choices even though everything is less than five pounds. Nearly new leather coat, still no more than five pounds. Designer evening wear, three pounds fifty.

Kathleen thinks they should price higher and said so once. She won't again, not after Bernie got all high and mighty with her.

'Ah'll tak hid here,' says Kathleen. 'Then I must be away hame.'

The Canadian woman had asked her opinion about all the scarves she'd tried around her neck, it was for staying warm on a trip to Westray.

'Nothing special for you. But it gets me excited just the same, boat travel always does. You know the staff at the hotel have been so helpful making arrangements. They're just so nice over there and they told me about all the good work the money raised here does, so I had to come over and have a look.' She'd leafed through the newcomer scarves to the layers beneath and pulled out a gauzy primrose number. She'd held it up to her face. 'You're right, I can never pull off yellow. Green, yes, but yellow makes me look like a ghost. You'd be the same. Not that you don't have wonderful skin. You can hardly believe the age of people here. What am I saying, now how about this?'

The woman had held up a voluminous fuchsia scarf with silver-grey detailing. She'd pressed it to her face and smiled.

'Feels like silk.' She'd checked for a label. 'I feel bad having it for so little.'

The woman had pressed a five-pound note into Kathleen's hand and insisted she keep the change. I suppose, thought Kathleen, if you're staying at the hotel, then you can afford to pay more.

The sports car parked at Skulstad makes Kathleen draw a deep breath. She exhales slowly, and becomes battle ready. As soon as she finds Andrew he is thoroughly cross-examined by look and word.

~

Meanwhile, Marcus Macrae is off island, heading south. Caithness is drizzle-swept from the east, the moisture soaking into the rusty peat beside the road. An hour further down the A9 in Sutherland the trees are losing their green, and circular hay bales stretch like an architect's dream across the fields. After a hairpin curve, where tragedy once threatened a bus full of children, the firth opens up before him and soon he's over the bridge and onto the Black Isle.

The A9 courses towards Inverness. Marcus crosses the Kessock bridge and breaks from the herd towards a suburb on the far side of the city. The half-finished new builds are starting to block the view. After he's parked, he re-reads the text he thinks Esther sent him and tries to think of a reply confirming their next meeting.

He takes a breath and leaves the shelter of the car. The cul-de-sac watches as he waits quietly for his wife to open the door. He rings the bell a second time and this time a figure in white approaches the glass.

'Canna get a lift to the airport? Leave the car?' says Marcus.

'No, you bloody can't,' says Helen.

She is blessed with an even temper, straight up and straight down.

Briefly there's a tableaux of a family, the mother sharp and highland beautiful, a small girl in a unicorn T-shirt with her arms wrapped around her scruffy father's knee.

Helen doesn't budge an inch. When Marcus leaves Katie presses a pink plastic horse into his hand, as a token. The mythical beast rides on the seat next to Marcus as he drives to the airport, then he slips it into his travel bag.

The plane drones, accelerates and heads through the clouds and Marcus is up in the air. He remembers flying to the award ceremony four years ago, the fluttering nerves and satisfaction he felt at being nominated. Today, an unknown child presses and kneads his seatback. He sits and takes it. It's the least he can do after what happened with Katie. He must pay the price like everyone else.

He'd felt something sharp, but it wasn't anger. It was of something irreparably gone, that could never be fixed or replaced.

It had taken him back to his graduation concert twenty years ago. He had played flute solo *Syrinx* by Debussy, and recalled the river nymph pursued by the god Pan and transformed into reeds. Unknowingly, Pan cuts the reeds to make his musical pipes and kills his love.

His mother had come.

On her way back to Aviemore, the broad road had been scattered with hail, she had been tired. The lorry driver had been tired, and the road had been unforgiving. He'd been up all night celebrating and having a breakfast fry-up when the call came to tell him she had been critically injured.

The last time he played the flute was at her funeral, until Esther came.

~

Later in the afternoon in London, Marcus is on his way to BlackHouse Media and thinking about the message on his phone.

He wonders how he might get to know Esther better, especially if Claudette or her mother will always be there.

It's been decades since someone's mother has had him on the hop like that. Blood warms his cheeks at the thought as he walks away from Putney Bridge Station and past the crumbling parade of estate agents and convenience shops. Shades of orange and brown are spreading as the sun sets, the sounds are changing, a subtle, discordant alteration that touches his musical ear.

At an alleyway between a hairdresser's and a kebab shop he turns away from the main street. A young woman is on her break, pacing to and fro in a black tabard, cigarette in hand. He stops at the side door and presses the buzzer for BlackHouse Media.

There is no answer. He presses harder, longer.

'They're gone,' says the hairdresser.

'It's only the back of six,' says Marcus.

She stares at him puzzled, figuring out his pattern of speech then, says, 'Nah, they cleared out last week.'

Her vowels are flat, pasted on the roof of her mouth. She sees his reaction, the readjustment of the travel bag, the swing of the instrument case. He's not bad looking, even with that long face, still there's the floors to sweep and dinner to get for the kids. She watches him slouch away, head bowed.

Marcus Macrae keeps trying Steve's mobile as a taxi takes him to a terraced street where he hopes they'll let him kip on the sofa. He is spending too much money, but he had to come.

~

There are four differently coloured wheelie bins in the tiny patch of ground between the bay window and the street. None have breeze blocks on top or bungee cords to prevent them being toppled by the wind.

Marcus tones down the Scots.

Things are different in the south, particularly London. In only a few weeks there has been almost a full turnover of tenants. He only knows one of the three men who live there now. His room used to be upstairs, tonight it'll be the sofa. It's seen better days and has been screwed around on plenty, but beggars can't be choosers.

'Been some cock-up with the arrangements with Black-House,' he says. 'You're good to put me up.'

A bottle of whisky is pulled out from the mass of bottles on the kitchen counter. Marcus has drunk finer, but he does not refuse a glass, and another. They're only half listening, nodding in that polite, bored way. The new tenants have no idea who he is.

'Aye, really gettin stuck into the writin,' he says. 'Fine to get some peace and quiet on the isles, clear the schedule of gigs for a spell.'

The television is left on all evening. When it's finally switched off and Marcus is left alone he thinks back to the night before. He remembers how the Orkney sky had mocked him, blanked inspiration with her brilliant star-sprinkled silence.

He'd gone along the top of the red cliffs on a path wide enough for a single footstep. A new route had been forged further back from the crumbling edge, but he chose the original. In the sea, Copinsay dragged its horse sluggishly through the water.

He'd taken the wooden steps down the cliff, touched shells that were being eroded out of the clay. It was only when he was at the bottom that he'd seen the danger from the overhang, and still it had not troubled him.

Not a tune came to his head, not a note. The feeling of emptiness was overwhelming. When he returned to Pipersquoy the only thing to do was pack up and leave. But he needed to tell Esther something. After all he'd taken the cheque—and more.

He's getting it now—they are both empty shells.

A copper-orange lid seals the streets of London with Marcus inside. He listens to the whirr of the refrigerator and watches the red eye of the television and thinks about the woman with the scars who makes his chest ache with longing. He wonders what she would say if she could talk, but then she would not have come to him if she could talk.

And even though he is exhausted, he cannot rest.

A feeling rises inside Marcus Macrae that he might write something about missing someone, a new tune.

~

It is not an easy night for Kathleen either. It's late before Maggie and Findlay stop talking and even later before their side of the wall goes properly quiet and the bed stops knocking. She glowers up at the ceiling as the thought flashes past that Esther might have needs apart from pills. She turns on her side and closes her eyes tight.

Grandpa George would sit in there above the shop, staring out into the past, seeing rows of bicycles propped up against the wall and following in his mind's eye the travel of a brown leather ball as it is knocked from one man's foot to the next. One afternoon, the boy from Padstow, who'd had lessons about how to cook from his mother, had gone straight over and snapped his leg.

When Ida had seen the injury she'd gone green as a frog. It had always made Grandpa George smile when he'd thought of that, which was quite often because his thoughts went around in circles, circles that eventually grew so very tight and small that they knotted him up inside. His world, full of flashes of memory that made little sense to anyone else, had eventually gone totally blank.

Yet, there was still a quality in him for which Ida would forsake everything.

Kathleen has seen Maggie, crowbar in hand, staring at the wall behind where the sewing machine had stood.

They'll not have another child. Maggie sees there simply isn't room.

It's done now. It's done. Who'd really have wanted her mother back anyway? Esther didn't know what she was saying. She doesn't know what it's like to look after someone, how it doesn't always work, doesn't always suit.

It had been a *lie* though, saying Granny stayed upstairs above the shop where there was no bathroom, and saying her fall happened for no reason at all.

No one had mentioned how she always climbed up to dust the tin mugs because no one else could be bothered, because for God's sake why would you bother. She fell because Kathleen had called her down.

Her mother had been startled, one hand on the shelf, one flailing about in mid-air. The silver ponytail had flipped as Ida fell to the floor. It could have been a lot more serious.

Kathleen likes to believe it wasn't revenge for feeling unloved, that it was a rational decision and that nobody else thought otherwise. That's what she likes to believe. Her mother's hair is now cut short, it is easier to manage for the staff.

~

Over the wall, cut grass lies waiting for turning and dry weather. It's not too late for bailing. Claudette runs her fingers through Esther's hair, gives her paracetamol and encourages her to drink water and lemon. They have the Valium on standby if things get really bad.

~

Ida sleeps, she wants to see Esther again. She wants to ask her to do something. Esther is made of tough mettle.

Dog hours

Rationally, I know they are gone, my medicine is dosing the septic tank. There is nowhere to go except the same toilet where the pills were flushed.

Claudette has helped me down the stairs, and is examining her reflection in the mirror while she waits. There is nothing flattering about the lighting in the bathroom, particularly in the middle of the night. Nonetheless, her reflection is still captivating.

After a minute or so Claudette turns on the tap, water splashes into the gum-pink basin. The sound encourages her body to release.

'You must drink more water,' she says, glancing down into the toilet bowl before I have time to flush. 'Force yourself. It will also help with constipation.'

– *You know everything, don't you.*

There's an echo.

– *Everything.*

There is a space between my thoughts and my skull where the unspoken rebounds. It's a shadow place, full of broken things.

– *Lord, it's a dark place.*

Pain throbs at my temples, hot and heavy. The nerve pain from my back reaches up through my thighs, twisting like ivy. My thin, tightly stretched skin itches.

'I have never found one,' says Claudette. 'But I did not search for long.'

She lifts the jar of groatie buckies and peers inside our family store of lucky shells. 'I prefer stones anyway.' She sighs then adds, 'My mother can never see that stones are important. I tell her they are much older than antiques.' She replaces the jar on the window ledge, then says, 'Time to take a shower.'

– *It's four o'clock in the morning.*

'Sweat contains toxins. You must clean the skin to feel better. Wait and I will fetch some new clothes.'

I sit on the toilet seat, head in hands.

The imperfections on the floor become little life-and-death landmarks. I lose focus for a second and when I look again I can't find what was important and I'm not even sure it's there anymore. I tip forward and rub my hands onto the linoleum to feel for what's hidden beneath and sink downwards onto the floor. My vertebrae merge lanes. The cracking sounds dramatic, but causes no pain. I observe that sounds get sympathy, scars and silence only occasional pity.

I'm nose to nose with the skirting board, on the bathroom floor.

It used to be a place to store cattle feed. Granny still calls it the 'new' bathroom even though it's been here for fifty years.

– *Take me away. Lord, life is a dark place.*

~

Claudette checks my pulse.

'This is different,' she says. 'Because I *want* to know about you, I like you. Before I knew too much that I didn't *want* to know. There was nothing I could do about it. I knew the medications people were on, people I'd known since I was a child. I knew who was dying but seemed quite well and had not told anyone. I knew who was healthy really, but made the most of a small complaint and liked everything done for them. I knew who cared when their children were sick or broke their arms, and who did not give a shit and just went through the motions.'

Hands go beneath my armpits to raise me up. My head is supported and I'm brought to sit with my back against the bath.

'It was the girl from the flats that was the last straw. I could see things were going wrong—I didn't have a problem with her mother, like some people—but I could see it coming. I could see it in the step-sister's eyes. And when they said she fell, I knew it was a lie. Who could I tell, though? The priest? The police? Why should it be me?

'It would be unprofessional. I never wanted to be a box for the town secrets. Nobody asked me.'

She wipes away the hair stuck to my face and smiles. The bruise on her cheek is faded to plum, less swollen than before.

'You can do a shower.'

She begins to remove my clothes, peeling them away from tacky flesh. She takes off her own shirt.

'Okay. The water is ready. Arm here and left leg to stand. Straight.'

A crimp in a nerve and a dart of pain shakes me, but she has me balanced. Legs locked, arms against the wall in the position of a strange vertical press-up.

She takes a body scrubber and squirts it with soap.

'Ssh.' she says. 'You are moaning.'

Water streams onto my forehead and lips, runs between my breasts and fans out over hip bones and into pubic hair. What was left of Marcus Macrae is scrubbed from my skin along with the by-products of Tramadol, ibuprofen and codeine.

'Bon. Fini.'

The water stops and she has me in a towel and sitting back on the toilet.

Blanks. There are more blanks.

'Maybe it hid other injuries,' says Claudette. 'Maybe that was her idea.'

A towel rubs my ankles with their fine dark hair. Each toe is dried separately.

'After,' she says. 'I saw it replayed every time I walked by. I thought for a while that someone should be told about the real way people die, and I had a responsibility to change things. To say something. But things happen and I cannot change people. There will be another antique in my room if I go back.'

She folds the towel onto her lap.

'I had to leave. Plus I like your weather.'

She smiles.

I hear and understand she has made a joke.

'Slide in,' she says, holding up a shirt.

Gentle, she does not mean me to have extra pain. I understand that.

When I am dressed Claudette fluffs my hair with a towel. Afterwards she takes up a supporting position on one side and we limp into the corridor.

– I want to go to Granny's room. I want to show you.

There's no deviation though. She takes me up to bed.

'Slowly,' she says. 'Blow out slowly, it will ease the pain slightly, let your body rest. It is going through a lot of suffering for you.'

– For me?

'Sssh. You are very tired of living with pain. I can help. I saw you needed me.'

A gentle hand.

~

Blank. Again blanks.

The unclaimed space in between pain and peace. Sleep, I fear you.

It is light outside, a quadrilateral of grey above me. The taste of salt is in my mouth, I have been crying.

– You stayed.

'You have tea and I have something your father calls coffee. But there is no time, I must go to work.'

– You haven't slept.

'I have given instructions to your mother and father. You will see Doctor Copik this morning. Give him this note.'

The pile of clothes has been cleared from the floor and the cardboard boxes are gone. The rising sun obliquely strikes the house back wall, shadows of birds bathing in the gutter fall onto

173

the bedroom wall. The jutting pipe is like an open mouth and the skirt of tiles creates the illusion of a yawning face. The birds chirp and balance, knocking against the wall. Then they are gone.

'We will plan together for next week,' says Claudette. 'Your body has metabolised, everything is finished. Gone. It is empty. Worse than empty.'

The tea must have been standing a while. It is lukewarm and slips down easily—Cinderella caffeine. Rags in the dust at midnight, you and me.

Claudette gets up from the bed and brings me something.

'Distract yourself.'

She puts the flute case beside me.

'To be good at anything you must practise.'

She glances at my mobile.

'I wonder what Marcus will do,' she says. 'His wife has thrown him out for good this time I think. That is why he is here. Not for writing songs. It is bannissement.'

– *Did you check for a wedding ring?*

There's a step at the door. My father enters, bringing the smell of melted butter.

'Comin wi yir toast,' he says.

'It's for Esther not me, thank you. You have a busy day ahead?'

'Aye,' he says.

'I must leave now,' she says.

Claudette bends and kisses me on both cheeks.

– *Thank you.*

'It was good to talk,' she says.

My father raises his eyebrows, a movement usually reserved for the expression of utmost surprise or a hammer missing the nail.

Claudette looks around, eyes narrowing with satisfaction, the emotion transferring into the room. Finally she turns to me, a soft enigmatic smile on her lips. She nods goodbye and leaves.

When she is gone I pick up my phone and write a message for my father. Something has occurred to me since my last visit to Granny.

– *What wedding?*

He stares at an invisible point between us for some time before replying.

'It's your Westray cousin Jamie, on the Slater side. He's marryin the shop lass. Your mither got the invite two weeks past.'

He shifts from one foot to the other, a hand searches for an overall pocket that isn't there because he's in ordinary clothes.

'She thowt it'd be too long a day fir you. Yir fairly sufferin.' He pauses, 'Too many of those pills is makkin you seek.'

– *It's lack of pills today.*

I type another message, '*When?*' A flush deepens on his cheeks, the broken veins stand out cherry-red on his nose.

'The morn's morn,' he says. 'He's a Westray man, so we've aal to go ower on the ferry. Ah'll hiv to polish me shoes and find a suit that fits.'

He shakes his head in half-hearted dismay.

– *I've nothing to wear.*

'Mind, here's Mither. Ah've a busy day aheed.'

They nod to each other. My mother keeps her eyes on my father's retreating back. When he's gone she says, 'Dinna ken whit he's so busy aboot.'

She nosies around the bedroom the same way she does Granny's room. But there is nothing for her to spy into anymore. Nothing to rearrange. No way for her to disguise that there is something on her mind.

Call it a plan

'Maggie's fund somethin in Granny's room,' she says.

My mother holds up a black and white photograph about the size of a matchbox. She turns over the image before I have a chance to take a proper look.

'Nineteen forty? If that's an eight then forty-eight. Hard to mind on.'

She flips it back around and shows the photograph.

'Peedie bairn.'

The features on the girl are familiar, rounded out because of her plumpness, but plain for anyone to see. The child is not like my mother or Grandpa George or any of his flat-faced ancestors, she takes after Granny Ida.

'Hid wis in the tin mugs. You ken the wans on the top shelf.'

The date is in the same handwriting as the airmail letters that I'd found as a child.

At eight years old it had been hard to make out the old-fashioned loops and curls and what I could read did not always make sense. No more letters appeared after the day she burnt them in the stove. Perhaps she stopped sending replies.

Years later, one had arrived written in a new style. This news had been shared with the family. I understood Granny would be sad when her cousin Winnie died, but she was so very sad I thought there must be more to it. As a child I had an acute sense of longing. I recognised it in her. I still do.

'Must have been forgotten aboot,' says my mother and tucks it into her pocket. 'You'll need tae get ready because wur seein the doctor early.'

~

There's no need for me to dress, Claudette has clothed me in blue and grey, I am protected from the elements.

Quick movements make me reel, everything must be slow, slow. Slowly.

– *Get off, I can do it.*

Holding the banister I descend, then take the passage towards Granny's room. Inside it's totally bare. The floor has been cleared, only the wounded walls are as I left them.

Maggie smiles at me. Full of admiration for her empty room.

– *Who are we now this room is gone?*

I remember the thin blue paper crinkling in my hands, the exotic red and blue striped edge. It was kept safe in the sewing machine because my mother had no interest in stitching cloth, Granny did it all.

I try to try to see the room as it was, but it won't come.

I can't let myself become desperate, it might be the end. My energy is so often taken up with simply being, nothing left for doing.

– *I hate what you've done.*

There's rustling behind me, my mother stands waiting.

'Time tae gae, Esther.'

She hands me my coat.

– *I'd like a new chauffeur if the agency has one available. This one has stopped wearing her hat.*

She doesn't laugh.

During the journey she hardly speaks, just remarks at how the ditches haven't been dug and that the grass is high in the kirkyard. Something is on her mind.

As the car comes over the brae into the town my attention is pulled towards the slate-blue spire of St Magnus Cathedral. The car turns and the crows fly on. The spire sinks behind rooftops.

A low roaring noise goes on and on in my head, a crashing wave that never ebbs and over the top rides the high-pitched squeals of nerve pain.

The sound of the foil bubble splitting was something to look forward to each day. As time went on, it became a choice between the terrible taste or the terrible wait.

The disability ramp has a rail to steady people like me.

Doctor Copik is there, waiting for us at reception. He has pinned a red ribbon on his chest since yesterday.

'Kathleen, please to wait here. Plenty of magazines or watch screen.'

He gestures at the monitor scrolling local adverts and health information.

My mother lets go reluctantly, as if I am a treasured possession being taken against her will.

It's funny that she does that.

'Miss Esther, you take all time you need. Today, we have double appointment.'

The consulting room door closes. The chair redistributes my pain.

'I have news,' he says. 'I have done research. It is an irritation to some, but there must always be new things. So, as my cousin Pavel is working with the rehabilitation of the voice with musical therapy—so there is also at the same time developments for persons with Tramadol dependence. Dependence, addiction—is rose with same name, same thorn. Many benefits with Tramadol, hard to take dangerous amount, mostly you will be sleepy, not too excited, euphoria is minor compared to alternatives; is fantastic solution for pain relief.

'And who cares if is addictive? I am coffee addict, every day must have at least four cups. Does not prevent me from being good doctor, does not damage my relationships with other people. As a matter of fact, it is one thing I have in common with my ex-wife. And coffee does not ruin me financially—best blend is from cheapest supermarket.'

He turns around and takes a mug from his desk, sips then smiles.

'Expensive not always best. This my wife trouble to teach me.'

He puts down his coffee and begins a physical examination. Carefully, he checks my throat, my neck and behind my ears.

'I could take blood sample to make sure drug is out of system, but I think devil was really in father. Your mother, she is honest.'

The note from Claudette crinkles in my pocket. I take it out and hand it to him. The handwriting is tightly rolled and unmistakably European.

'Remarkable,' he says. 'You receive best care possible.'

– *I can't remember.*

'This is next stage. There is new device—produces electrical pulses, helps withdrawal and retrains nerves, blocks pain. But we also have option of Gabapentine, non-addictive and can help with your type of pain. It will need patience before we see if it works.'

A hot and itchy sensation flares around the skin on my ankles. It grows into a tingle that spreads upwards onto my shins. I rub and scratch the fabric of my trousers,

Doctor Copik leans forward. He stills my hands, and covers them with his own.

'It will pass,' he says. 'Will be better.' He waits for a moment then says, 'The worst is from missing codeine. How can I help you today?'

A paper and pencil are placed on my knee.

Tears come into my eyes, a surge of emotion from nowhere filling the emptiness. I'm not used to the sensation, not straight up, not without anything to shelter behind.

'Sssh…take tissue.'

A year. It has been a year. My life is empty.

– *Nothing will help.*

'Maybe I will tell you something about myself,' he says. 'In all years, since I was young man, I think one small saying is true, "Be careful what you wish for." So yesterday I wish with whole heart to be reunited with my boy, my son. I have given tickets for visit and so happy we'll be to see each other. But I know this—it will not be so.

'There will be something, like I spill coffee waiting at airport or he is losing baggage or yes, the flight is delayed. And even after this when we have first embrace it will not be perfect. There will be disappointment.

'You think I am depressive? Or pessimist? Or dramatist? No, that sort of complication I leave to my wife. I must be realist or disappointment will feel greater. It will stop me from doing anything in the future.

'In point, the case of my wife. I wish many, many times that she will leave me alone and go to the other side of the planet. Now, this is true. But am I happy? Not completely.'

– *What's this got to do with me?*

'So, now we are wishing you to be no longer taking Tramadol.' He raises his voice slightly, emphasising each word, his accent heavy. 'This we can do. You can do. We will find alternative. It is struggle and willpower and must be wanting to change. It is taking flute lessons. It is driving *in* car. It is *driving* car. But what then?' He leans forward. 'If you have success, will you be satisfied?'

There is a pause.

'Or will you be disappointed that still you are waking every morning in pain and first thought is remembering what it used to be like, how easy life was with Tramadol. And you know this memory is a lie, a trick of the mind. This is the reality.'

He glances at the picture of his son.

'You must be with clear expectation. Not depressive or pessimist.'

He reaches over and pushes the paper and pencil forward an inch.

'How can I help today?'

This time I take them up, then I turn the pad so he can read.

– *Is there hope?*

He smiles, then gently nods his head.

'There is great hope for you, Esther. More than for many other people. Because you know that you do not know.'

His gaze meets mine, a sparkle of good humour in his deep brown eyes

'Make new appointment. We can try Gabapentine? Less addiction. Maybe better for you.'

I shake my head.

– *I cannot be trusted.*

'No more codeine. Pharmacist will not sell for you any more. Do not worry. It is normal to cry. We wait. Give small time and start again. You are brave to try this way.

'Come to see me whenever you need. If I am not here then I cover for hospital emergency. Doctor Carnegie is retiring now, so I am here more often.'

I nod.

'Stan is mid-air,' he says. 'What am I to do with him here?'

He shakes his head affectionately and then offers a hand to help me from my seat.

'Drink plenty of water and tea, paracetamol may help, small meals. You must eat. And prepare for lack of sleep to continue for some time. Do not be disappointed.'

He holds my arm like the father of a bride.

'Keep breathing too,' he says. 'That is point of flute lessons. You must breathe, relax and breathe, strengthen.'

– I make a lot of mistakes.

We walk in silence down the corridor, I think he is proud of me.

In the waiting room my mother is in conversation with a man—a Westray man—in a flat cap and round silver spectacles. His mouth is a river of sound. The delivery is so fast and rolling it's hard to catch on, each word a piece of jigsaw. At my arrival I see a hint of disappointment on my mother's face.

'Here is your daughter returned,' says Doctor Copik. 'She continues to surprise.'

'Weel Laurie, Ah'll be sayin cheerio. Mind how you get on.'

I refuse her arm and walk without support.

When we're in the car she asks, 'What did he give you this time?'

I open my hands and show her they are empty. No Nurofen Plus in my pockets either, nothing.

– Go on, search me.

'No need fir the chemists then,' she says.

This makes her happy because there's no affinity between my mother and Claudette, some adults aren't good at sharing. So she drives me around to Stembister House.

'Wait in the car if you like. Yir lookin tired.'

– Claudette watched over me. There are times I don't remember.

With effort I unbuckle myself. I have noticed that my mother helps less when it is something she does not want me to do.

At the front door there is a note taped over the keypad, 'PUSH DOOR TO OPEN.' It is stiflingly warm inside, the air laden with moisture, as if there has been excessive breathing overnight. When we're in the door my mother kisses Granny's cheeks, then leans over and pulls the window closed.

– Why? Why do you do that?

'How's you today, Mither?'

'Och, fine, fine. Whit you botherin aboot me fir? Haven't you enough tae dae? Thowt you'd be at the hairdresser.'

My mother ignores the comment and keeps searching around the room.

'Is thir anythin you want washed at hame? Ah've got tae tak Esther back this efternoon because she's no feelin weel.'

'Whit's the matter lass?' says Granny.

I go and sit and hold her hands. They are often cold, but she never complains, never asks for them to be warmed. I cover her soft silver-blue fingers with mine.

– *I'm detoxing.*

'Yir comin good. Aren't you lass?'

My mother abruptly becomes still, and then remains still, her task totally abandoned. Without a word she has our full attention.

– *What is it?*

'Maggie fund somethin,' she says.

Just started crying

A blush appears on Granny's cheeks when my mother produces the photograph, even before she sees the picture I know she's recognised what it is from the size and markings on the back. Her face relaxes and fills with pleasure when my mother puts it in her hand.

'I thowt hid wis lost,' says Granny.

My mother moves around the room busily again, presentation over.

'Andrew's been tellin Findlay fir months to shift stuff oot intae the trailer, but he's no energy left efter work,' my mother rattles on. 'No doot hid's easier to hiv a skip rather than dae aal those trips tae Bossack. Maggie's gettin on wi the job noo. She spotted this in wan of those terrible auld tin cups.'

'Hadds a cuppa as weel as anthyin,' says Granny quietly without taking her eyes off the photograph.

The girl is in a simple smock with a round collar and stands alone by a table with a cloth and flowers, loose dark curls fall past her shoulders.

'Slater by look o the chin,' says my mother, snooping around the drawers for items of clothing to clean and repair.

'Aye,' says Granny.

Carefully, Granny slips the photograph down the side of her chair.

– *Who is it?*

Meanwhile, my mother has found a grey cardigan with a loose button.

'Can't say I dinna look efter you,' she says.

'Give hid awey,' says Granny. 'This place is hellish warm, an I dinna ken when I wis last ootside in the air.'

'Ah'll check the bathroom,' says my mother.

When her back's turned Granny looks at me, her eyes steady, trying to communicate something.

– *Do I really look that bad?*

I take up her hands again, but she looks restlessly out of the window.

– *I don't understand. I need more. Please.*

A wave of tiredness and sickness washes over me.

When my mother comes back tears are running over my cheeks. I have to rest my head on Granny's lap. My heart is running a marathon.

'Why're you greetin?' says my mother.

'She's no weel at aal the day, Kathleen.'

A hand flutters over my hair.

– *Can I stay here with Granny?*

'Thir's ups and doons,' my mother replies.

A hand pats my shoulder, for a moment all three of us are linked. It's hard, hard to take comfort, because it is only ever for a short time and then I have to go back to the painful place where I stay.

'Ssh,' says Granny. 'Bide.'

Glowing blobs fade and grow on the back of my eyelids. Obscured behind them, I see the little black and white girl. She's trying not to smile, finding it a challenge not to speak or move. But she has to stay absolutely still because she's in a photograph and it would break the rules.

The touch is gone from my shoulder. The tears are drying up now and the girl is gone. I sit and take a tissue.

A rattle of dishes comes from the corridor, followed by the glutinous smell of chicken soup.

– *It can't be lunchtime already? What kind of place is this? Something's wrong here.*

'Aren't you lucky tae have so many visitors Ida?' says Helga. 'Whit like Kathleen?'

It would solve a lot of problems if I stayed here. I'd never have to ask for things and I could stay inside all the time. No one would call me a recluse here. Maybe Marcus Macrae could come and give everyone flute lessons? Wouldn't that be nice, one afternoon, to have some noise, some breath, some life…

I'm only joking.

'No bad the day,' says my mother. 'Takkin a few pieces tae wash an mend.'

The implication that everything is not as clean as it could be hits a sensitive spot with Helga. She gives my mother a steely look.

Granny starts to speak. 'Mither used to tak in washin durin the war. Mendin as weel. I'd help efter school, earnin a few pennies fir the weekend. Cousin Winnie came doon an lent a hand if we had a great deal. I'd the job o cycling oot to the stations, deliverin.'

Helga offers a cup filled with green-grey tea.

'We hiv tae be off. Esther's no feelin weel,' says my mother.

'Hid was a way tae get a glance at Grandpa George,' says Granny. 'He wis the best lukken of aal the beuys who came tae the parish fir the war.'

'No gettin eny voice back yet?' says Helga.

'No yet,' says my mother.

'Stayed long enough to be smitten,' says Granny. 'That's whit they said. The radar came in an he wis sent awey. The search-lights were no manned so weel at the end o the war.'

– Why have you taken the photograph Granny?

My mother puts a hand under my elbow.

– I'm not ready to go. Granny's telling me things.

'Ah'll makk some soup at hame,' says my mother.

My muscles cramp as the damaged disks shift and I forget what I had been figuring out. Thinking and pain do not mix well. Thinking and Tramadol do not mix well either. Things flow better with Nurofen.

– They do.

– I remember how it used to be.

– What were you trying to tell me?

Iron bars press down on my head, it feels like my skull will burst from the pressure. A packet of Nurofen would go down a treat, it'd make the day worth living through.

'Mind the bed,' says my mother. 'Ah'll no see you till Sunday noo Mither.'

'Aye. Off you go tae yir waddeen. Ah'm no gaan anywhar,' says Granny.

186

'Ah'll drop by the kirkyard an see to Fither.'

'When am I gaan?'

'Hid's a poor day the day. Let's see next week.'

Granny stays sitting, cold hands on her lap, gaze cast down as we leave.

In the corridor my mother runs on about Helga taking against her doing Granny's laundry, 'Some folk cheust canna let go o their burdens.'

My eyes start to water again.

Because I used to go with Granny to the kirkyard. She'd talk on as if Grandpa George could hear. And now she can't even go and visit his grave. And all you can think of is laundry and how the keypad is not fixed.

When my mother leans in to pull down the seatbelt I push her arm away. She says nothing, but deliberately leaves the passenger door open and goes around to the driver's seat. Slowly, I manage the actions of seatbelt clipping and door closing myself.

The wave of sadness wanes. In the car anxiety rules.

– *Why can it never be plain sailing?*

Is Claudette pleased I've not come today? Relieved?

I feel like someone else, a replacement. I don't even recognise my clothes. Whose are these jeans? This white shirt and this wraparound cardigan? I don't know where they're from.

– *Did you dress me Claudette?*

There are no messages from Marcus Macrae.

Why would there be? Why would I care? I'm not attracted to Marcus Macrae and he is not attracted to me. Not in the least.

– *Not in the least?*

The rush of adrenaline, the pounding of blood in my ears from passing Accident Corner echoes the pleasure found in the cool, damp bed with Marcus when sleep nearly came. A tingling sensation on my skin flees deeper into the tissues below. I rub my limbs to bring relief.

My mother looks askance at me, then slows. She puts on the indicator for the Redland turning. I flick it off and point ahead.

'She widna ken,' says my mother and puts the indicator back on.

– I will.

I cancel it again, reach across and hold the wheel straight.

'Hid's aal very weel fir you Esther. Ah've things tae dae.'

A car is coming towards us from behind. I brace my arm so she cannot turn.

'Grandpa George widna ken.'

– I will.

The tension goes from our opposing forces on the wheel. My mother harrumphs, then changes down a gear and we go on towards the kirkyard.

The sun could be anywhere behind the layers that gloam and shift above. Meanwhile, an iron hand grips my skull, trying to find its cracking point.

– Not found it yet.

The indicator is tick-tick-ticking and we're onto the straight road, past a thicket of pines surrounded by yellowing syca-mores. A rare stand of trees.

There is no church nearby, funerals are held in either the kirk over towards Holm or at St Magnus Cathedral. The kirk-yard is simply a set-aside field, instead of animal haunches and heads domes and crosses rise above the stone walls.

A lozenge of light blares in the southern sky, in places the clouds are cut through while others darken in relief against the bright glow.

There's a series of hills sweeping in waves from south to north, water gathers in the lowest dips. On the hill opposite there is a post and wire enclosure to stop animals falling into a hole left by an archaeology team. One post tilts drunkenly inwards, indicating the direction of prevailing wind.

With lips pulled straight and eyes staring straight ahead my mother parks in the layby, turns the keys, then fastidiously buttons her coat. I don't think she was a daddy's girl. She definitely isn't a mummy's girl.

The wind is going about its business, worrying the stalks of last summer's cow parsley, flicking up the tongued leaves of plantains.

– *Granny likes being out in the fresh air.*

I bend awkwardly and fiddle free the latch at the bottom of the gate. Without comment, my mother pushes the opposite side open and trudges past.

– *Why don't you want to be here?*

There's no answer, the first part of the ritual has begun, reading familiar names with fresh offerings.

Even before Grandpa George died Granny went regularly to the kirkyard. She'd bring me and we would lay flowers on other graves. Later, I brought her, whenever I had time. Of course I wish I'd done it more, made fewer excuses.

– *I've never loved anyone like that. Maybe I won't.*

The headstones run in lines over the shallow rise of the land, like hunched shoulders bending in prayer. Some are tall with a grand base and a Celtic cross, most are more humble. One or two have a bit of a lean, and one's laid flat on its back staring up at the sky.

The grass is lush with daisy, buttercup and moss. I don't think it's too long, it'd be unkind to keep the place shorn to its flanks.

'Yir better tae stay at hame,' says my mother.

– *Would you come on your own?*

'Maybe I could get a photograph,' she says. 'Tae go in her room.'

She speaks without kindness.

'He wis a difficult owld man. Niver lettin anyone sit doon or get on wi things. Aal the time gawpin oot the windae, half the time seein whit wisna there. While I wis runnin the shop doonstairs, lookin after you twa, wi your fither awey fixin everyone else's machines.'

– But Granny loved him.

The headstone is the same red as the cathedral, tall and narrower than most. The inscription in the upper half reads, 'George Young, 1925–2008, 9th July, Aged 83 years.' At the bottom, fringed by the grass there are the words, 'In my heart you will live forever.'

I take out my phone and take a picture. It captures the lettering clearly, white on red stone.

– It's better than nothing.

If Granny was not with him, she'd be making him something to eat or mending a piece of his clothing. She kept hand washing his clothes in the great white butler's sink no matter what my mother said about the machine.

The sink has been moved and filled with marigolds, but the nail where the servicemen's washing list was hung still pokes out where it always used to be.

My mother folds her arms under her chest and then stares for a short while at the blank space left beneath reserved for Granny.

Weak at the knees from standing still I move on, it's the only way to stay upright.

Each grave has a unique pattern of lichen weathering of stone. One where I have stopped often is small and made of pinkish marble. The inscription is smeared, as if streaked with salt. 'Alice Harvey, born 1944. Died three months.' And at the base, it reads, 'Taken to live with the angels.'

The baby was the child of Granny's cousin who left for Canada after the war. We regularly place flowers on her grave because in all her life Winnie never returned.

My mother reminds me of the story. 'Thir wir terrible outbreaks o meningitis durin the war. No cheust bairns that died fae it.'

I lift my phone and take another photograph. My arm drops heavily from the exertion, and my heart is beating greyhound fast.

A ragged skein of geese cuts across the sky. The ground starts to tip and sway.

The grass glows and rises, pink and green edges distort the small gravestone.

'Steady,' says my mother. 'Time tae get you hame.'

She leads me back to the gravel by the gates where hearses park. In the far corner a single tree shelters behind the stone shed built into the wall.

'Tak a peedie rest.'

I lean against one of the entrance pillars. Sweat breaks over me, I am febrile and chilled to the bone. Tears drizzle onto the shoulder of my mother's jacket, she holds me up, stops me from falling.

Your hands on my hope

There are no short cuts for Esther. Her mother drives her around the long way. They pass the Border Leicester sheep, like giant rabbits with snuggled down bodies and long ears. A flock of starlings join and break with each other, then come to rest on barbed wire. They know the trick is to keep moving and roll like a wave.

Respect has been given and duty fulfilled, but there is no balm for the stings of Kathleen's childhood. Even on her birthday, when candles burned on cake in the dark she'd notice her mother and father staring into each other's eyes rather than looking at her. Always fixed on each other, Kathleen imagined the synchronicity of their hearts. It'd been unnoticed by her younger sister Elspeth, too busy with her own affairs to suspect anyone of neglect.

They were the two girls who sat in the shop on rainy Saturdays, one absorbing the ways of trade and the other daydreaming. Two girls with the same straight fringe and matching woollen coats, both sewn by hand. Kathleen with her solemn flat face, none of her father's charm, and none of her mother's intensity.

In the war there were handfuls of men for every girl on the island, even someone like Kathleen would have been in demand.

As it was she had waited, like the fly traps hung in the shop. It was a case of patient planning, and she'd be damned if the copier repair man got a warmer welcome elsewhere. Whenever Andrew came she made sure there were fresh pancakes on the griddle, and farmhouse cheese and floury bannocks better than for sale anywhere. One December the weather was on her side. The *Ola* would not sail for sure and there were few places to stay. She'd said a camp bed could easily be put in the shop and the fire was stoked with peat.

George related his experiences to Andrew about how he'd kept the Meadows generator running on the searchlight stations during the war. They'd taken a dram or two and Andrew had heard about the nights George found a welcome at Skulstad and learned how Ida's family had run the store and served tea to servicemen. He'd heard about the natural turf of the football pitch being torn up to extend the radio communication camp and how of all the impositions this was the hardest for the local men to withstand. Temporary pitches were set out in other places marked by horse and plough, with driftwood used for goal posts.

Andrew had liked George, he liked the workshops out the back of the place.

It was a comfortable bed and generous supper that Andrew thought back on fondly as he drove away.

Whether Kathleen would admit it or not that difficult old man from Portsmouth, her father, had a fair hand in securing her a husband.

~

Andrew himself is away from Skulstad when Kathleen and Esther return, although the red van is parked in its usual place. Kathleen cannot find him anywhere. Not even propped up against the vegetable stand talking away the afternoon with Willie. Close to the byre it smells of the earth and dust that joins life and death, and many contented afternoons are passed that way between the retired men.

In the end, Kathleen gives up and goes to chop celery.

There is no comfort for the unspoken expectations of a mother for her daughter. She had never meant to punish Esther for her own mother's coldness. But in the end, it was Esther who left.

Now Esther lies on the sofa, tremors running through her body. She tenses her muscles to stop the shaking, they ball and threaten to cramp. She can't stay still.

A little pink grave dances before her; when it stops the world around becomes pockmarked with craters then disintegrates into nothing.

Normal function has been forgotten by her cells. They've got used to a different way of life and are not at all happy with the reduction in their comforts. Delegation after delegation besiege Esther's exhausted willpower.

At three o'clock Maggie leaves her renovations and calls out to no one in particular, 'I'm gettin the boys.'

Esther finds her feet and puts them squarely on the floor, a favour in mind to ask her sister-in-law.

She can move quickly when she wants or needs.

~

Things are not panning out in London for Marcus Macrae. The morning has been spent trying to find the new location of BlackHouse Media. It has moved from above the hairdresser's to a narrow house on the South Circular. The chimney is tilted like a gravestone and behind the plasterboard lurks Victorian asbestos. There is no sign outside the door to indicate a business at the property.

'Yeah, come in Marcus,' says Steve. 'Didn't think you were coming down.'

Steve's vowels slide like dirt from a shovel.

'Where's the studio?' says Marcus.

'More efficient to hire something by the hour.' Steve runs a hand though his thinning hair. 'Better to have people working at home too. Cover more gigs that way, you know, more locations, more reviews and exposure for advertising. That's what it's all about, yeah?'

Someone is running a bath upstairs. The hallway is cramped with a bicycle leaning against the wall.

'Let's get out of here and go for a coffee.'

Marcus shoulders his bag and case and they walk together. Steve keeps talking. After being in Orkney the noise of the traffic interferes with his concentration on what Steve is saying.

In truth, most of the BlackHouse Media business plans are fictional anyway. It doesn't feel like October at all under the milk-white sky.

The cafe has wooden benches and plants; you pay double for coffee *and* quiet.

Once their drinks are in front of them Marcus tells Steve about the bow.

'Why d'you let her have it?' says Steve.

'I'd been playin. It was just lying oot.'

'And it wasn't insured?'

Marcus shakes his head. Everyone says they should do it, but few on the folk circuit ever bother. There's a sort of faith that if you love something enough then it won't be broken.

'I'm strapped for cash,' says Marcus.

Steve nods, expression neutral. No comment.

A woman in high boots and tight jeans comes in with a sleek baby carriage. It's her sort of place, carefully constructed bohemia, down at heel with French pastries and Italian coffee. Two men, one with a violin case, fit perfectly.

'What about your fiddle?'

'What?'

'It's a Peresson. Sought after you know.'

A bitter taste begins to spoil Marcus's barista brew.

'You're jokin. Of course I know.'

'Sort of gigs you're doing, no one's going to tell the difference. You could borrow something for session work, yeah. The bow'll never be the same. Would it? Even if you got it fixed.'

It is a practical solution. It would release thousands of pounds, give a man freedom.

'Fuck off,' says Marcus.

He pushes his chair back.

'I came here for Hendry because he taught me respect for what I do. And what do you do?' His voice is harsh, the Scots broadening, that quick temper surfacing. 'Tell me to sell my fiddle? You canna even keep a fuckin office runnin.'

He swings up his bag and crashes it into the baby buggy. The child wakes with a high-pitched and insistent cry. It reminds him of coming back late from gigs when Katie was a baby. His throat tightens. It's the same feeling he had when he played the Debussy for Esther and Claudette. Every nerve is tender.

'Helen not giving you anything these days?' says Steve.

'Fuck off.'

The young woman turns and glares at him. It wasn't the knock, it was the swearing, the strength of his emotion that caught her attention.

The bell on the coil rings sharply. Marcus leaves, violin case held stiffly at his side. The child's cries are hitting close to top C. Fiery little lungs, with a chest smaller than a fist, but how the sound carries. It's still echoing in his ears at Clapham Common tube station.

When the tube gets rolling Marcus places the instrument on the seat, resting a hand on it like he would on a woman's knee. The scream of wind and metal tunnel roar reflect his interior world.

The air is laced with exhalations, expectations and disappointment. It's a place where Marcus Macrae does not matter. He's just that guy who slept on the sofa and drank more whisky than his hosts wanted to pour, who spent a whole evening going on about his broken bow and... told them about a woman with a scar who he'd shagged, and get this, they'd never even spoken. How's that work?

A few days and they'll forget he was even there. And the story of the bow and the woman with the scars will be forgotten and no longer matter to anyone.

Sell the violin?

Change it into money, then beer and eggs and petrol. Steve's logic gnaws away at Marcus. But right there and then he begins to accept that the bow is broken forever. Back ends of terraces go past, stained with hundred-year-old soot, and his anger turns to grief. The reflection in the window is a man who's much older than the photographs on his sleeve notes. That's all he is. That's all he sees. No one will believe he wants to be on the album for any reason except the money.

He squints past his reflection and observes the ivy growing downwards in long tendrils over purple-brown brick, and rushing behind a river of three-eyed windows and the blank backs of commercial buildings. The endless running wires, maroon bricks and white graffiti blur together. After a while the introspection wears thin, his attention moves back inside the carriage.

The young woman sitting opposite has two dragons tattooed on her neck, one green-scaled with a long tongue, the other red and breathing fire. Her hair is all matted dreadlocks, swept up from a delicate face, eyes and lips outlined in black. Marcus begins to notice the rips in the tattooed woman's jeans and how they reach up to her inner thigh.

He feels done with London, done with BlackHouse Media, done with being Marcus Macrae.

He slides out his phone and reads over again the text from Claudette masquerading as Esther seeking another lesson '*ASAP*', then begins to search for flights to Inverness.

He must arrive by mid-afternoon to have a chance of catching the *Pentalina* from Gill's Bay.

~

There are tricks Claudette has developed to get through days when she has not slept, to stay alert. She takes a vaporizer refill from the shelf, scans it at the till, pays and then walks out of the rear door of the shop. The sun is dropping, reflecting in the windows as it sinks in the western sky, cutting beneath the clouds and spreading a delicate geisha glow on their underside. She loves it here.

Two boys are being walked across the car park towards her. The woman holding their hands is wearing heavy boots, her fleece smeared with dust and dirt. She clicks and encourages the children as if they are animals. The older boy has delicate features, a fine nose and familiar sea-blue eyes.

When the automatic doors open, Claudette follows them inside and relieves Susie Gordon at the till.

Maggie asks for two packets of Nurofen Plus.

'It's for my auntie. We've to get them before we can go home,' says George.

'Granddad flushed her pills doon the toilet,' says Erland, jumping up and down, chin nearly cracking on the counter.

'These are different. She'll be allowed these ones,' says Maggie.

Every light is noticed on a black hillside

The shadow of Willie's barn has eaten the square of orange fire on the living room wall. The window is cool on my forehead. Two massive tyres lean against its wall, big, black, empty zeros.

Findlay and I watched when they knocked the old roof timbers down. We leaned against the petrol pump and saw the new, bright-yellow timber bolted in place, ugly as sin and deserving of a corrugated roof. When it was finished we'd fooled about with the hose, filling empty pellet buckets then spraying each other, then sliding on a tarpaulin.

Later, our mother gave us a strike of the wooden spoon for wasting a whole bottle of washing-up liquid on our makeshift waterslide. We'd slipped about like eels.

Findlay had caught a cold that went to bronchitis and I was to blame. For weeks there was an evil cloak around my shoulders whenever I caught my mother's eye.

I transfer weight onto my hands and the sill, my arms covered with goosebumps.

– *Bits of the past are real.*

– *Try and think of those.*

Fledglings found on the ground.

– *Don't feed them milk. They will die.*

– *We did that too.*

The base of my skull is squeezing shut, crushing the neuronal worm that crawls into my spine. Nowhere is safe from the cymbals of pain.

Something is missing. Missing. Gone.

There's a blank space where something should go. Something that was there before and I miss it, like when someone dies and they're not there at the end of the line anymore and you keep wanting to call.

The voices have gone, the angels with bat wings that sang in my head. Although I enjoyed listening, it wasn't the music of a healthy mind. It isn't any good like that.

Upstairs, the hairdryer stops. A few minutes later the smell of conditioning shampoo announces my mother in the room.

'Maggie'll be back soon,' she says. 'Sit doon and Ah'll makk a cuppa.'

In the window's reflection an aquamarine pillow is given a friendly pat.

My forehead leaves the glass and I'm about to step back when headlights catch my attention. They're coming past the old school where my mother went, past the bungalow with pampas grass and swing set where my one-time friend Kathy Taylor lived—not speaking isn't good for relationships.

People take it personally.

The nerve impulses to the larynx were disrupted they said. Later, they gave me leaflets about the physical and psychosocial causes of voice loss. The effects of post-traumatic stress on the voice are well documented.

Psychosomatic is a word often used to describe my condition.

If I clear my throat on impulse the sound is natural, it's the act of will that changes things.

Psycho.

The car headlights are closer. A small car, not Claudette's because the lights do not hug the ground in the same way, the beam flashes over the one-legged postbox and the car pulls in beside the skip.

A short-bodied hatchback, the same make and model I was driving the night of the accident. There's an airbag fitted, it saved my life.

– I can go back in time.

I remember striding to the car, cursing my mother, my whole family, cursing Simon and twisting the keys and then jamming the car into reverse, swinging back and away.

I drove out past the byre, dropping into potholes opened up by early autumn rain. The outlets were blocked so water flowed onto the tarmac, black streams reflecting the lights of oncoming traffic.

'Is that yir fither back? says my mother.

The car comes to rest and the headlights switch off. I'm back in the sitting room, standing by the glass.

'Who's taken him?'

– *No one. He's driving.*

My father waves when he sees me at the window. There is a smile, the expression of a job completed. My mother leaves and there are raised voices next door in the kitchen, a disagreement.

A new car crouches on the forecourt, hungry and ready to pounce. The urge to flee takes hold of me, but I cannot move, I cannot save myself. Where is Maggie? I need her.

– *I was wrong. It's too much. I can't go back.*

The door opens and in comes my father. The image of him scooping up the pills and throwing them down the pan is miraculously preserved in my mind. Funny that, when so much else is thistledown.

A car key is in his hand, he handles it in a way that expresses a high level of expectation. Here comes my mother behind him, cheeks blotchy, eyes wet.

– *Why?*

My mind is not working well, sleep and other deprivations taking their toll.

Yet, just before he speaks I know what he's going to say. My throat tightens and it becomes painful to swallow.

'Thowt havin the same model would makk hid easy,' he says, and holds out the key.

I shake my head, lips pursed. Everything blurs.

Simon is pissing me off on the train, then the glossy brochure arrives and I buy an expensive dress in the boutique. The key is put in my hand. Granny lies dying and I'm searching for her in the dark, and I know I'm not going to find her. Did she know the room was vandalised by her own daughter?

For the sake of an inch I failed to kill myself.

Quicker, quicker, through the air all these thoughts. Ticktack, tick-tock. Like the man at the races. Tears rise and I lean forward, crudely pushing the key up to my father's face then slashing it through the air.

There's a loud cry of pain.

It's not him, it's me.

'Ssh,' says my mother. 'Ssh,' she says and holds my arms. 'Stop. Stop now. Maggie'll be here soon.'

'Whit the hell's wrong wi you?' says my father, his voice skirling around the room. 'I canna dae anythin right. Canna keep peace, no matter whit I dae.'

– How could you?

'If you dinna want it Ah'll just tak it back! God knows whit's gaan on in your heed.'

My mother is leading me to a sofa drowning in cushions.

– You could smother a baby, if you didn't want it any more.

There's more lights coming into Skulstad, higher and wider. I free myself from my mother, go through to the kitchen and throw open the front door.

– Did you get them Maggie? Did you? Outta the way boys.

Maggie strolls towards the house, casting a casual eye over the skip and the new car. A hand slips into her pocket, but she doesn't smile. The ground is wet though my socks.

I swallow, my mouth is watering as she pulls out the packet. It is plain with red corners and simple black lettering. Paracetamol, 500mg.

'Yir allowed these wans,' says George. 'Not the other wans.'

There's genuine warmth in his grin, he thinks I will be pleased.

The car key is still in my hand. The slim metal tool flashes like a knife.

– Here I go.

Scoring through the paint feels so damn good that I continue all the way around the new car, every panel. There's a buzz of adrenaline when I stop.

'You wrecked it,' says George.

– *Let's savour the moment.*

Erland begins to follow the trail running his finger along the scratch line. My mother, father and Maggie stand under the outside light.

Grandpa George watches darkly from the upstairs window. I see him quite clearly. Findlay arrives, car stuttering to a stop.

'New car?' he says, climbing out.

'Come inside boys,' says Maggie.

'It's scratched,' says Erland.

'Is that right?' says Findlay. 'Same as your old car, Esther. Gaan to tak it fir a spin and stop treatin Mum like a taxi service?'

– *I never asked for this.*

He smirks and turns away.

'Come on Mags. Whit's fir supper? How's school the day boys?'

Maggie takes George's hand, but his head stays turned and his eyes fixed on me until he reaches the doorway. My father's face is stony, he puts his hand to my mother's elbow and guides her into the blaze of the kitchen. I want to call out to them, but there is no way I can do that now.

My charmless weapon is thrown away. There's a click and slither as the key lands in the skip and settles into a resting place.

Inside, my route through the house is all clear.

On the stairs I stop to let a wave of weakness pass. Granny looks through me, her eyes on the man behind the camera. She is a strong woman. She'd never throw herself away like this.

A few more steps and I'm in a room with clear surfaces. I leave the light out and inhale the emptiness then produce short panting exhalations to keep panic at bay.

– *I want to be in the present.*

The flute case is on the bed, nestled on the covers, giving the illusion of a rectangular black hole.

I release the catches and run my fingers over the cool smooth pieces, the head piece that's heavier than its dimensions suggest, the cool curves and hidden felted undersides that muffle the button's quiet little clicks. As I steady the body of the flute against my chest. My fingers shake and it's almost impossible to line the two pieces together.

– *Say please. Say please.*

It slides and joins. To add the end section I hold the whole thing upside down between my legs, and go on failing and repeating what I need to do over and over again until the piece fits into place. The drill sergeant shouts.

– *Stand up or die here.*

– *I'm exhausted.*

– *Blow.*

A high-pitched screech pierces the air. My sound. My call.

– *Again.*

– *What if someone hears?*

Hourglass

Nothing feels right about the mouthpiece position, or my fingers crabbed on the keys. It's a challenge for muscles habitually tensed against pain to obey. The lips should be relaxed and the body upright.

I lower the instrument, there are no scribbles on the walls, no angels in the shadows. The automatic outside light switches off and the darkness deepens. It was a bad scene outside. This will not be the end of it.

– *This will not end.*

The desire to make noise ebbs.

Why didn't Maggie get me what I asked for?

I close my eyes, feel the weight in my hands, the differences in temperature where my fingers have moved. The resistance from my lips encourages the abdomen muscles to work harder, to actively move air. A weak sound like the breeze through school railings comes from the flute.

Making my lips softer and drawing in more deeply I blow again. Nothing.

– *You used to have determination.*

There are secret spaces inside, that can stay closed for a long time. Scars grow, invading the good flesh. In my mind's eye I picture the dome of the diaphragm separating my body in two. With the next breath I will it downwards, to yield just a little

– *Esther, concentrate.*

Somewhere a muscle loosens. The breath moves deeper. A pulse of emotion passes through my core. It spreads through the centre of my body into my throat.

These are tears from another place.

I hear my mother say, 'Findlay was easier.' She says it again, 'He was easier to love.' This is the first knot to be untied.

My hands tremble, fingers shift out of place like spider legs, sore from the unfamiliar position.

– *Do what you're told.*

I inhale deeper and then draw up and push out warm and heavy air. It brushes past the aperture of my lips and into the silver tube.

Making any sound was a feat, something I could not manage voluntarily before.

This time there is nothing. I lower the flute and rest, tear-streaked.

– Why does it mean so much?

I try again, but the flute will not yield, not until I concentrate again on the same place inside. I close my eyes.

The band of muscle below my ribs moves a little lower. In my mind's eye I see my brother sitting in a banana box in Granny's room, with a biro moustache and a floppy cardboard sword. My mother's there and she's smiling and clapping her hands. And I want to laugh with her, but I don't. I stop myself because it feels like an intrusion, like I shouldn't be there.

There's a change low in my pelvis, a tightening in the groin, it moves up gradually to my stomach as if my whole body is breathing, moving up through my chest to my neck and the back of my throat. The flute takes the breath, savouring the firm, steady pressure flowing from my lips.

We are in no man's land, between the lines, between the waves of craving.

– I have found space to breathe.

Eyes open and the space folds away. I can no longer feel the tension in my internal muscles or sense the moment between the inhale and the exhale of breath, there is simply nothing, no will and no need.

I cannot stand the nothing for too long, it is such an empty place.

Panic strikes and I'm hit with the sudden urge to see something real. I switch on the lamp and everything is shocked into place.

In the mirror I study my reflection, she is real. A woman with deep blue-black eyes and a streak of silver in her hair that falls in waves on her shoulders.

Scars run over her eyebrow and across the bridge of her nose and cheek. The upper lip has a narrow white line that might be a corrected abnormality.

– *No, I was not born this way.*

With backwards logic I make tiny adjustments to the way I hold the instrument, I remember how Marcus Macrae used his hands to guide me. I remember his gentle hands clasped tight around my wrists.

That moment we connected wasn't long.

Long enough.

It is strange studying myself so closely after studiously avoiding the sight of my face for so long.

I lower my eyes and focus on the breath. I don't want memories, just breath and sound.

– *Does there have to be nothing?*

This time when the diaphragm sinks down it releases feelings held deep in the solar plexus. Another memory comes.

I am seven, performing in the Christmas choir in the Redland community hall, too young to stop myself from singing high and loud. It's a song with actions and I am having a ball, waggling my hips and clapping my hands.

Out of all the audience there is only one I want to please, and she is standing at the back so I have to sing very loud. But when everyone sits down she is not there, gone away to the clatter of tea cups behind the shutters at the back.

'Why're you so pootsie?' said my mother afterwards, seeing my dull face.

I didn't answer. She knows full well.

'Thowt aal the bairns did a fine job,' said my father.

He smiles proudly and pats me on the head. I try to stop myself from crying, I know it is silly to cry.

'The only person yir Granny ever loved is in the kirkyard. Yir foolish to think anythin else,' says my mother. 'Granny wis thir tae dae the tea and no to listen. I dinna ken whit you expected.'

I feel the nothing. The breath flows, and the note I make is soft and clear.

– *She does love me. Loves us.*

Happy memories are the worst, a trap, and the way out is no longer being sold freely over the counter.

– *Why all these tears?*

I look in the mirror, the woman with tears running down her cheeks also has a small smile on her lips, ever so slight.

– *This has been successful.*

I remember my mother's sharp, clear footsteps on the stones outside as I lay with Marcus on the bed. The smile creeps wider.

– *Be brave.*

I lift the flute and prepare again, but the process is interrupted by a buzz from my mobile.

Do not be disappointed

A message from Marcus Macrae, '*Busy Sat with gig. Meet Monday? 11? Sorry. Marcus.*'

There's really no need for a reply. I toss the phone away and start to dismantle the flute.

– *What was I thinking?*

Whatever the next note might have touched is lost. There is something powerful about holding the instrument. I handle it nervously and hurry to pack it away, fearful of where it might take me. The barometer is falling.

– I must rest.

I lie on the bed, light on, present in the moment, heart beating, head aching and caught in the need again.

I know you've got problems of your own Marcus Macrae, but they are not the same as this.

– I'm sorry.

Claudette has prized out my secrets like limpets.

I turn onto my side. In my mind's eye, there's a girl swinging a yellow bucket, barefoot, pebble in hand. Only rarely were limpets allowed.

We dropped them into boiling water and ate them with lemon and pepper. The tiny eye stalks made me remember that they were living things, but Granny would never cut them off.

'They had them as bait in the war,' she'd said. 'Once Grandpa George came back wi mackerel enough tae feed his whole station.'

She must've been thirteen or fourteen when they first met, from that day he was imprinted on her.

My breathing is deepening, inhale…exhale…inhale… exhale…

The bedroom door pushes open and I am brought back to the present, pain included.

'He's gone all day to collect a car an noo you've made damn sure he canna tak hid back,' says Findlay. 'Yir some ungrateful witch.'

– You're just pissed off because he's not been making your shelves.

'Whar's all yir clutter? Is this whit that Frenchwoman did?'

The habit of asking questions is not the only way he takes after my mother. Flat-faced and pale-eyed with long limbs, he might have been strong if he ever did physical work.

There's nothing for him to snoop around or disarrange, no distraction from me on the bed.

He sneaks a look back through the open door then reaches into his pocket.

'I thowt you might want these.'

The box flashes in the light, a shiny silver packet with orange logo.

I sit up on the bed and pull up my knees.

– *Yes, I do want it.*

'Maggie telt me that Frenchwoman widna sell her any. Keep a packet at work,' he says, 'fir headaches.'

The box is still sealed. He's not just offering me one or two.

He smiles and it's not a kind smile. The pills are not being given because he wants to take away my pain.

– *She said you were easier to love. I don't see it.*

'Weel, I canna stay here aal night. Bairns to put to bed. Maggie's gettin wur claese ready fir the morn. No been tae Wastray fir a peedie while.'

He throws the packet onto the bed. Thirty-two tablets.

For three days use only. Can cause addiction.

– *Please take them away.*

'Canna help thinkin it serves you right some o this,' he says. His smile twists and hardens. 'See that? Yir no better than the rest o us.'

He turns and walks away, deliberately leaving the door wide open.

A cardboard box cannot blink. It lies where it is thrown and waits to be picked up. The box wins every time.

I reach out, take up my phone. I type quickly and press send. The signal isn't bad in the upstairs of the house, not so good downstairs. There can be delays of hours between messages being sent and received in Orkney.

– *Help.*

I am engaged in a stand-off with the box of pills. The compulsion to take them is stronger than hunger or thirst. It feels life and death.

There are footsteps on the stairs, I stretch forward and seize the box and get to my feet. My father comes into the room.

'Esther? Wis that message yirs?'

– *Please forget I sent it. I've changed my mind.*

He sees the packet in my hand. Abruptly his expression becomes serious. Silence slides from the flat surfaces of the room.

'Whit I did before was wrong,' he says, 'flushin away the pills. I shouldna be tamperin. Shouldna got the car withoot askin.'

The cardboard sides flex between my finger and thumb.

'If you need them, you should hiv them,' he says.

The online forums are full of tapering plans. They'll ease the way I feel, just a few, just while I'm getting used to things.

'Remember the time,' he says, 'I found you in the windae o the shop among the jars o sweeties, been chowin them doon. Pleased as punch you were. Whit a belly ache you had. Granny threatened to boil up some moss and dose you like a coo.

'Then whenever you hid a belly ache everyone would laugh an say you'd been back at the sweetie jars and hid wis your own fault.'

He shakes his head, then holds out his hand.

I move the packet from one hand to the other. The room waits for a decision, the spiders circle around my knees.

Briefly the box forms a bridge between us.

He takes it quickly and pushes it into his pocket, then turns his face to hide his expression. Then he turns back and opens out his arms to me and steps forward. I rest my head on his shoulder and feel his strength as he holds me tight.

– *I'm sorry about the car. It was too much of a surprise. I'm not ready. It's too soon.*

He kisses the top of my head.

– *I love you.*

I feel all this at the same time as wishing he would hand back the pills back and say, 'You have this. They're yours.'

But he doesn't say that. I cry even harder.

'There noo lass,' he says. 'We'll think fresh on it the morn.' He sighs. 'Sooner be at home than gaan tae Westray,'

He pulls back and looks at me.

'Ah'll stay home if you want. Canna understand half o whit yir mither's family spaek aboot. Canna stomach the home brew. She'll represent us fine if you'd prefer me tae bide.'

He holds me close again. Deep inside a knot unties and there is a small, calm place. When we finally break, his cheeks are flushed.

The big light is put out and the bedside light put on. I feel I could sleep.

In the doorway he pauses and says, 'Doon the toilet?'

– *Aye.*

I nod and he smiles in return. Right now, I'm breathing through the pain.

Memories spin together: scratched metal, pill packets, bruised arms, bruised Marcus, Findlay winking, Granny and that look she gave me.

The sounds I made.

The next thing I know, my phone is jingling. I've not heard the ridiculous ringtone for a long time. It sets my heart racing. It doesn't make sense for anyone to call so late and I don't recognise the number, yet I press the red icon and answer.

'Esther, it is Claudette.'

In the background, I hear chairs scraping, glasses clinking and laughter. The thud-thud of someone tapping a microphone quietens the room briefly, there are strains of fiddles tuning and a flutter of notes from an accordion. A glass comes firmly to rest in the foreground and I hear Claudette tut her lips apart, ready to speak again.

She is not in a hurry. She knows I will not interrupt, although I could always hang up.

'I came into Catcher's after dinner,' she says. 'My housemates did not want to come because of a football game on television. I cannot understand the attraction. For me, that is always a pointless pastime.'

I imagine her elegantly dressed in deep colours, sipping a drink. Her accented words roll like gentle swell on cerulean water.

'I have been thinking about you today. The woman who came into the shop, your sister-in-law, I expect she told you what happened when I refused to serve her. She did not like the word 'no.' In fact she needs to understand that when someone is saying 'no' they are not going to change their mind, no matter how late it makes little boys for their supper.'

Music begins on stage, an accordion playing light and fast in a traditional style.

'If I have any concerns over the suitability of a product or its intended use, I will refuse sales.'

Her speech is rapid, less accented when she relays facts compared to the description of her confrontation with Maggie.

'When you came in for the Tramadol I felt I wanted to...' She pauses, searching for the right word, then says simply, 'I saw you needed help.'

She sighs.

The accordion is in full flight now, conversation in the room has quietened. In the muddle of sounds I can hear the bleep of a kitchen timer behind a bar stocked with local whisky and gin.

'It is a good line-up this evening,' she says.

I can picture the main room in detail, even though it has been a year since I went out anywhere. Many of my movements have been outside my control.

The list of acts is chalked up on the board between the windows that face the cathedral. It is possible to see from the Mercat Cross over to the Earl's Palace, a line which used to mark out the shore.

Either side of the chalk board, posters promote albums of local artists or visiting musicians, and long, black curtains form a simple backdrop for the stage. A stout metal bar hangs from the ceiling for speakers and stage lights linked together with wire spaghetti.

A fiddle strikes up and slips into the tune, weaving in and out of the notes in a companionable way.

'I think you'd like it,' says Claudette. 'If you came.'

– *I was selling this sort of thing, not buying.*

The music circulates over the lacquer tables up to the elegant plasterwork that has soaked up decades of music. The ceiling used to keep me entertained while I waited for Findlay having guitar lessons upstairs. I never wanted to learn. He never could.

My attention drifts. I remember the performers, arms over the backs of chairs, empty cups of coffee before them, passing the afternoon easily while people scurried past fighting the wind.

Another fiddle joins the set, distinctive as a song thrush at dusk.

'Listen,' says Claudette. 'It's Marcus.'

Fresh energy fills the melody, it's a higher, faster-paced sound, the notes sharp and clear. In the short spaces within the tune percussive notes are added. The lines of music run and twist, build, then turn and slide into a skiffling beat. More strings enter, the plucked notes of a mandolin, a new ribbon of sound weaving into the strokes of the fiddle. They dance, bow

214

and turn their backs then meet again, the fiddles taking the tune together, then one with a merrier voice skips into a new melody and all the other instruments chase after.

The musical parade is accompanied by the tapping of feet on the wooden floor, the hubbub of conversation, glasses lifting and falling onto tables.

The four walls of my room disappear.

I imagine Claudette with beads around her neck, eyelashes curled, lips pale pink, short chestnut curls on the nape of her neck. A shiver runs though me.

She is smiling, holding a phone to her ear as we listen to Marcus Macrae.

I can feel his eyes are on the band, bending their play to his will. His bow is twisting and curling, making an invisible figure of eight in the air with its tip, but his body is rooted to the spot.

A new lilt turns the tune and I feel as if he is looking at me, slowing and simplifying the melody so that what was a moment ago a field rippling in the breeze becomes a single ear of barley swaying in the wind.

Gradually, the other players drop out. Silence gathers around the notes, the audience's glasses are still, their conversation gone. There is a lump in my throat, a deeper release.

In our lesson, he told me that the signs used for silences in music are called rests.

– *Music for me.*

– *Silence for me.*

I imagine Claudette's eyes shining, her body also drawn like an arrow towards him. A natural sigh escapes my lips, rising below my ribs, passing over my heart and rolling out in a wave of gentle sound.

Claudette smiles. She doesn't speak.

The tune rises up into a final tender refrain, then the sound melts and holds. Finally there is silence.

Marcus nods to the band and looks beyond his circle of light, into the dark world where the music rolled and danced. The moment is electric.

He has that thing, that power to make each person feel he has played for them alone and given them everything. The music is a personal, private gift.

Then applause.

'Thanks for lettin me step in,' he says into the microphone. He nods to Jimmy Dingwall, his neighbour, who is paused to begin once more on the accordion.

There are footsteps as someone walks over to Claudette and me.

'It's Esther,' says Claudette. 'She was listening.'

The phone, warm against my ear, becomes real again. It takes a moment to realise where I am. There are the bare surfaces and black rectangles of night in the windows, small lights shine in the distance over Redland.

'Tell her I'm sorry to cancel our lesson, I've no plans to go south again,' says Marcus. 'Can I get you another drink?'

'Okay,' says Claudette. There's a pause, then she says, 'He's gone. I wanted you to hear him play.'

– *Thank you.*

Another tune has begun in the background, two accordions dosey-doe-ing each other in a new dance.

– *But I'm at home, sitting on the bed. I am not with you. Either of you.*

'I will see you soon,' says Claudette.

The telephone icon on the screen turns red and she's gone.

O

While Marcus and Claudette enjoy their drinks and the band plays on, Esther lies on her bed.

The memory box has sprung open.

Esther remembers the shop as it was when she was a child, a 'No Smoking' sign yet plenty of cigarettes, and packets of Drum, Golden Virginia and Old Holburn. She sees the lighters glowing like Christmas tree lights, waiting for their miniature Flotta flare to be lit.

The days of the local shop are already waning, but in the glass counter there are Jacobs crackers, Dairy Milk and neat rows of Trebor mints. The bananas and apples are kept in the wooden boxes used for putting deliveries around to houses. Her father put wheels on one and painted it red, so she could pull it along to help.

Small again, she's peering through the top of the freezer, eyeing the baskets of ice cream balanced on bags of frozen mince and white pan loaves.

A carton of new items is being unpacked by her mother; she is heavily pregnant and it is an effort to reach the top shelf. Watching is like seeing someone doing shopping in reverse. Up go the tins of custard power and a pair of Pot Noodles, a carton of fabric softener and six tins of pet food—Mrs Finnie comes in twice a week when it's too wet for her to drive to town. She has three dogs.

'Canna hiv a sweetie?' says Esther.

Her Orcadian accent was stronger as a child after hours spent listening to her mother yapping all day in the shop, to local people coming and going.

It was London that smoothed off the edges. After all she was of mixed heritage, Grandpa George was from Portsmouth and her father was from Caithness. The way someone speaks isn't always the truth of where they come from.

'Bring the bottles of Iron Bru fae the back.'

Esther does as she is asked.

'Canna hiv a sweetie noo?' she says.

'Sweet enough already,' says her mother.

But Kathleen reaches over and unscrews a jar of soor plums in the window and pinches one out between finger and thumb. Esther sucks the sweet and skips in circles trailing fingers over the counter and around the shelves until Willie senior comes in wanting *The Orcadian* and a packet of tobacco papers.

Esther doesn't catch all Willie says, but her mother understands. It's worse if Granny Ida's on the counter and out of the earshot of Grandpa George, she's as Orcadian as anybody underneath. Mostly it's talk about past times like when the mine went off on the beach during the war. She's heard the story a hundred times.

In the end, Esther goes through to the back room, rolls around on the floor and nearly swallows her sweet. Granny comes through and gets up on a step stool to dust the tin mugs while no one is looking.

Ida has a way of looking kindly at Esther when she's not noticing, trying to take in everything about her granddaughter, because never mind what it looks like to other people she loves her aafil dear.

~

Back in the present, flat on her bed, Esther can almost taste the soor plooms. Tramadol also comes in a lollipop, but it's never been offered. The slow-release capsules were meant to keep her going all day. Just because it's hard to overdose does not mean it is a trustworthy drug.

Simon was not trustworthy. But he did exist, didn't he? He was going to stay. But there was some reason he didn't. That's what she told everyone.

She wonders if her father has flushed away the pills that Findlay gave her.

He has.

He did it straight away. Then he stood in the kitchen and tore the box to shreds. When the bin flapped shut he'd passed a hand down over his face, covering his eyes for a moment. He'd looked out into the night, over the rusted pumps and the byre. Now he goes through the back corridor and past his mother-in-law's old room.

He goes into the room that was the old post office and finds Findlay drinking a beer and watching television in the make-shift living room, rather than come through and sit together. He sees a game of cars went on between the grandbairns before bedtime and the floor is scattered with turned-over wrecks.

Andrew speaks to his son. 'You'd hiv been better leavin Granny's room till you'd done more on the shop.'

The bottle pauses a second.

'Maggie wanted tae dae hid,' says Findlay, eyes fixed on the game.

It's not the clutter and mess of the boys that Andrew minds at all. What would they do without them about the place? It's something about his son's attitude to Esther that puts him on edge.

For a calm man, Andrew is just about as angry as anything has ever made him. His hands are closed tight in his pockets.

'Niver gaed me a car,' says Findlay.

'No,' says Andrew.

'Niver gaed me money fir gaan tae business school in London. Whit a waste *that* was.'

Findlay doesn't take his eyes off the screen.

'You've had just aboot everythin else,' says Andrew, gesturing towards the house. His voice is low and quiet, matching the volume of the television so what he says cannot be overheard. 'And I'm tellin you to leave your sister alone.'

'Whitever you say,' says Findlay.

Andrew turns his back and withdraws down the corridor, more than ever he doesn't give a damn about the scratches on the car.

It's hard for Andrew to understand why Kathleen always had their son as a favourite. Many times he's thought about getting to the bottom of it all, but it's not the sort of conversation he has with Kathleen.

They'd let Granny Ida choose their baby daughter's name, and once it was said there was nothing anyone could do. She'd recited verses she'd learned at Sunday School and told them Esther was a 'Gey strong wife fae the Owld Testament.'

Esther 4:25
Come to our rescue, O Lord. Help me; I am all alone, and have no one to turn to but you.

The connection had always puzzled him, but the name fitted the bairn.

What's in a name, though? She'd have been the same child whatever she was called, thick brown hair falling in curls and a terrible, curious urge to wander. Wilful as sin her mother called her. There was never any confusion at school, Esther was the only one with her name.

Now and again as the years passed, Andrew has wondered how things might have been different if Esther had been a boy. There's plenty of time in the workshop for wondering while hands are at work. The name Ida would have chosen would have been George, and dreadful spoilt the boy would have been.

Andrew stands at the laundry sink, looking towards where the lawnmower waits half-assembled.

Willie, who drove over to Orphir to pick up the car they'd spotted on Merkit Place, is taking a dram and wondering how it's funny that a lass who used to talk the legs off a goat has been stopped silent for a year now. He doesn't know how Andrew manages.

~

Beyond the dyke, over the old football pitch, a chalky half-moon is rising into a dark bronze sky. Through the clouds the ragged halo casts streams of light, tinted with green and red. Andrew has seen many such a moon before. It'll grow small as it rises, swing, sink and swell until the golden glow of the rising sun catches the moon's mountains and edges them in crimson.

In the town, the rising moon has less majesty, but Claudette sees it as she dresses for going to Catcher's and notices it again high and cold as she switches off the light in her room. The darkness takes a long time to settle. Caffeine and whisky, and the sound of Marcus Macrae's breathing keeps her awake. She is determined to sleep, though, a second night without rest will make for a long day tomorrow and they have an early start.

~

In Stembister House, Granny hears the groans of Mrs Rory next door and the ding-dong of the button for the night carer—all Mrs Rory wants is someone to say, 'Ssh dear, just a bad dream.'

Ida's hand moves to the lamp and light pools onto the bed. She takes a black and white photograph from under her pillow.

'Poor Winnie,' she says, gently touching the wrinkled surface. 'Her poor peedie lass.'

The bright eyes of a child look back at her.

Ida pictures herself in a knee-length skirt, carrying home-made lemonade from the shop. The glass bottles were stoppered with greased marbles, and collected once the boys went back to play the second half. She goes around asking if they've finished, doing her best not to blush when George's hand touches hers and his friends laugh when she walks away.

She had only just gone up from Sunday School to Bible Class, but she felt a woman in her straw hat with its turned-up brim, pinned with a corsage of roses.

Once Ida's pleats were cut she didn't look any different in years to Winnie, who was nineteen and already had a serviceman walking her home before Stuart Harvey arrived.

When the war came and Stuart Harvey enrolled in the Canadian Navy he'd promised his mother he'd visit the old croft down by Clivie Bay. He was a second cousin of sorts, whose forebears had left Orkney two generations ago. Winnie had been collecting a basket of eggs when he walked up the brae. She had been ready to fall and so had he.

Once Winnie was married it wasn't long before she was wearing a coat that flared at the back. Everyone had seemed pleased for her. More than likely a boy would be born. Harvey men always had boys, too many for a small croft to support—that's why they always went overseas.

Stuart had been posted away on a ship built by the British and worked by a Canadian crew. Winnie had less need for her skirt and polka dot blouse. They'd fitted Ida sweetly.

The story was that a mine washed up on Mussaquoy rocks put Ida in George's arms for the first time. They had stayed until dawn at a dance not to break curfew and walked back together, the red of her skirt coming true as the sun rose. The truth was they had already stopped for a long while in the byre before the detonation.

Ida and George came together often in those long summer days and dusky nights. But the new radar technology meant the searchlight stations inevitably needed fewer men. When summer passed George was redeployed.

They'd never made any promises to each other, simply broke their hearts in two when he'd said goodbye.

Afterwards, Ida sickened with grief. Outwardly you could not place what was wrong with her, yet being in her presence gave a person a deep melancholic feeling. So, as Winnie's time grew near she was spared from the shop and forgiven school to go stay with her cousin and help with the new baby over winter. After all, they were close.

With the photograph in hand Ida slowly drifts into thoughts of Brek, the old farmhouse overlooking the cliffs of East Mainland. She remembers rubbing Winnie's back to ease her tired muscles, and if they both couldn't sleep they would watch the bright searchlight beams scouring the sky and the sparks of tracer fire as German planes were chased from Scapa Flow.

~

Veronica Harvey has taken a night drive, parked her car in the dunes, then made a short uphill climb away from the sea. It's not quite the same view as her mother would have had, but it is very close.

This is where I come from, thinks Veronica.

For her it has been a pleasure, coming to understand the boundaries between the Orkney parishes, and how important they were and still are. The names of farms, fields and lanes hold the past and present in a way she has never known before. In Vancouver she knew areas and districts, some better than others, but it isn't the same—a single apartment block could hold the whole population of Deerness, a handful could hold most of the city of Kirkwall.

The air is fresh and cool above her, the sky clearing and becoming a truer black. The moon, high and small, makes silver trails of the empty roads.

The farm down at Clivie Bay that was too small for her great-grandfather's brothers has been taken over by a couple from the north of England who have ideas of growing organic vegetables. They were interested in her photographs and knew some of the old family had gone to America. Veronica politely corrects them, 'No, it was Canada.'

They are incomers themselves, still finding their feet.

But tonight she is at Brek, where her mother lived and where she was born. Moonlight strikes the slates, glossing them pewter, while the walls guard the empty space within.

She was right, night visits bring the past closer.

The warmth from Veronica's exercise is leaving her body, her feet are cold and there is whisky back at the hotel. It will help her sleep, help her defy the last remains of jet lag. It won't be long before she must be awake and dressed, ready to leave.

This place, an island with little to recommend it on the surface, thrills her.

Won't someone take me dancing?

I know there is a second bow, but he grieves for the spare. Yet, the audience didn't seem to care, only the connection of music and body and sound was important.

– Are you thinking about your face again? The scars he saw?

The thought flashes past and goes round and round my head, sinking and rising. Pain is streaming after me like a locomotive and the pills are in the drains, flushed away. I can follow the thread of events that's brought me here.

Sex after the London launch left me staring at the tangerine-grey ceiling, wishing Simon would vanish and that I had a clean empty bed. My intuition about his decision to abandon me for a holiday cut deep; any choice against me cuts deep.

Now I have an empty bed.

Above Skulstad, the moon is leaving its roost. I leave my bed and see the pearlescent light reflected on the corrugated roof of Willie's byre.

I remember Granny's story about Grandpa George. The sound of an explosion made her leap into his arms in terror for her life and they ran into the barn.

I rock back on my heels so only the sky above is visible, tilt my neck back into radio-crackle pain. The stars are fading, shimmering in the deep ultraviolet sky. I remember Granny, and that look she gave me as she slipped the photograph away.

– I understand, it's time to leave.

I pick up my phone and go quietly downstairs. In the hallway I lift two jackets from the coat hooks then slip the latch and let myself out of the back door. This way I will avoid setting off the outdoor lights. My eyes are already adjusted so the abandoned skateboards pose no threat.

Towards the north, the land curls back on itself and cuts inwards, a pool of water is growing as the tide advances. The inlet is alive with the squabble of geese and the squeaky trill of migrant birds. There's a rich texture to the darkness, the expectancy of a long journey ahead.

Willie's barn squats heavily on the other side of the lane, more palpable because of its fullness, the fields have been emptied and the kye brought home.

– *So this is goodbye.*

The landscape breathes deepest in the early hours.

'Whar are you gaan?'

George stands behind me. The moonlight catches the dinosaurs on his pyjamas, their mouths full of sharp teeth. When I realise who it is my heart settles. I raise a finger to my lips.

He checks back towards the empty house then walks forward.

'You went roond the back,' he says. 'So the light didna come on.'

He points upwards to the stars and I look up.

'The inside of the Earth is hotter than the surface of the Sun,' he says.

But he sees I'm not really interested.

He steps forward and takes hold of my hand. He wants me to stay.

'Auntie Esther?'

– *Please let go of my hand. I am walking away.*

George's face is alabaster, serious, hardly like a boy's at all. Then unexpectedly he just lets go and stops by the skip.

– *Isn't this what everyone wants?*

'Is it time to go?' says George.

The glint of something in the skip catches my attention. I reach into the piles of debris and fish out a tin mug that has caught the keys I chucked away. I place the mug and keys on top of the roof of the new car, they can take it to Westray.

At the last moment, I can be thoughtful. My father's heart is in the right place.

I walk towards the silver bubble. He follows.

'Can I come with you?' says George.

I shake my head and take the keys from my mother's coat pocket.

– *You don't understand.*

I open the door and get into the driver's seat. He comes and stands close to the window, watching as I adjust mirrors and put the key in the ignition. It's like being a learner all over again.

My limbs feel watery, every effort to do things correctly only makes me more clumsy, and I am in pain. Yet, I am undeterred.

When the car is ready I open the window. George leans forward and I kiss his cheek then start the engine. For the first time in twelve months I drive by myself, panic rising and heart pumping out blood and fear.

~

The moonface boy is left behind. Skulstad is left behind with my mother and father, Willie's barn and the petrol pump.

A blackbird is trying to get clear of the field, struggling to get lift from the low cold air.

This close to panic I feel high. A polka runs through my head.

Dah-de-dah de-dah-de-dah-de-dah-dah-dah.

There is no way of unlearning, forgetting maybe, but not un-learning. The car and I move surely along the single-track lane. I know where I am going.

Each minuscule decision fights against baffled, dull thoughts. It is difficult to explain how hard it is to keep going.

A car overtakes me on the brae past the airport, accelerating towards town.

I used to sing along to the radio in the car, full volume, not caring because no one could hear. But in London, where there was always someone listening, there was no place where it was safe.

The night of the accident I'd turned up the radio, I'd wanted other voices, anything except my own. At the last second as I flew around the corner and tractor lights filled the windshield, I realised I did not want to be silenced.

The trees are the same bone white with a handful of tattered leaves. The edges of my vision start to pull inward, the road is caught in the fish-eye lens of the past.

A year ago I was wearing high heels and scent.

Simon was skiing with his father, maybe already laying in ground-work with the chalet girl.

I'd been searching for the car keys, hot-faced from blocking Maggie's entrance to Granny's room. It wasn't respectful and Findlay should have told her.

Then there had been a call from Helga at Stembister House saying Granny was getting worse and needed to go into the hospital for fluids.

All I was really trying to do was leave. I had to get to the launch, these family things were not what I came back for.

But my mother went on speaking. There was nothing I could do to stop her, she couldn't understand that this was not the time.

'....niver came to the hospital when you were born, widna close the shop. Livin in the same hoose an she niver buthered aboot you. Niver wanted tae hadd you or babysit so me and yur fither could gae oot of a night. And you still thowt she wis everythin. I dinna ken. Bringin her flooers and she paid you no regard.

'I canno mind Granny ever haddin us except to makk us still. Couldna bear to. I wis put aside, left to bide on my own until thir wis Elspeth fir company.'

Why tell me? Is it because Granny is dying?

228

The door opens, rain is flying into the kitchen. I'm thinking plenty, but there's no time to say any of it because I have to leave.

'The only person she ever loved is in the kirkyard. She can bide in Stembister noo.'

She had put her arm across my path. Her voice low and hard.

'I dinna love your fither the same way as she loved Grandpa George. I dinna want a man like that. But you. I tried tae love you. And you left us aal.'

'You tried?'

'Findlay wis easier.'

Then I was gone.

Visitor book

I have to stay out of the past because I have the wheel. Control the vehicle, keep your head up and do not be sick, lock your arms.

– *Hold on by your fingernails if you have to.*

The road ahead is clear. The antennae on Wideford Hill stand up black against the swathe of dark cerulean blue. Further west the moon is dropping and the sky is the colour of flesh and stone.

– *Only gae doon if you've energy tae cam back up again.*

There you see Mother, there's dialect in me.

Headache-bright light streams from the supermarket windows. The sky is still dark over the street lights. I'm way ahead of the crows.

I take a turning into a lane between two plain houses and pull into the car park for Stembister House. The first part of the journey is done. I breathe through the tears and let them fall.

Behind me, a creamy blur stretches in a line around the horizon, blocked to the north by a sweeping shaft of cloud. A light is on over the entrance porch surrounded with ageing plastic fittings, the rails and handles are useful to keep me steady.

The out-of-order notice is still there, but I enter the code anyway and hear the click of an automatic latch. It shouldn't allow visitors to enter except between nine and five, so I suppose something is still not working. Good.

I have to concentrate on dampening the sound of my footsteps because I must avoid detection, detection will mean trouble. The fire doors are spring-loaded and could flick me away like pin ball.

A pain ball.

A pin pill.

A pin, a pill, a pain.

A long febrile moan comes from behind a door, fading into muttered one-sided conversation. Poor Mrs Rory.

Inside Granny's room, I close the door carefully. She is asleep with her lamp on, the photograph of the little girl tucked between her fingers.

I begin to get the clothes she will need and she stirs. When she opens her eyes she takes a quick look around, making sure of the photograph, then smiling at me.

'Whit a good thing tae see you,' she says quietly.

Everything is ready now.

I ease back the blankets and she sits upright. She doesn't want help getting dressed, but I try to speed her along where I can. There isn't much time if we want to get everything done.

'You can spaek tae me if you want,' she whispers.

I place my hand on her cheek.

– *I know.*

She allows me to comb and clip back her hair and asks for a necklace to be fastened around her neck. The pendant is a gold bird, smooth-winged, delicate and strong. I haven't seen it before.

The only footwear I can find are slippers. They are sheepskin with a hard sole and will have to do. She slides in her feet.

'The other shoes were guttery efter wur visit tae Newark. I dinna ken whar they are noo,' she says.

It was six weeks ago, but where has the summer gone? I remember the pictures on the noticeboard, the wheelchairs and blankets, the bewildered faces wondering at not being able to run on the sand anymore. Granny was stood apart from the rest, zipped into a grey coat, white shirt collar peeping over the edges, her gaze searching the water.

My mother's coat is too large around the shoulders, it takes on a mannish style that suits my grandmother better. She puts her hands in the pockets and pulls out a small fabric purse with a metal clasp, heavy with coins.

'Yur mither's alwis prepared.'

She leaves the purse of coins on the bedside table, then turns ready to go.

'Early fir the boat are we no?'

I shake my head, then hand her the photograph.

– *We've a busy schedule Granny.*

In the corridor she takes my arm and we do our best to keep steady. We are upright in our own fashion.

The heat and the smell, she needs a break from the heat and the smell. We all do.

The interior keypad does not operate at all, but a series of twists, pushes and pulls releases the catch and we're outside. Granny makes no effort to draw her coat tight or bow her head to shelter from the cold. She is smelling the air, eyes seeking the glimmer of dawn. It is still some time away, but it is coming.

I've got Granny and we're taking a trip.

Two gulls are raising the alarm, parading on the chimney pots, squeaking and squawking.

We lever and lower ourselves into the car; it takes us both a while to get our seatbelts fastened—it is a slow getaway, but we slip from Stembister unnoticed.

By my side Granny takes stock of the small changes in town: the new traffic bollards, the demolished builders' warehouse near the supermarket.

I have an urge to tell her about other things she might be interested in and take a breath, making an effort to let my diaphragm sink. It finds the space inside, but silent tears rather than words are unlocked.

A cool hand rests over mine on the wheel, fragile fingers with sunspots. She pats lightly.

'You dinna need tae spaek,' says Granny.

Ahead of us, the dawn is lengthening.

A skein of geese receives a disapproving tut.

'Niver used tae be so many. Used tae be an excitement tae see twa-three togither.'

Shooting geese had been part of the *Island Fling* plan. The gun club was interested in the work, refreshments of local produce would be provided in a wicker basket. There would be island charm to the experience, and dead geese. Win–win.

Simon has more than his fair share of charm, just ask the chalet girl.

I feel Granny's hand on mine, breathe in the smell of roses and see the dawn breaking. My heart is huge and hard in my chest, as I go past the bone trees.

– *I stayed, I did not go back to the past. I am here.*

We pass the turning for Redland and head over to the low eastern hills and the turning for the kirkyard. The sky is clearing, the band of light broader, brighter and tinged with peach and summer rose.

Granny sighs.

'I dinna want tae see George the day,' she says.

My foot lifts from the accelerator.

– *Why not?*

'Will you tak me somewhare?'

I nod.

– *Where?*

'Follow on. Ah'll say when.'

So, I drive onwards.

There are only half a dozen miles before the end of the land, before cliffs and fisherman's debris and the Pentland Firth. We head past crofts and byres, buildings in the creases of the land where trees shelter in the lee of their stone walls. When we're closing in on the pinch of land at Dingieshowe, Granny speaks.

'This een.'

There's a track before the dunes, the left side partly washed away, exposing fist-sized stones and potholes filled deep with water. It's further back from the cliffs than the one heading up to Pipersquoy and has fields on either side. Bales loom darkly waiting to be collected and wrapped.

Three-quarters of the way up the track sits a low stone building, the windows blank, the door worn by farm dogs, wind and rain.

The fields are dotted with decomposing crofts that are uneconomical to repair. A new farmhouse overlooks Clivie Bay further up the hill, perfectly positioned for a picturesque beating when storms come through. They have kept the name of the place; a shiny wrought-iron sign on a pole says Brek.

Granny points to the abandoned house. The gate is open and the silver car bounces over the ruts then slides to a standstill.

Slippers are not going to do well here. But a woman who keeps a purse of coins in her pocket also has other useful things stashed about. There are wellingtons in the boot and they fit over Granny's slippers. The open tops waft around her knees and catch her skirt, but she is satisfied.

We go to the door.

It's the house of my great, great grandmother. Where Granny was born.

'Gae open the door,' says Granny, gesturing.

– *Please don't fall over anything.*

The door is still solid on its hinges and swings open. Inside, the partitions have been felled and it is back to the original single space. It smells of rats and peat smoke and is intensely cold. I use my phone as a torch and light the way, holding Granny's arm.

'The baby wis born here,' says Granny, pointing to the darkest corner.

Neglect and sadness seep from the walls, a feeling springing from more than material ruin.

'My auntie delivered the bairns and helped wi poor peedie Alice,' she says. 'She wis niver strong, peedie lass. Broke all wur hearts when she passed. Meningitis. Took hold wi the servicemen too. Poor Winnie, I feared for her, she was so stricken wi grief.'

A shiver runs through me, I remember the low pink headstone where Alice lies: 'Taken to live with the angels.'

'Couldna go anywhere fir the snow that winter. Mind, it worked oot fir the best, fir both o us.' Freezing air slips in through the open door, the temperature is lowering before the dawn. 'Whit a chance Winnie had. All passage paid fir by the Canadian government.'

Brek

Somewhere close by an animal scuttles. The light outside is beginning to reveal shapes in the distance. I put pressure under Granny's elbow, anxious at the passage of time. She doesn't move, doesn't seem to notice the cold.

'I was hellish depressed efter George wis sent away, then nine months later there I wis waving Winnie off on the *Ola*. First, bound for Liverpool and then she took the *Mauritania*. Seemed the whole island was taen apart. Hid wis no an easy time.'

– *Come on Granny.*

'Aye,' she says. 'Hid wis gey hard tae go back tae me mither's house.'

She responds this time and turns to come. The greys are multiplying, becoming complex shapes, shades of carnation pink are beginning to light the underside of clouds.

Across the bay I see Pipersquoy, and there's a space where the car should be.

'Whit wis that?' says Granny.

– *Sorry, it was involuntary. I was looking for him.*

She shakes her head.

We leave the heavy lintels and uneven stones, and the roof ragged with moss, and hobble down the overgrown path back to the car. Dockens are shrivelling and browning, broadcasting their seed.

The tyres cut into the turf as I edge the car backwards. There are fifteen minutes to get back to town, easy if I drove like I used to. What I had thought was the most important evening of my life does not matter any more. All I wish is to take Granny safely to where she wants to be.

Granny raises her hand onto the window, pressing her palm into the glass, her face stays turned towards the deserted farmhouse. As we move her whole body leans, resisting the descent to the road. She keeps her eyes on the lichen-smeared stones and Brek's poor unkempt scratch of ground.

When we are about to turn onto the tarmac road she grips the door handle and I fear she's going to pull it open. There's something left behind, some memory that she cannot bear to leave. I feel her longing spread and grow, imagine the fast, desperate thump of her heart.

– *What takes you away from the kirkyard and brings you back to Brek?*

Slowly, I unclasp my left hand from the steering wheel and cover Granny's knee. It's like hanging one armed from a cliff. But I do it for her.

I know she would have hated leaving Skulstad for Stembister House. I could feel her deep distress, even when I was the prodigal daughter in London.

– *Why did they not feel it?*

When we round the next bend Brek disappears from view, hidden by a green shoulder of land. Of all the places she could go to, it was Brek that called her back. Finally, she gives up her hold and surrenders to the seat.

The car and me, we've dropped from sight. A wound has been exposed that she's always kept covered. She is falling from a high place, streaming through the air and no one can save her.

– *I'll take care of you.*

Her eyes are full of tears and waves of sadness flow from her small, weary body and fill the car.

– *I'm taking you. I'll take care of you.*

I have always known that my grandmother needed me. And I knew that my own mother did not.

She once said it herself, 'Findlay wis easier to love.'

The dawn proper is breaking and the windows of high farms in the west are golden. Skulstad will be empty. Young George will be quizzed if he betrays witnessing my departure. My father will be wearing polished shoes and driving a scratched car.

Granny's attention is returning to the present. I move my hand back to the wheel. The light is coming steadily, silhouettes breaking and taking on depth and colour. Granny glances at the turning for the kirkyard.

'Yir mither always puts the radio on,' she says as we enter the town.

We drive past the top of Clay Loan. The shrubs that were a mound of fresh green and frothy pink in the spring look like brushwood waiting for a match. A few brown petals still cling to the tiger-lilies, but most have flitted their stems and lie like scraps of yellow cloth on the grass.

The miniature tour continues as we head to the harbour. The road bends gently to the right and is renamed a crescent, the houses are grand and made from precisely cut stone rather than ones reclaimed from the shore. Past the Episcopal Kirk the road widens and the descent becomes steeper before the space opens up again, green on the left with tall trees and the remains of the Earl's Palace, and on the right hand side the red umber giant, St Magnus Cathedral.

'Could've danced every night o the week,' says Granny, smiling. 'And the things we kenned fae the WAAFs,' she chuckles. 'Don't spaek.'

We're passing The Catcher now. The doors are closed and it's too early for a light on inside. A sign has been left out from the night before, a round-faced man with metal glasses and a plain expression is holding an accordion on his knee, 'Jimmy Dingwall and friends, followed by open mic, 10pm.'

Granny hums a polka, *Dah-de-dah, de-dah, de,-dah, de-dha-da-da*. The same I had in my head when I left peedie George standing in the dark at Skulstad.

We turn to the harbour. Work is being done on the sea wall, wire fences are up opposite the Kirkwall Hotel and there's a bollard blocking where you used to drive. The turning onto the quayside has moved. I have to follow the new signs for access to the pier.

Herring gulls squabble over the marina, their black-tipped wings and white fuselage bodies making them stand out against the grey sky. Over the low hills of St Ola the rising sun picks out the boxed shapes of the distant houses. Two wind turbines spin.

A great wave of fatigue sweeps through me.

'Mind oot,' says Granny.

She points to a man on the pedestrian crossing. I brake hard.

I stare at his yellow trousers, high-visibility vest and hard green hat. He examines the ground as he walks and speaks into a mobile phone. In his other hand is a carrier bag. I didn't see him at all.

– *The beacon hadn't caught my attention.*

Granny waits for me to move on.

A car comes up behind, lights bright in my mirror. Step by step I have to go through the procedure for moving away. It isn't safe, me driving. Me.

– *What am I doing?*

Panic starts to swell, my mouth is dry. It should be Tramadol time, I should be taking pills not be behind the wheel. A horn sounds and a car goes past, driver's hands waving. I crawl in first gear past the ferry terminal and toilets.

– *This was Tramadol time.*

Only a shallow lip marks the edge of the inner harbour basin. The sight of it turns my stomach. I blow out slowly. There are pedestrian routes marked out in yellow on the pier, but it's a no man's land for cars.

– *This isn't safe.*

The pier widens into a broader section of marked-out asphalt where we must line up to wait for the inter-island boats.

Half a dozen cars are already waiting for the Westray boat.

Maggie and Findlay are at the front in the four by four, my father and mother in the scratched car behind. My mother is talking rapidly into her mobile phone, my father watching the shore hands at work. No one notices when the silver bubble joins the end of the queue. Before us in the queue there is a red sports car. Claudette is leaning against the driver's door, vaporizer between her lips. She sees me at once, waves and smiles.

Marcus is standing close beside her. His gaze is raised to the top of Wideford Hill, his jaw held tight.

– *You weren't at home.*

Then the penny drops and I realise all this time since the concert they've been together. My legs turn to water, my stomach drops away. I had no idea how much store I'd set in you, Marcus Macrae.

– *I can be very stupid Granny. I believe too easily.*

Claudette strolls over and knocks on Granny's window. My fingers are trembling, my heart running on like a curlew's call.

Granny smiles and presses the button to lower the glass. The smell of ozone and diesel fumes carry on the damp morning air. The icy sound of shrieking gulls flies inside the car. Claudette looks from Granny's face to mine. I turn the key back and the engine dies.

– *What? Surprised?*

Westray or bust

It knocks Claudette out to see them together, and that Esther is behind the wheel. Isn't that everything that she's been hoping for from her patient, come friend, come protégé? There is a similarity not just in appearance, but manner as well, a kindredness. The same bright expression is in both of their eyes, the thirst of an explorer.

'You are going to the wedding?' says Claudette.

Ida nods.

'I brought Marcus,' she says. 'His car was parked overnight behind the cathedral. It is unreliable anyway.'

Esther is looking past Claudette. Marcus concentrates his attention on the mottled sandstone buildings along the harbour. It's hard for him not to turn and look. It's hard because he would very much like to spend more time with this woman who has a streak of white hair and who took something from him that he hadn't quite been ready to give. But now he is.

Marcus had a choice last night, he's always had a choice.

Claudette looks towards two men in navy boiler suits leaning by a stack of plastic trays filled with bread and crates of beer.

'Did you book the car on?' she says.

Esther has forgotten this sort of detail. All she had in her mind was taking Granny to see Grandpa George's grave and going to the wedding together. After all they were both invited—it was decided by others that they were not fit to attend. Nothing had been booked or paid for.

Esther shakes her head.

'I will settle things for you.'

Claudette leaves the window and walks over to the men. She's in skintight jeans and an oversized yellow cowl-neck sweater. As she passes Marcus he turns to stare at the ground by his feet. What he needs to do is becoming clearer.

While Claudette is in negotiations his gaze turns towards the silver, easy-to-park, low fuel consumption, low road tax car.

In his mind, he strides over and opens the door. He takes Esther's hands from the wheel and brings her gently to her feet. Then he kisses her, like the way he wanted to up at Pipersquoy when they had held each other's gaze in the mirror.

But Marcus does not move. All he dares to do is lean on the car and glance in her direction. There is no chance for small talk with this woman.

'What kinda buddy is he Esther?' says Granny inside.

She is looking at Marcus.

Esther's mind stutters, there is no easy answer. She shrugs her shoulders.

'I dinna ken him as a Westray man.'

They hear the clang of the stern doors opening and the ramps lowering. The top of Esther's legs itch through her jeans. She sees her face in the rear-view mirror, very pale, cheekbones high and white, hair swept back.

Meanwhile, Kathleen has gone against Andrew's wishes and got out of the car.

A car that goes missing Andrew can smooth over, but not a missing mother. Kathleen emerges and her hair is blown helter-skelter in the wind as she goes to the four-by-four to speak with Maggie and Findlay.

'Oh, Maggie, you'll niver guess.'

Out of the corner of her eye, Kathleen sees the worse-for-wear Marcus Macrae walk away from the Frenchwoman's car as if he has a purpose in mind.

She hopes he can keep a wedding dance moving. She can't think what that Frenchwoman is talking about with the shore men, why are they laughing with her? Of all the mornings for her mother to go wandering she would have to choose this one.

Kathleen sees where Marcus is heading. Her stoical smile slips to a tight frown. She has a head start though, and Kathleen's strides will bring her to Esther well before Marcus.

What the hell was Esther thinking?

~

Veronica is wearing a fuchsia scarf. She watches everything, sees the tall man abandon the red sports car, a flash in his eye, and then Kathleen overtakes him with no trouble at all, and he stops in his tracks. Veronica frowns, this is not how she expected this morning to be. Although you can never tell what families will do.

~

Kathleen is speaking to Esther, 'For the love of sin whit are you daein?' She breaks off. 'Mither? Whit the hell are you daein here?'

'Comin fir the weddin on Westray,' says Ida.

'You need…you've tae gae back tae Stembister Hoose. They're callin the police because no one kens whar you are.'

'Ah'm here,' says Ida, 'and Ah'm gaan tae the Westray waddeen. Used tae be fine home brew in Westray. Proper stuff.'

Esther turns her head. Marcus was coming their way, but he has turned around and his head has dropped.

Kathleen comes around to Ida's door and pulls it open; the mud-covered wellingtons are the final straw.

'Yir gettin oot this car an gaan back right noo.'

There is no hook for Kathleen to grasp, she cannot imagine what her mother and daughter have been doing together or why they are here.

Two men break away from Claudette, shaking their heads and leaving her with smiles. Above Wideford Hill a curtain of cloud is coming, backed by a coarse wind. A small pallet-lifter driven by a man in a flat cap takes the ramp onto the boat, clunk-clunk on the bridge of iron, carrying bread and beer.

'Okay, beuy,' he calls.

The first car is beckoned forward. Maggie is coming to see what is going on and George is running after, catching his feet and stumbling on the black and yellow rumble bars.

'Can I help, Kathleen?' she says.

She is met with an uncanny, unblinking stare from both Ida and Esther.

George passes his mother and bustles around to his aunt's door.

'I didna tell anyone,' he says breathlessly. 'They musta guessed.'

He grins broadly, then takes a keek at his great-granny Ida wearing his granddad's big wellingtons. George thinks, she'd be better off wearing his boots because she's so tiny. It makes him giggle.

~

The first of the cars is marshalled forward and Veronica tidies her scarf and starts the engine of her hire car. She has a trunk full of presents and wonders when she'll have a chance to share her gifts. To tell the truth, she is nervous about how they will be received.

The moving queue transforms the situation, there is a compulsion to follow and not be left behind, to sort things out afterwards. Andrew and Findlay already have their engines running. Marcus has folded his long legs back inside the sports car and is waiting.

Kathleen hurries away, her hips rolling like boulders as she marches with a mobile pressed to her ear.

'Helga? Dinna worry aboot Ida. I hiv her here wi me. Some confusion with my dowter aboot who wis gaan to tak her the day. Aye. Westray. She'll be back by half-past seven no doot. Aafil sorry fir the confusion.'

There's no need to give Helga Gordon the full details. She fills in the gaps and thinks her friend Kathleen has been unlucky with that daughter, and never a word of thanks. They never should have let Ida choose the bairn's name. Esther is not a local name.

Before Claudette joins Marcus she stops again at Esther's door. Rain is sweeping over the other side of Kirkwall Bay.

'They're not full,' she says. 'Payment is possible on board with cards.'

Again, Esther has not thought about this. Her mind is not working at normal speed, although it's true that she is feeling more, thinking more, but the gearing system has been knackered by mu-opioid inhibitors. So much can be blamed on withdrawal. Also, she is broke.

The empathy between the two women, which from the start has been unusually close, allows understanding from the smallest change in expression.

'They will accept my card,' says Claudette, quickly. 'If you will let me pay.'

Esther nods.

Claudette strides away, legs flashing in the rain. Marcus is in the passenger seat, eyes forward, hair brushing the roof of the car. The neck of his fiddle case pokes up into the back window.

Well, Claudette had him first, didn't she. First come, first served.

~

The rain repels the dawn backward into murky half-light. Houses that briefly stood out in the landscape retreat. In the old homestead of Brek, creatures are seeking dry corners, forced together by circumstance they both flee and attack.

Brek saw everything, a rich war and then a poor peace. It left a hollow feeling that the family could never name and felt they didn't have a right to own. They were alive, they had made it through, so why hark back? The old folk passed on.

~

The radar vane above the bridge spins around and around like a twisting bird as the boat's crane arm extends over the quayside and takes its last load. Drips of rain slide over everything, over the men in blue and neon yellow who don't seem to mind any more than the hills. The giant parrot's beak bow doors are held aloft by shiny hydraulic arms in rusty casings.

A gentle roll comes ashore, enough to rock the lifeboat in the basin. The cars rumble between the black bars and clunk-clunk onto the boat.

Ida's gaze is on the red car.

'He's gey tall,' she says.

Esther had not thought of the complications of driving onto the boat. If she had, she wouldn't be here. She wonders if Findlay has any Nurofen Plus. She wonders how many he takes. How many he carries.

'Yir doin fine,' says Granny. 'Did you see yur mither when she saw wur boots?'

Ida catches Esther's eye. They both laugh out loud, and then Esther has to concentrate and steady the wheel to guide the silver bubble onto the ship. The car is so light with her and Granny inside that there's hardly a clunk as they cross over and pass under the huge, hinged prow.

Passengers' minds are turning to coffee and bacon rolls, although Veronica has butterflies in her stomach because of who is on board and what will inevitably happen soon.

The four-by-four makes a sold thunk as it drives over. The boys wave at the shore men who've got together to form a group around one of the hydraulic arms. One leans back on his heels and throws a handful of syllables into the air, making other heads nod in earnest. Another tilts his hat back and looks up into the rain, then over to the pink buoys that mark the safe channel out of the harbour.

It is only the very slightest of bad omens, as four generations of the same family roll aboard. They're all heading for a wedding on Westray, held in the chapel on the hill overlooking Pierowall. It will be celebrated with dancing in the school hall, and bairns have been invited to bring their swimming suits and to use the community pool.

George is high as a kite.

'I didna ken Granny wis allooed oot,' he says, pushing his head and shoulders between the headrests.

'Course she's allooed oot,' says Findlay.

'You never tak her oot. Hasna she any shoes? She's wearin Granddad's boots.'

'Course she's got shoes,' says Maggie.

'An you said that Auntie Esther wouldna ever drive again...'

Findlay is watching the woman ahead of him as she lifts a bag out of the back of her car. Her clothes look more cruise boat than Westray boat. She has a vivid pink scarf wrapped around her hair like he remembers Granny wearing when he and Esther were bairns. It's a funny thing, memory.

Maggie snaps him back to reality.

'Fetch that bag o stuff fir the boys tae keep them busy,' she says.

'Is she gonna start spaekan too?' says George.

At this Findlay turns around.

They are nose to nose, much closer than Findlay expected. George's eyes start to cross slightly as he focuses on his father's nose. He wonders why adults find driving onto a boat stressful when it's just exciting and why they don't realise it's fun running about.

'No,' says Findlay. 'She's kept hid up a long time. I'd hiv thowt if she wis gaan tae spaek she'd hiv done hid by now...'

'Oot boys. Get coats,' says Maggie.

'I want twa bacon rolls,' shouts Erland as he steps out and skips away, entirely forgetful of cars. He wants to catch up with Granddad who'll have sweeties in his pocket, and even in his best clothes smells like his usual self.

~

For Veronica, the salt and iron and diesel throw her mind back to family trips to Vancouver Island. The scale is many times smaller here, there's no highway, no queues of recreational vehicles. They'd be all crammed in the back, her brothers were a high-spirited bunch, she was an anomaly among so many boys.

When her mother had first arrived in Canada it'd been shock to discover no inside toilet or running water in her home. Veronica remembered her saying even Brek had a freshwater tap. The house had also been made of wood, and the sound of the timber creaking under snowfall got on her mother's nerves more than the wind ever did.

Winnie said she hadn't regrets, no use to have regrets.

Stuart had been surprised when her parents agreed she should go, but it was what he always wanted—the prospects at Brek were small compared to the land he'd in mind when he returned from the war. Veronica's brothers all share their father's character—they work hardest when working for themselves. She is different, more giving.

When Veronica has everything gathered up she hurries to avoid the rain. She checks behind to see if anyone else is coming and sees Ida and Esther. The deck is slippery and big wellington boots are not helping.

Veronica's heart flutters. She's so happy she can't believe what's happening.

'Please, let me help.'

She holds open the door for Esther and Granny to step over the lip inside.

~

Andrew waits, collar up to the rain, watching the deckhands. There is a delay closing the prow. A hammer is being applied with increasing force to the stuck hydraulics. There's a pause and it is handed to a man nearly as wide as he is tall with a full red beard. He looks at the tool carefully, then turns sideways on and delivers a glancing backhand blow.

The mechanism is in business again and the men in overalls cast off lines and secure the deck.

Kathleen is still on the phone.

Andrew raps on his wife's window, he doesn't look in because he kens the kind of look that she'll be giving him; well she's giving it to the whole world really and he's usually included in that.

~

The skipper has been watching the squall pass over the town and the lifeboat rising and falling in the basin.

'Okay, beuy.'

It is time to leave. There will be seven short blasts in the event of an emergency.

Swell come ashore

I reach out and still the tremor in Granny's cold fingers.

– *Both of us, together.*

The woman with the North American accent who held the door stays and keeps it open for my mother and last of all, my father. All five of us are together in the small corridor. It is quiet and close, like being trapped inside a nut.

There are four wall-mounted seats with wipe-clean covers, and signs that forbid smoking and e-cigarettes; Claudette is going to fall on hard times.

'Whit like Ida?' says my father.

'No bad Andrew. Yoursel?'

'Pickin awey,' he says.

'You can sit doon here,' says my mother, gesturing to Granny.

The woman with the pink scarf takes a seat one from the end; I hold Granny's arm and settle her by the stranger's side and ease myself beside her. The only place left is the other side of the stranger. My mother has nowhere to sit and she can't bring herself to give me a row in front of a stranger.

My breath is short, nerves jangling.

'Bacon roll?' says my father.

'No cheust yet,' says Granny. 'Esther, will you hiv wan?'

I shake my head.

'Esther disna want wan either,' she relays.

– *You're a top interpreter.*

My mother looks at us, from one to the other. And I feel a tiny bit sorry for her now. She has been defeated by her own elderly mother and painkiller addict daughter. We're a disreputable pair.

My new clarity of thought is not to her benefit.

My father opens the door down to the galley with my mother's handbag strap wrapped around his wrist like a lead. He holds both rails, leans back then steps down and gradually disappears from view.

'Do you think it will be a good sailing?' asks the American woman. 'I haven't heard a forecast this morning.'

Her vowels are short, the rise and fall of her tone gentle.

'Esther disna spaek,' says Granny.

'Not at all?'

'She used to,' says my mother. 'Post-traumatic voice loss the doctor says. I canno mind the forecast, but they widna go if hid wisna guid enough.'

'Aye,' says Granny.

'It's my first visit to the islands and I must say...'

My mother interrupts.

'Weel Ah'd better get me bag or he'll be loosing hid. And Maggie will need help wi the bairns. Bide here wi Granny, Esther.'

She tugs the door open. Once she has hold of the rail with one hand she turns about and descends backwards and the door closes.

'They'll no be much o a view jammed in here,' says Granny. 'Would you tak me oot? They'll be no wind this side.'

I share her desire for the distraction and push up to stand.

'Please, let me help, dear,' says the American woman. 'I'm Veronica by the way, most people call me Ronnie.'

I nod and Granny smiles.

I help Granny negotiate the raised metal lip while Ronnie holds the door. A brief flow of warm air greets us from a vent with the gritty smell of diesel engines. The sheltered seating area has a single bench along its length and is empty apart from ourselves; the rectangular space is set back into the body of the boat and has a waist-high rail. The roof overhead is the floor of the upstairs passenger lounge.

The masts of the boats in the marina are passing by, they cluster birdlike along the jetties rocking to and fro in the breeze. A low spit of land emerges as the squall slides away and the sun, still barely risen, spirits a rainbow over St Ola before the next cloud comes across.

Granny's eyes are bright, checking the landmarks as they pass by. My stomach muscles tire quickly from the effort of steadying myself and soon the roll and pitch of the boat make it difficult for Granny to stand and we leave the rail.

The old coastal batteries that guard the harbour hold her attention for longest. The concrete cubes have slits like the visor in a knight's helmet and sit as if abandoned by giant men gone to war. Men would wait hour after hour manning the batteries, just like Grandpa George in his searchlight station, dying of boredom and cold and willing the minutes to pass until they could be somewhere else.

Although there is plenty of space the three of us sit close together. The sway and pull of the water draws us together like coins in a purse.

Granny holds up a finger and points to the battery.

'No hame comforts fir those bueys out here,' she says. 'No football games or country dances.'

'It must have been terribly lonely,' says Veronica, in a soft Canadian drawl. 'Such a long, long way from home.'

Granny nods then reaches out her hand and places it on Veronica's knee. Veronica covers it with her own.

– *Granny?*

'George wisna so lonely,' says Granny, softly.

Veronica smiles at her. There is an intimacy between them.

251

'You know I've lived *all* my life in and around Vancouver,' says Veronica turning to me. 'Except for the first few months. I found out they were spent here.'

She rubs Granny's hand, smoothing the thin skin to encourage circulation. It's what I do.

The wavelets rise and fall in tiny peaks on the swollen back of the water below.

– *I'm listening.*

'I don't recall anything about it now, of course,' says Veronica, 'although I was told stories of Orkney customs, the Ba' and ploughing matches, I know about them all. And I got to recognise the postage mark on the airmail envelopes, of course.'

Our bodies are shuffled closer again by the motion of the boat, occasional spots of rain fly into our nook swirled up by the wind.

'Hid wisna too late,' says Granny.

Veronica smiles. The fair hair that sits softly around her features suits her, but her eyes are dark and it's easy to imagine she was once brunette. She has the same pert chin that runs in the Slater girls, a family likeness.

'I thowt it wis too late when they pit me in the owld folks hame,' says Granny. 'You ken thir's a limit on yir time remainin when they pit you in Stembister.'

Granny frees her hand and pats Veronica's knee, then she reaches into her coat pocket and slides out the black and white photograph.

The skin of the paper is criss-crossed with tiny folds.

'Hid's aal I ever had,' says Granny. 'George didna ken. No even at the last. Hoo could I tell him efter aal those years?'

Veronica takes the photograph gently and holds it between her fingertips.

'We had another the same,' she says. 'Much larger, in a frame over the fireplace. My father thought it an extravagance to have a portrait taken. But my mother insisted I should have one of my own as soon as they could afford. There was always plenty of food on the table, but money for taking photographs was not easy to find. There's barely a single one of my brothers. Mind you, they all look alike.'

She laughs, the sound is musical and soft.

'Winnie kent she'd no come back,' says Granny. 'Told me the day she got on the *Ola* and you were hidden in a basket, quiet as a mouse. I ken she loved you like she loved her own.'

~

The sky flattens, there is a sea change. A pause in my heart.
– *What did you say? Granny?*

Veronica puts her arm around Granny and holds her close.

A memory returns, a fragment lost for thirty years. Not everything was burnt that I'd found hidden in the sewing machine. Granny saved a photograph from the range.

Granny fusses with the Canadian woman's scarf, making it tidy after having being messed about by the wind. Body warmth grows between us.

A baby died, her name was Alice on the grave. But another baby was taken on the *Ola*.
– *Your little girl?*

Veronica glances at me over Granny's head, then she begins to speak.

'I always knew Brek was the name of the croft my mother came from. One of the helpful women at the Archives pointed it out to me on the map. Isn't it funny, when I got up there it was as if I'd seen the view a hundred times already.

'I already had the address of the shop and Skulstad from my mother's letters. One night after I arrived here I came and parked outside and I waited for a long, long time. I just couldn't go in. Which is silly, because that's why I came.'

Veronica takes a small, sharp breath.

'I found out I had been adopted only after my mother died. I discovered the letters and found out I had a sister, two in fact, Kathleen and Elspeth.'

She pauses, a bittersweet expression crosses her face.

'I lost one mother and found I had another, and two sisters all in the space of a week.'

She glances at the islands floating past in the rain, then pats Granny's hand. Side by side, rocked by the boat we're hammocked together.

'I wis alweys close wi Winnie, so it wis natural I went to her when her time came near. Told my mither I'd go up tae Brek an help luk after her through the winter. Her folks were gey owld by then, and I kent auntie would see us both through. She'd been a howdie wife.

'I wis fit an well and no one kent I wis carrying a bairn when I left the shop for me auntie's farm, cheust when I'd got to a point where I couldna hide what had happened wi George much longer, an I thowt he wisna comin back.'

Granny's face is pale, her eyes glow bright with memory.

'Where did he go?' says Veronica.

'Tae France,' says Granny, coming back to us. 'You ken searchlights wisna as important as radar by then, so he went. He wis a prisoner of war in the end.'

Veronica tilts her head to one side and smiles sadly.

'Winnie alwis wanted a daughter,' says Granny. 'She kent hid wis unlikely when she married a Harvey man. Alwis sons wi Harvey men. You could have knocked us down when peedie Alice wis born, red scrap o a thing.'

Granny's voice falters for a moment.

'You were hale and hearty, even though hid took twa days o heavin and pushin tae git you oot. Alice wis so peedie that you were big as her in no time at aal.'

A wave rolls the boat up and down, welcoming us to the open water.

'Efter Alice passed away auntie wis so faerd for Winnie and hoo depression hung on her. Hid wisna Winnie who asked fir you, hid wis her own mither who thowt o hid. She kent you could swap babies in the cradle an the men would never ken.

'Stuart Harvey was aal the time posted awey and makin arrangements to take Winnie to Canada, so she never telt him Alice was dead.

'The snow wis meltin an I had no reason to stay at Brek anymore. An hoo would I explain bringin a bairn hame?'

She shivers. Veronica and I draw nearer.

'So you were kept up at Brek until Winnie boarded the *St Ola* and left fir Canada. My milk dried up queek, and Winnie kept hers. All my mither kent wis that I took a fancy to wearin stays when I came hame.'

The boat tips and dives. Granny and Veronica slide towards me. I push my feet more firmly onto the decking and hold us together.

'I wanted tae gae back to bein a girl, an no be tied to the shame o a bairn. I wis too young and shoulda kent better whit I wis doing wi George. But I couldna resist, he wis alweys jokin me an makin me laugh. Whit a fool I wis.'

– *You're not a fool.*

'I visited the graveyard,' says Veronica. 'I found Alice and I found George. My mom was upset to hear of his passing. She told me it would be hard for you to be without him after all this time. Dad never knew I wasn't his daughter. She kept her peace and let him have the daughter he never expected.'

'Aye, she wis a guid wife,' says Granny.

'How is it that I wasn't called Alice?'

'Winnie promised she'd use the name I'd given and tell Stuart it wis a middle name she forgot to put on the certificate, but liked better because Alice wis so common.'

Veronica looks down at the photograph, then Granny continues.

'I couldna let you be another Alice efter watchin her pass away.' Granny moves a hand to Veronica's cheeks. 'Winnie's fither went oot to fetch a doctor, but he got lost in the snow an came back wi no one. She wis aal red cheeks and pouty lips, a rag doll in yir arms, poor peedie hert.'

'It must have been just awful,' says Veronica.

'Alice had to bide in the cradle twa days efter she died while we waited fir the blizzard tae pass. Winnie fed you at first tae ease the pain o her milk no bein taen, hid wis the only time she stopped weepin. When her mither spak the idea aboot me givin you over I was mad as hell, but there didna seem to be any other wey. The funeral for peedie Alice was hardly noticed wi the commotion o the war. Stuart was niver telt an hid's no the kinda thing folk bring up wi a man doon the years. We burnt the death certificate the mornin she took you hidden awey tae the pier. Everyone believed you wis born in Canada.'

Granny looks out to sea, face in repose. There's nothing but the drone of the boat engine. I lean over and kiss her on the cheek.

– *I won't tell anyone.*

'Aye,' says Granny. 'I wis barely more than a child. Hid was unfortunate tae fall so hard fir George. Winnie and Stuart did a handsome job.'

Veronica has tears in her eyes.

'He never raised his voice to me, always let me learn from my mistakes.' Veronica laughs.

'And Winnie loved you an awful lot,' said Granny.

The phrase hangs in the air.

~

The rest of the story of Granny and Grandpa George is family lore.

After the war was properly finished, the Nissen huts were dismantled, the radar stations and telephone exchanges were taken down and the island settled back down to work. Thousands of men and women crossed the Pentland Firth for the last time, leaving Orkney's open horizons and star-strewn nights. Only much later did Grandpa George come back.

He'd gone to the shop. He'd just walked in and asked for a lemonade. Ida's mother had called into the house for her to fetch a bottle from the back.

Granny had seen his silhouette caught in the brilliant light. The bottle dropped from her hand and Grandpa George caught it before it met the floor.

She knew, all the time she knew there could be no one else.

They were married six months later. Two years afterwards my mother was born. Their second child.

My mother's sister

Veronica leans over and whispers something into Granny's ear. She's not like an oldest sister at all, not like my mother, she has more comfortableness.

She takes her arm from around Granny and delves into a large white handbag.

'I have a gift for you, Esther,' she says. 'You know, dear, I have a more than a dozen nephews, enough for a soccer team if you line them up, although Philip and Aaron would rather be in the library. All Harvey boys, not a single niece.'

– *Really, you don't have to give me anything.*

'I already found out a bit about your accident before speaking to Mom. I was getting sea-sickness pills and couldn't help overhear someone talking in the pharmacy. You're doing so well.' She opens the bag wider and peers deeper inside. 'I spoke to the young man on the hotel reception, that's James, he knows your brother and he told me about your vacation company—it's such a good idea. There, I have it.'

The ring box is mauve and edged with gold, immediately recognisable from one of the local jewellers.

'I hope you like it,' she says. 'Ida helped select it from the brochure.' She passes the gift across Granny's knee then laughs to herself. 'I'm sorry, you see how I'm still getting used to calling her Mom.'

Granny smiles broadly, a satisfied blush on her cheeks.

I flip open the lid.

A gold ring stands up proudly on the purple velvet; it has an intricate design of two dragon heads facing one another. The pose is such that it's impossible to tell if they are preparing to fight each other or release some other irrepressible passion. The precious metal collects the dull morning light into a bright, buttery shine.

– *It's beautiful.*

Veronica's gaze is intent on my face.

I open my lips and mouth the words, 'Thank you.'

I breathe deeper and find a pocket of space inside. Something releases and tears well up in my eyes. I try again and this time control the air as it passes over my throat. I move my lips as the warm air flows out, and produce a hoarse, barely audible whisper.

'Thank you.'

The sounds are immediately stolen by the sea. I wipe away my tears and pluck the ring from its cushion and slip it onto the middle finger of my left hand. The lustre is rich against the paleness of my skin and there is a liquidity to the dragons' forms—as if they are alive and their half-moon eyes about to spring wide open.

I put the ring box in my pocket then slide one arm around Granny, holding out my other hand to show her the ring. Veronica beams.

~

This is how my mother finds us when she pokes her head out into the wind.

'Mercy. Whit in heaven's name are you oot here fir?'

It's less sheltered where she stands, taking spray as the boat cuts through the water.

'Get Granny inside,' she says, boosting the door open with her hip. 'You canna even be trusted tae bide still. You'll hiv the blame if she's seek efter this.'

– *Don't speak like that. Open your eyes. I'm doing this one thing for her.*

Impatiently, she cuts off my mime.

'There's a swell moving across,' says my mother loudly.

She beckons with her hands to Granny.

– *This woman is not a stranger.*

'Hid's much better doonstairs.'

When I stand up there's a surge of jolting pain down my legs, from tailbone to backs of thighs and to my ankle joints. I was far too long sitting in one position and pain is a jealous, spiteful, revengeful, needful thing.

Granny's boot slips.

'You must let me help,' says Veronica.

She goes the other side of Granny's arm and leads her. The world tips, rises and dips.

– *I am not fit for this.*

Granny rests her weight on my arm as we go through the door. Slowly, she navigates the metal lip and enters the boat. Veronica insists on holding the door and closing it behind us.

The motion of the boat is amplified inside the cramped space. The seats are fixed, but I shift and shuffle to keep my feet still, and the signs for muster stations blur and dance. Small jarring movements bump my knees against the lifejacket box.

My mother feels Granny's hands.

– *They're always cold.*

'Hid's no good enough,' she scolds me, then turns to Granny. 'Let's tak you doon to where hid's warmer. Has she even had breakfast?'

I shake my head.

She glowers, then makes her voice kind for Granny again, 'Come on, let's get you a cuppa.'

Veronica catches my eye, she's biting her lip, an anxious shadow flitting across her face.

'It's quite rocky, dear,' she says to my mother.

'Hid's no so bad.'

Veronica moves sideways and partly blocks the door to the galley. They stare at each other for a moment. Veronica is half an inch taller than my mother, younger looking too, but what can she do?

Granny is quiet, hunched over, the animation gone from her face after leaving behind the skittish salty air.

Clear thinking, I must be clear thinking. There is something I must to do here, something I must say. It's important. Hold on.

Hold on.

– *That's it. That's what I need to say.*

My mother blinks at me, Veronica's face is hopeful.

– *No way. No way is Granny going down there.*

'She needs warmed up,' says my mother curtly. She lowers her chin and bends her forehead as if heading into the breaking sea. She speaks to Veronica. 'If you howld on the door Esther can go afore and Ah'll come doon efter.'

'Why don't you let me go first?' says Veronica. 'If she really must go down.'

There is a small pause and a look passes between them.

My mother's unspoken meaning is clear. 'And who the hell are you? And why are you interfering with me mither?'

She senses there's a connection, but she forbids it being spoken. She forbids it becoming part of her life.

But she's wrong. Every secret has to have a beginning and an end.

– *I will go first.*

I open the galley door and turn around backwards. The ring clinks against the rail as I take hold, two dragons holding fast about my finger. Pale-faced, Veronica holds the door open while my mother fusses over Granny, turning her around so she can go backwards and down. The boots are clumsily onto the first rung. It's not really a ladder, just steep stairs with open backs.

– *Please don't make her do this.*

I concentrate and match my movement to hers so she can lean if she needs rest. The noise of the galley below is distracting. After the confined space above the openness below draws my attention. The smell of bacon and sausage float in the humid ceiling air.

Claudette is counting slowly in French like a teacher: 'Une, deux, troix...'

A boy tries to repeat the sounds she has made. There's laughter and high hopes heading for a wedding to see the promises being made.

The head mob are overstimulated and under-medicated, a free-for-all of sensation jangles recklessly through my limbs.

– *It's a struggle to keep thinking straight.*

– *When is Tramadol time?*

– *Soon!*

For a second, I glance away from Granny's back into the seating area below. The floor-fixed tables blur, the polystyrene cups and sauce-blotted napkins dance. The chef, a barrel-chested man with red beard, is behind the serving hatch and dressed in spotless white.

– *Where is Marcus Macrae?*

Blood roars in my ears. There are too many impulses, too much strain.

The boat rises.

The effect of gravity from the upsurge makes my body heavy. Granny sinks backwards, unable to hold on and I take her weight. The boat tops the wave, then dives. For a second we are weightless, featherlight and floating upwards, my arms the ropes of a swing.

The boat and everything inside, together we are swung.

I'm sinking again, a deeper, longer fall.

Pathetic muscles, barely used for months, stretch and give, my fingers slip and open.

We fall, Granny Ida and I.

It's not far.

A quiet second in the air.

Crump.

The knock of a head against a hard surface.

Then silence.

~

It is dark and there is petrol in the air. The radio is still playing and warm liquid spills onto my cheek, down my neck and beneath the expensive dress. It annoys me that the fabric will be stained, and that the night is ruined because there is no way I will make it on time now.

Thinking stops.

A terrible aloneness descends.

Pain runs unstoppable. It pushes me to the edge, into voids of endless blackness, fierce and relentless, coming and going without warning, then growing monstrous, beyond bearable, until there is only void.

Then there is cold.

And now nothing. A place with no hope of rescue, the only hope is that everything will stop. Whatever it was, it is now accomplished.

If there is salvation there is no control. Let go.

Bright stars bring the sky lower

There's no bridge, no tractor or car, no shattered windscreen. It's a hard landing onto a galley floor, tailbone, then backbone and bull vertebrae until finally my head cracks back onto the floor. I'm pinned by weight on my chest, my feet rest on the last step.

Someone uncovers my face and I can see up my mother's skirt, the tan gusset of her tights. I see her foreshortened face, mouth open and eyes wider than I've ever seen.

Granny has disappeared from the ladder, dematerialised. Instead there is a weight on my chest restricting my breath.

– Am I drowning?

My mother's sister is coming, forcing my mother to move aside as she descends.

Veronica kneels by my side.

'Mom,' she says. 'Mom, Mom....'

– I'm not your mother. I'm not anybody's mother.

She keeps on repeating the word, each utterance more heart-rending.

Granny's head is resting on my shoulder. It does not feel right. There is something about the position that is not right. The weight makes sense, I'm holding her. Granny's hip bone next to mine, she lies diagonally over me, but something is not right.

– I see now. I understand.

I nod when somebody says my name.

– Nothing broken. Nothing.

I reach out and find Granny's hand and bring it over and across her heart, holding her in an embrace.

– I love you.

My mother is with us, and Elspeth, and my father and brother. Family are above me and around me kneeling. As the waves rise and fall they rock and sway, all steadiness has gone.

Veronica speaks. 'Mom,' she says. 'All the time I felt it and I never knew what it was.' She leans closer and kisses Granny's cheek. Her hair tickles my face. I turn and see the closed eyes, the life fading. 'I missed you my whole life,' Veronica whispers, tears falling. 'It's been my privilege to meet and to get to know you. I know you let me go out of love. You didn't do anything wrong.' Her lips close into a courageous smile. 'I love you, Mom.'

She smoothes Granny's white hair.

My mother stands and wrings her hands and turns from face to face then back to Granny and me. Elspeth kneels beside. Ida watches Veronica closely, her eyes softly aglow.

– *She looks peaceful now.*

They drink the moment together, Granny's expression preserved as life leaves.

The boat swings up and round, carrying us over the water, our bodies held in the swell. The scent of roses fades.

~

There is movement and voices, the living and the dead must be separated.

Claudette is touching my limbs here and there, feeling my neck.

'Ssh…' she says.

– *I'd rather hold her.*

A frown passes over her brows. I try again, forcing air over my vocal chords, to make some sort of sound. Her expression clears as she understands.

'Non, cheri,' she says softly. 'Non, I will stay with you. Your father is here also.'

They brace themselves so I will not slide, my father with his back against the wall on one side and Claudette on the other.

They are fearing the worst, but I can move my toes.

– *Where will Granny go?*

~

The baby that was born by one woman and given to another has always somehow been part of our lives, part of who we are and how we loved.

Fingers feel my wrist then my neck.

There *was* someone else, a daughter and a sister and an aunt, who was always missing and she never knew what it was like to sit on the rug, never knew the sewing machine and the row of tin mugs.

'Esther? Cheri, can you hear me?'

Cold sweat flushes over me. My father's voice takes quick turns with the chef.

'Lifeboat's doon aboot Muckle Skerry. We'll turl aroond to Kirkwall.'

'Aye.'

There's a rustle, the red-bearded man is tucking me in with tin foil like I'm about to be baked in the oven.

'This'll keep you warm. Peedie bit o shock, that's aal.'

The tannoy sounds.

'Hi folks, we've had a serious injury on board an as such we'll be returnin back tae Kirkwall. Thir's a bit o chop so we'd ask you tae stay in yir seats. There's no entrance tae the galley at this time. Thank you.'

The boat engines are on full and the swell easing, we are travelling away from the Westray Firth. The chef whistles a fragment of polka, slow and falling away.

De-dah-dah de-dah de-dah…

It sticks in my head, and plays out with the rhythm of the waves as chills pass over me. Damn polka.

Damn Marcus bloody Macrae. All I wanted was to be numb.

– *Going now.*

The engines labour and the waves tumble, but there is quiet in the galley. A deep silence presses against the laminate wood panels. Tears fall and slide into my hair. The silence holds fast the pain, there's no distraction, no other way to forbear. Now and again a handful of rain is thrown against the high narrow window, that is all.

When I open my eyes the coolness on the left side of my body tells me my father is gone.

Claudette is tapping out a rhythm on her knee, it skips and returns impatiently. The bruise on her cheekbone is like a stain on her skin. Gone the playful smile, the confidence that builds and heals.

Slowly, I turn my head and look past where my father sits.

There is Granny, lying on a bed of coats, a ferry blanket spread over her body. The handsome nose and gentle curve of her lips stand out against my mother's shins.

They have lain her between the benches, and are sitting gathered around. A new smell is in the air, peaty and sweet.

I slip my hand from Claudette's grasp and roll into my side, supporting myself with my arm.

'Non. Mon Dieu…non.'

I wave her away and push up.

– *Let me go.*

It hurts like hell, like I've been rolled in a barrel over the fields. There's no way to tell what's real, what's old pain or new pain or the body's loathing of opioid freedom.

– *After all this.*

– *Is that all you can think about?*

I teeter forward trying to get my balance and rise onto my knees.

'I will help,' says Claudette.

By the time I'm on my feet everyone's attention is on me. My father comes, but I wave him away and with Claudette's help I move forward.

'We opened a bottle,' says Findlay. 'No gaan tae makk the weddin.'

Drams have been poured, glass tumblers materialised for the occasion—there are ways of sharing grief without passing words.

'Aye,' says my father. He throws Findlay a silencing glance.

It is Veronica who moves aside to make a space. Her eyes are red-rimmed, her face wearing its age heavily. She has an empty glass in her hand.

'Please be careful, cheri,' says Claudette. 'You should not be moving.'

She does not release hold until I am seated and even then she stands behind and guards over me.

Erland grins across from the other side of the galley and under his breath sounds, 'On, duh, twa…' There's a pile of sweetie wrappers on the table beside a sick-looking George.

My mother and Elspeth sit opposite, their shoe tips touching the bed of coats.

I picture three girls in matching clothes walking the lane from Skulstad to Redland Loch. But they were never like that; everything would have been different if the baby had come home to Skulstad.

– *Mum?*

Between the small breaths I use to keep everything at bay, I take a deeper draw. I control the air flow over the roof of my mouth and find a small vibration. There is barely any sound, but there is something.

'Kathleen,' says Veronica. 'Esther has something to say.'

My mother turns, that slow stoical turn.

The muscles in my belly, chest and throat tighten. Now she's looking at me. It's gone and I can't find it again. My lips close and a wave of love swells and bursts.

All I wanted to say was sorry.

Leave us on the dockside

This time there are no stuck hydraulics. Ropes are thrown and caught, pulled through and heavy lengths wrapped secure. Robotic clunks sound across the quay, creaks and scrapes, but there are no voices.

Gulls on warehouse roofs watch, heads turning this way and that as the paramedics board the ship.

The shore marshals silently direct cars to disembark. Men in boiler suits come and drive them onto the quayside. They park them at the passenger pick-up point so they are out of the way, but handy. Most people leave their keys in the ignition.

The shore hands and crew cluster together by a stack of pallets wrapped in cellophane, their hands in pockets, their heads dipped against the wind. Yet their posture subtly different.

It is a strange sight, the boat prow open and no activity, no loading or unloading.

There will be no relief when the last passengers disembark.

Here comes the fiddle player Marcus Macrae, who last night held an audience in his palm on a student fiddle worth less than his shoes.

He holds the door.

Next comes little Erland, hand held by his father. Findlay gawps at the empty deck, then sees Maggie's car parked on the quayside and feels small-minded—but wasn't it only natural to worry about where their vehicle had gone?

Behind them is George, his hand inadvertently released because Maggie is on her phone trying to get through to her second cousin on Westray. She sighs and wishes the signal was not so shite.

None of them speak to Marcus.

Another squall is coming, but the warehouses and sheds of Hatston are dry, they still have a little time.

Now comes Claudette, her short hair tucked behind her ears, expression serious.

'I am going with her,' she says to Marcus. 'Will you stay?'

'The wedding's going ahead,' he says.

Claudette frowns.

There's no time for further exchange because the paramedic with a blonde ponytail must come through. She is guiding Esther's unsteady steps, her body stiffening with pain as adrenalin and emotion withdraw, leaving a dumb high-tide line on her mind.

The survival blanket on Esther's shoulders shines like silver leaf, snagging as the wind tries to wrest it skywards. The paramedic has given her a paracetamol. She cannot feel any effect at all. There is only one thing that eases the pain properly. Might she be allowed to have it for a little while? Might she?

They have told her that the doctor may have some stronger pain relief, but he will not have Tramadol in his emergency bag.

A car has pulled up by the loading ramp, parking in a most inconvenient spot. When the shore hands recognise Doctor Copik getting out they are not surprised. More than likely he has done it on purpose. More than likely he will not have codeine in his case on purpose too.

The group on the car deck continues to grow in number, sheltered by the high sides of the bridge over the boat that looks through the flipped-up prow. Rust lines drip earthwards across the white paint and curved metal.

Andrew comes through next. Good suit creased, hat rolled up hard, the life being squeezed out of it as he looks towards his daughter. She wasn't quite strong enough, he thinks. It'd help her if folk didn't believe other people were as strong as they make out. He glances warily at Marcus Macrae, then sees Claudette and nods.

She wasn't strong enough.

The sensation of being present and yet everything not feeling real is spreading. The solidity of Kathleen's face that has been a relief to watch as they came into the harbour now seems absurd. But there is no mistaking her. Never has been.

Yet, people change. They are not who they think they are.

Claudette watches Esther carefully. She touches the arm of the paramedic.

'She wants to wait,' she says.

The paramedic thinks twice, this is only the start of Saturday and it can be a busy shift, but she understands that it will make little difference if Esther's treatment is delayed. This is a memory that will last.

Inside, the operation to carry Ida up from the galley on a stretcher has been successfully completed. The chef, shiny-faced above his beard, holds the stretcher poles behind his back in thick strong hands. Ida is not heavy. It was giving her dignity that made the work so hard.

Her body was lifted from the coats to the stretcher. Elspeth tucked the blanket around, turned down the top into a neat fold. Veronica tidied her mother's hair with the tips of her fingers. It was a reverence she knows the wind will undo, yet she did it gladly anyway, like a mother would for a child.

Kathleen had been there, and yet not there. Her mind whirred, replaying the past, recasting the times her mother was distant and sad, and how she hid it all from her father. Perhaps her mother transformed when her father entered a room for more than one reason.

It had haunted Ida, the strength of her feelings, frightened her at times. The truth is they'd left the dance early that night and spent it together in Willie Senior's byre, lying on the soft, new-cut hay. They couldn't stop.

The exploding mine hadn't thrown them together, it had woken them in each other's arms. The kye had thrown up a rumpus and the hens gone to panic. In the commotion no one had seen anything amiss about Ida being out of the house at dawn and George was quickly away to see the mine down on the shore.

That was the way it had been.

Veronica had cried with laughter when Ida had retold the story during one of her visits to Stembister House.

'It's only fair you ken hoo you came aboot,' said Ida. 'Yir fither couldna makk a promise the way things were. But he came back tae me. He wis my man.'

Even though Veronica *might be* a distant relative Helga Gordon had still refused her permission to take Ida for a walk, never mind a trip to Westray, especially if Kathleen did not see fit that Ida should go.

It needed someone like Esther to steal Ida.

There aren't many people like Esther.

~

Ida is in the blowsy, billowy air, the wind tousling her white hair.

On the other end of the stretcher the second paramedic is bald and slight, conscientiously looking down to make sure Ida is doing okay. It's a habit that overrides logic.

Esther takes hold of the edge of the stretcher, gripping it tightly as her father squeezes his cap and walks by its side. A procession of three sisters follows: Elspeth, Kathleen and then Veronica.

Under the bridge they go, and up the ramp towards the waiting ambulance and Doctor Copik.

On deck Marcus closes the door, last to leave.

All he knew was that someone was injured. He sat out the return journey on the upper deck on his own, not knowing who. He'd resisted sending a text message, nothing would have made sense written down. Only said, only face to face.

He wanted to have the right to ask after Esther's feelings. When Kirkwall Bay came back into view he wanted that chance again.

The decision he made last night, when he unfurled a sleeping bag on Claudette's floor rather than sharing her bed, had significance. Music, whisky and opportunity have always been his Achilles heel, but he wants to change. A better ending with Helen, and to be there for Katie when he can.

Strangest of all, he wants the privilege of grief.

To the west, a rolling grey wall is approaching. Rain lands on the empty fields, runs into the grass-filled ditches and sinks slowly towards the salty water.

The rude clatter and clunk of the quayside ceases.

A big open silence spreads up and out, filing the sky above, and even though footsteps go on, heartbeats and car wheels go on and people talk and come and go in places out of sight, there is silence here because none of it matters right now to these people gathered here.

They are in the wide, empty silence, caught in that edge of understanding, a place where they have a brief chance to be courageous and admit what they do not know, and that right now the mystery of life and death holds them and binds them.

The rain is coming now, dropping into the tired sea, finding the flat, sad faces.

The procession halts.

'This is very, very sad,' says Doctor Copik to Esther. 'Come to car. I will examine you. Shore men can wait. Boat is not in hurry now.'

Mind and body numb, Esther follows.

Everything is exposed on the dry bed of grief; the guilt of leaving; the guilt of not being there for her grandmother; the guilt of not helping her mother when she found it hard to cope; the guilt of letting go.

Esther has been self-righteous, conceited and vain, and she never cared who overheard or was hurt.

Yes, Esther has loved the easy road.

She wants to change. Hard things are not impossible.

No longer ghost

The cabinets at the airport are like a miniature museum, encapsulating the essence of a place in half a dozen glass shelves, just as the shop at Skulstad once did. There are handcrafted pieces of jewellery, Veronica has bought and gifted plenty of those.

On one shelf there is a pair of leather moccasin slippers, embroidered with intricate beadwork and part of a small display celebrating the connections between Orkney, Canada and the Hudson Bay Company. But men went to farm as well, to raise pigs, to start new lives. Their first litter from a Duroc was her father's biggest source of pride, next was the need for a bigger barn, and then the slow passing of knowledge from father to son that is rooted in the land. There were costs and benefits. Winnie could make lemonade and watch her husband and children flourish, even if she lived a long way from the sea and the island where her daughter briefly rested in her arms.

Veronica looks briefly in the cabinets, but they do not hold her attention as they did on her arrival. She has been accompanied to the airport by her Orcadian relatives. She embraces each of them, squeezing the little boys tight, holding Esther with care.

It is impossible to go back in time, but not place. Here, Veronica feels the echoes of the past and touches hands with those who stayed. She sees there are costs to staying and leaving, and now she must leave.

She passes through security, stripping and then re-assembling herself. She thinks of Kathleen—stripped of certainty, her face fallen.

Her sister, still beneath the waters of grief, had softened as the final days passed. They spent more and more time in close proximity, drawn together physically without the need for conversation.

'Good morning ladies and gentlemen, I am your captain… flight time today to Aberdeen will be thirty-five minutes… relax and enjoy the flight.'

It is the beginning of the journey back.

Veronica feels that beneath the surface, something has settled; it had risen softly like blood from a clean cut when she'd found her mother's letters. It rose at night and made her heart beat faster and her insides light and hollow as if her existence was a mirage. It stayed that way until she was honest with herself; she did need to know. She needed to find the family that had lived without knowing her, or her knowing them. She thought of her friends and how little some of them knew or cared about their families, yet she could not do the same. She had booked the plane tickets and felt the lunacy and honesty of it. It made her feel lightheaded, but she knew it was the right thing to do.

Now she was leaving, and she had the sensation of having eaten a nutritious meal, something long and slow in the preparation, satisfying to consume, like the whisky she had been getting to know.

In the empty seat beside her, Veronica pictures Kathleen. One day might she come and get to know the family who has cared for her sister all these years past? Would she be curious to see where the seeds taken from Orkney grew?

Veronica looks out onto the tarmac, its patchwork of black, brown and speckled grey mimicking the golden fields. The low, curved buildings have a military aspect and beyond is a bay, Inganess. She took a walk down there one evening, the return climb left her breathless, but she looks on it with affection now, and with the promise of return. The calls of the gulls, curlews and oystercatchers had brought her attention to the silences in between. The sunlight reached into the shallows and elusive shades of blue and ivory flickered as the brightness reflected around the bay.

The scattering of rural dwellings that greeted her arrival each now belong in its own parish, each piece of land is named and carries a history, Skulstad was only a word before, now it is people and place – and the unlikely heart of it all is her niece, Esther.

The propellers spin and throb, and the aircraft increases in speed. Takeoff brings her into the air, that medium of transition, of life, that is breathed in and given out without thought or thanks. Today Veronica gives thanks. Thanks for the low clouds that decorate with dark shapes the pewter water below, for the shadows that give scale and solidity to the islands floating serenely over the deep ocean. The plane rises through denser vapour and a second later the view remains only in her mind.

Veronica remembers her mother, and how she said, 'You wir gone out o sight, but niver wance oot o me mind or hert.'

It was a love that grew, and was silent. And now another silence has begun, after a goodbye that was sudden, sweet and sad.

How absurd death is, she thinks. There is no end, her mother is simply out of view.

Veronica wipes her eyes.

She smiles down at the field of wind turbines in the ocean. What power there is to be harvested from the air, if only we can work out how.

~

Kathleen doesn't have to be the big sister now. She is surprised how much of a relief this is. She has lost her mother, and the duty of her care and her affection has been refreshed and revitalised in a way she never expected by grief.

She is beginning to see Esther as herself, not simply a daughter to be dutifully maintained, like her husband cares for his lawnmowers. Oh, she's seen him mend machines over and over again when all hope was lost. She was always concerned with the maintenance of people. She picks up and oils and greases until there is order again.

Could she help having a favourite in the child who makes less risky decisions, who has less ambition and will never leave her? But Esther has her own qualities.

Kathleen thinks a great deal about the jealousy she had of her father and mother. It was a need to be loved and listened to, only natural. The thoughts seed new ideas and interpretations; she works at her grief like she's turning out the kitchen cupboards.

Perhaps she will find some new freedom now she has Veronica, someone from outwith the community, who listens with love and without judgement whenever she wants to talk—and the time difference allows. She is open to a new relationship. She has more time.

Three times a week she is at Peedie Hoose.

'Whit like the day, Kathleen?'

'Pickin awey. Niver kent I had an older sister tae miss afore.'

She holds up a badly worn pair of children's jeans, broken through at one knee, washed pale.

'Niver kent whit me mother did.'

'She wis gey strong,' says Bridget.

Kathleen looks over to the baby clothes.

'Poor peedie Alice, I've been pitten flooers on all these years past.'

Bridget nods. She's missed Esther, such a bonny lass, scars or not.

This week Women's Aid will get profits from the raffle. Prizes include a bottle of whisky, a hand-knitted scarf and a fresh batch of tablet Kathleen cooked up late on Sunday night. She'd stood, standing and stirring, watching the light in the byre where Andrew and Willie were setting the world to rights.

An old tune passed through her mind, one her mother used to sing about the harvest, it's as if she can hear a voice humming in the backroom. But it can't be. There's only herself and Esther in the house.

The range, Maggie found out, is almost impossible to remove. There have been a lot of men in boiler suits standing, shaking their heads and drinking sweet tea to get to the conclusion that it's better it stays. Maggie's started making plans to put in a television and move in George and Erland's toys. Esther has compromised on allowing the toys, but not the television. More than once, Kathleen has watched her smoothing the damaged walls with sandpaper. Andrew has begun to dismantle and clean the range.

Kathleen responds to the rhythm of the old harvest tune as she works. It pauses, repeats then fades, and when it stops the memory rests in the silence.

The tablet becomes creamier, wrinkling on the surface, releasing a sweet buttery smell that reminds Kathleen of cut grass and meadowsweet. She thinks of the year past and the year to come, then she judges the time is good and lifts and tips the saucepan, delivering its caramel contents into a tray. Kathleen's hands are warm and content as they perform the same actions her own mother made. She takes a clean spoon and smooths the surface. When she is finished she raises the spoon, and licks it clean.

'It'll no harm ye,' she says to herself.

~

Ida was buried in the same plot as Grandpa George, a few stones away from peedie Alice. Afterwards, the wake was held at Skulstad. Andrew spoke a few words after the first drinks were poured.

'To the best mother-in-law I ever had,' he said and had raised his glass. 'When I first met Ida I had no clue me feet would be under her table fir quite so long. But bide here I will, and I will be taking things apart and putting them together out there as long as I am able. If anyone kens how to fix the carburetor of a twenty-year-old Honda lawnmower you're welcome to join me in the workshop.'

Kathleen had folded her arms across her chest and given her husband a wry smile.

'Dinna worry Kathleen, we'll be back noo and then fir a dab and a bite, and sooner or later Jimmy will start playing his accordion.' He raised his dram and the gathering drew breath and followed his lead, 'Ida.'

~

The key is in the ignition. Esther has adrenaline running through her veins, heart pounding fit to burst. But it's not from pain. She wonders how much is pain simply a memory of pain? A cycle repeated in nerve cells and in the mind. Claudette agrees with Dr Copik, a mind that is determined to self-protect can prevent the process of healing. It is miscommunication.

There is a powerful connection between head, heart, body and breath. Don't forget breath.

It can be miraculous.

Walking the line

It is November, early morning. I drive east from town. Hail flies across the windshield. The sun, half-covered in slate-grey cloud glows orange on the hillside ahead, breaking through for a moment and there comes an extraordinary rich golden light.

The land below is green-grey, the sea dull and insignificant compared to the dramatic sky above.

My mother's sister has taken her leave. She's called Ronnie by everyone now, except my mother who insists on Veronica. She said in the airport lounge it was a name she'd always loved.

Two dragons meet face to face on the ring on my left hand. The gleam in their eyes playful. Had everything not happened as it did I would not be here, not at this time and place. It is a better place.

Today, I have slept then risen of my own accord, although I miss Tramadol and my father is watchful. I think this is a one-way journey. I am building willpower.

I have already kept an appointment with Doctor Copik. We have talked about Pilates and the importance of sleep, and that I must take the help that is offered.

His son Stan came to meet me and shook my hand.

'Esther is doing the hardest of all things,' said Doctor Copik. 'She is trying not to be disappointed.' The twinkle in his eyes had brightened. 'I disappoint your mother constantly,' he added to his son. 'It is bad habit.'

'She's very high standards, Pops.'

The young man's way of speaking is distinctively American.

'Gabapentine for moment is working for you. Side-effects are lessening. But come back in one week,' he'd said. 'We have still much to improve.'

I'd breathed deeply; taking the cue Doctor Copik had leaned forward.

'I'm feeling better.'

The words are quietly spoken, the timbre of my voice is altered, deeper.

'Good,' he'd replied. 'Still come back in one week. I am keeping my eyes on you.'

Stan had said his father was a great doctor. I'd smiled and made some quiet applause. Doctor Copik beamed and performed a bow.

Later today, I'm choosing paint with Claudette for the spare room in her flat.

Do I need to say I am bound to her? Do I need to say how much she loves the sound of my voice? No.

~

A claw of quickly moving cloud steals the gold disk on the horizon and only a soft yellow-green glow remains. In the southern sky, veils of cloud are closing over the eggshell blue until the towers of cloud join into one single giant mass.

There's a flash of electric blue, a rip in the grey. Hail rattles on the windshield, covering the sound of the radio.

Accident Corner is coming, and I cannot stop the panic rising, but I breathe and ground myself in the present. Even as stiffening begins in my spine, my heartbeat rising, I concentrate on the feel of the wheel's stitching puckered beneath my fingers. I inhale slowly and deeply and there is the soft, sweet perfume of rose oil sprinkled in the car and with it the memory of Granny.

The bridge and the bone trees are here and I have to pass.

I find my vibration, concentrate on the fizzing on my lips, keeping my attention on the present. A tickle of sound travels up into the roof of my mouth.

'Hmmmm…mmm.'

I soften my tongue and open my lips.

A sound is released, and a new breath flies in.

Easy as that. Nothing terrible happens, and the car travels onwards. I drive towards the silhouette of a house held aloft from the sea by crumbling red cliffs.

The creamy streak of dawn to the east blooms, growing whiter and more intense, until just before the sun is revealed it becomes golden and the whole sky is a sheet of yellow.

There are no tyre marks for me to follow, the tarmac is white where hail has fallen. Still, I know the turning I must take, just after the narrow pinch of land with the quiet sea of Deer Sound on one side and crashing waves on the other. The houses and farms that bide in this landscape have stories that deserve to be heard. We all do.

When the sheets of hail finally clear the sun is whitening and becoming pearlescent, shrinking as it breaks free of the horizon, exhausted of colour.

Up by the fence posts at the top of the brae there is a movement, a man breaks from the line of the hill. Sunrise over the

North Sea has tempted somebody outside despite the storm clouds.

The man is wearing a hat, gaze turned to the earth like a farmer, his movements methodical as he climbs up and over the gate towards Pipersquoy. The sound of the car's engine is hidden by the wind and he does not look in my direction.

He lengthens his stride and enters the low cottage with its pile of stone chips outside. A space has been left for my small silver car.

When I step out the cold is invigorating. My joints ache and protest, yet every movement is thrilling.

Across the bay, the sun is touching the fields, throwing shadows behind the round bales. Brek stands abandoned and alone. It's been there my whole life, a marker of days passed by. It never held more sorrow or joy than any other place until a month ago. Someone has turned over the potatoes in the vegetable patch, their pink skins shine like newborns.

We are having to change the way we think. Haven't we all been guilty of thinking my mother was stronger than she was?

She wasn't. She isn't.

She's now the one at Peedie Hoose with Bridget, sorting out the second-hand clothes—many of mine are amongst them.

~

When I reach the front door it opens, the timing quite by chance.

'All fine?' he says.

I nod.

He stoops and arranges his muddy boots on the steps. Things have altered at Pipersquoy, grief is no longer a permanent resident. It can feel open and free on the high cliffs, the sea's skirt dancing below.

Marcus has not heard my voice yet. An understanding is slowly growing between us, and for the moment there is no hurry to confuse ourselves with spoken words. He is composing tunes for flute, and he doesn't know where it will lead.

Doctor Copik's music therapy and withdrawal plan continues. I have a flute case hugged against my chest, and a schedule to follow. The quality of my silence is changing.

Epilogue

Confess or don't confess, the fire will be just as hot

The link between the contemporary fictional narrative of Esther Russell and the epilogue historical fictional recreation of a witch-craft trial transcript lies both in the power and powerlessness of silence. Constructing this short historical piece was part of a process of understanding how silence can be interpreted and misinterpreted. Both narratives also interrogate the response of society to the perception that physical health and mental health are linked to personal deserves; there is a tendency to see other people's character as constraining their outcomes whereas our own fortunes are determined by structure and circumstance. In other words, when bad things happen to us it is beyond our control, but when it happens to other people it is, at least just a little bit, their fault. The sick and suffering are blamed in some way for their condition, and furthermore they become an infectious risk to society. This idea persists within contemporary concepts of the deserving and underserving poor, and many other categories that are imposed on individuals based on invisible value judgements.

These judgements are formed by social norms and values and affect the dispensing of resources and compassion to the individuals who are affected. It is a complex issue. If we try to interrogate the decision to feel compassion for someone we are required to examine our own values and their origins. There are individual, familial, social and institutional foundations for these core beliefs. Within these layers of experience there grows an internal decision-making process that guides our feelings and actions towards other people.

Within an institution, professional principles offer practitioners a set of guidelines to follow, these might be legal or medical. The spirit with which they are carried out has a meaningful impact on the individuals with whom they come into contact. Dr Copik blends his professional responsibility with a humour, compassion and self-awareness that allows him to meaningfully connect with Esther and her cycle of drug dependency. He is able to empathise with her, despite lacking her particular experience. In fact, this is true of much more. It is impossible to fully experience another life as if it is our own, but by imaginative extension of our own experiences we are able to gain empathy, and this is a gateway to compassion. Dr Copik may not have ever been addicted to pain killers, but he is cognisant of his regular caffeine requirements; such an everyday list could be extended to alcohol, television, pornography—anything that offers the regular physical and mental alleviation, anything that is a daily, inevitable comfort.

Outside the professional principles of an institution it becomes a more personal and arguably a more courageous decision to act with compassion. Bridget, the quiet stalwart of Peedie Hoose, places herself in this role. She responds instinctively to the person in front of her as they present themselves there and then. She responds openly and simply, with kindness and without judgement, in the same way as when sorting through the bags of donations she receives. She accepts what is given as a sign of good faith, even if it has no monetary value that can be realised. The essential thing is the giving.

Beyond the behaviour of our institutions and individuals there is the wider body of society and its building blocks—the family, in all its forms. The seeds of how society at large develops norms that define 'the other' are sown early. The categories are innumerable, but it is possible to list a handful touched upon in the contemporary narrative: speech/lack of speech, accent, mother tongue, occupation, social role, appearance, physical health, mental health and gender.

It is possible to speculate how both the contemporary and historical narrative would change if 'he' and 'she' were reversed. If Esther were Marcus? If Claudette were Simon? How would that change the power dynamic and expectations of individual behaviour? The possibilities are dazzling.

It is also notable that age is a category highly loaded with expectation. It is not a matter for dramatic concern that Ida remains secluded, medicated and adventureless in Stembister House, but Esther's existence at Skulstad can be viewed as tragic. Their parallel daily life and passionate nature bind Ida and Esther across the generations.

The use of silence can be viewed as the ultimate show of strength—the right not to self-incriminate, the right to not speak. But silence is also the death of self-expression and creates vulnerability; uninvited persons may speak for and make decisions for someone who chooses to remain silent.

In the scenario of the witchcraft trial, *The Case of Esther Russell, 1643,* the plaintiff or 'pannell' is constructed through a series of accusations. She does not herself enter anything into the record. The accusations are domestic and intimate, brought forward by close family members. The accusations are presented as damning whether good or bad comes of Esther's actions, or whether there is a link established between cause and effect. They seem to carry the same weight, regardless of whether prurience or self-righteousness motivate the accuser. The construction of 'the other' through the manipulation of social expectations and norms lead to the persecution of an innocent victim. Let's be clear—witchcraft does not exist, and painkiller addiction is not something deliberately sought.

The fictitious witchcraft case was constructed after detailed reference to notes of the proceedings of the Orkney witchcraft trials, which in fact compete in number with the more infamous events in Pendle. Anyone wishing to read further on this dark period of Orcadian history may refer to the following: *Special Edition: Commemorating the Victims of the Orkney Witchcraft Trials, New Orkney Antiquarian Journal, Vol 9, Published by Orkney Heritage Society.* The periodical includes a list in memoriam of Orcadians who were victims of witchcraft trials.

The framing of *The Case of Esther Russell, 1643* within the 'Miscellany of the Priorsfield Club' sets the context of how the trials were presented to the public—albeit a limited literate circle. In the pages of an exclusive gentlemen's club periodical the case study is listed amongst articles such as *Descriptions of an account of the last moments of Queen Anne of Denmark* and a *Burlesque Sermon of the Fifteenth Century.* In this way it becomes fixed within an institutional framework, with its own somewhat biased guiding principles. It is a bureaucratic sleight of hand that transforms the original hypocrisy, greed and heresy into legal argument and legitimate judgement. A woman's life is taken, exposed and destroyed. She is made 'other', and in uniting against her the community is strengthened, warmed by her fire.

There is little record of the voices of persons such as Bridget or Dr Copik; although these persons did undoubtably exist, their dissent is silenced. This key feature—dissent, and the refusal to blithely categorise 'the other'—is essential to protect everyone in society. A person does not know when they might be redefined by some aspect of their person or behaviour. It is in showing compassion and protecting other people that we show compassion to and protect ourselves. In a sense, Claudette is dissent.

The language of the trial is challenging, necessarily so to convey the mood and metre of past events. It is not intended to be off-putting, rather to induce curiosity. What do we see of ourselves here? The epilogue seeks to place Esther's story in a wider social and historical context. There is no Frenchwoman or folk musician to nurture Esther's silence into sound. This is another key to protection and compassion—looking outwards to other communities and ways of thinking and doing—it is essential to generate change. By trying new approaches, welcoming others and listening to their experiences, there is a way to see beyond our own island shores and out across the silent sea; there is hope for both physical and mental health.

The Case of Esther Russell, 1643

MISCELLANY
OF THE
PRIORSFIELD CLUB

VOLUME VII

At the General Meeting of the Priorsfield club held at Kirk-wall, the 8th day of September, 1829, it was resolved to print a seventh edition of the Priorsfield Miscellany, the preparation of which was committed to the secretary.

THE
PRIORSFIELD CLUB
MDCCCXXIX

Francis Dixon, Esquire
Right Hon. The Earl of Gallowgate
Harold Gows, Esquire
Louis Gibbon, Esquire
Rt Hon Thomas Miller, Bart.
Howard Morrison, Esquire.L.L.D
Rev. Edward Stocken.B.A.
James Tennant, Esquire
Mark Tennant, Esquire
Kenneth Wanderer, Esquire
Robert Stevenson, Esquire
Francis Flemming. B.A.
Steven Gardiner, Esquire
Lyell Johnson, Esquire
Nathaniel Ralph, Esquire
Leslie Foubister, Esquire

PRESIDENT
James Baxter, Esquire

TREASURER
George Brown, Esquire

SECRETARY
Gideon H. Bain, Esquire

CONTENTS

TRIALS FOR WITCHCRAFT, SORCERY AND SUPERSTITION IN EAST MAINLAND, ORKNEY

VOL. VII

1

TRIAL OF ESTHER RUSSELL, FOR WITCHCRAFT, SORCERY AND SUPERSTITION

Intrat vpon pannell, Esther Russell daoughter to Andrew Russell in the stedding of Redland St Andrew's before St John Buchannane of Scottiferaig, knyght jufticiar, and fchireff-principall of Orkney and Zetland, to anfyer at the inftance of Robert Chalmers of Ryffany procurator fifchall of the fshireffdome for certain points of witchcraft, sorcerie and superstition; at the leaft behaveing hir felff to have fie fkill and knowledge, throw abufeing the people as follows:–

In the first ze, the faid Esther Russell ar indyitt and accufit for airt and pairt of vfeing, comitting, & practifing of the divelifh and abhominable cryme of superftition, witchcraft & sorcerie, in that at mid-fomer, she did tuik water and efter the flyting did put her brother into a barrel of watter where faid brother did roll doon the brae then efter* tuik seik and was fenceless and myndles for ane long fpeace. Quhilk, rank witche, ze cannot deny.

*Findlay Russell, present maid fayth that this first point of dittay was trew. The pannel deny it.

Secundlie, in that immediate efter the tyme forfaid the faid Esther Russell did concoct poisonous brews with flooers and herbs from the feildside and did feed it on a spoon to neighbour Jonet Finnie's* best cockeril and aught days after that the rooster died. Quhilk, rank witche, ze cannot deny.

Jonet Finnie maid fayth conforme to the point of the dittay. The pannell deny it.

2

Thirdlie, in that, the pannel did find a keepsake of her grandmother, Ida Young* hir had chanced in a tin cup where the keepsake lay without searching by eye or hand, quhik came to pas be your witchcraft and divelrie.

Ida Young did pass awey afore this trial commence. The testimony is from her daughter Kathleen Young.

Fourthlie, ze are indyted and accuifed for airt and pairt of the said abhominable fuperftition, in that yawself have craft and foreknowledge of death and accident in man and beaft. And did bid yaw own fither bide from a cold fhouir that wast raining and offer victuals to him and the next day efter his cart wheels did fail and his horse was killed. Quhilk, rank witche, ze cannot deny.

Fiftly, that ze do go to bed nightly, but do not rest. Night long a candle burns and there is the found of watter and pipes a great multitude of people laughing and gasping with a hissing noise. And Findlay Russell* did fwear that he saw the devill come to lay with the pannel and ze was taken up on the hills by a whirle of wind and thir ze masked yawself and danced with the devil.

*Findlay Russell, maid fayth that this was trew. The pannel deny it.

Sextly, in that in mid-fomer, the pellant was seen depositing flooers in the kirkyard by the graves of children, and came hame many times with red cheeks and crocodile tears. Quhilk, rank witche, ze cannot deny.

Item, ze ar indytitt and accuifit for the forfaid cryme of bewitching yaw nephew George Russell and making yawself invisible on occasion to secretly leave your homestead and lie

with the devill and carry out yaw abhominable crime of sorcerie. Quhilk, rank witche, ze cannot deny.

3

Item, in that efter harvest tyme having come hame bleeding and
bend double efter collision with William Finnie's cart that ze did
not die. That fince or thairby ze did curse yaw owne mother, and
mime & mimic to control the faid mother to do yaw will out of
bewitchment, including the provision of devilish herbs that further
drew the appellant into a state of staring and moaning and closer
communion with yaw mafter the devil. Quhilk, rank witche, ze
cannot deny.

Item, ze indytitt for the faid cryme, in that, last year yaw
craft and knawledge wis laid out to enchant this man Simon
Sands* into a debasement with his [guid and chaste]† maid,
who even though they laid together only wance, did conceive a
child under the duress of devilment.

*Simon Sands, maid fayth that this was trew. The pannell
deny it.

And Generally, ze ar indytit and accufit for airt & pairt of
ufing and practeifing of witchcraftis, sorceries, divinatiounes
and charmes.

And so possessed by the devil are ze that yaw own toong
is silenced except for hissing and groaning, and unnatural
curfings, and will not be loosened to fpeak a word of regular
speech. And yaw own eyes cannot bear the observation of yaw
devilish reflection in mirror or watter. And yaw body does bear

the marks of devilment on the face and bare back and even the most secret parts of the body that do burn for the devill yaw maifter to touche.

And thairfoir ze aught & fuld vndirly the law, & be adjudgit to the death thairfoir, in example of vthers to doe the lyk.

† These words are scored out in the MS. G.B.

4

ASSISA

The Affyfe paffing out of judgement, electit for the maift pairt Simon Sands in Chancellor: and returning, all in ane voice, be his mouth, FYLLIS the pannell in the firft, secunde, third, fourt, fyft, fext and alfo of the generall poyntis, as a commoun, notorious abufer and charmer.†

SIMON. SANDS.

Acceptis the determinatioun of the Affyfe, and continewis fentence.

XV October 1643

The judge ordains the pannell Esther Russell to be takin be the lockman hir hands bund behind hir back, covoyit to the place of execution Loan Head wirreit at a ftaik and burnt in afhes.

† The names of the jurymen are not given. It may be right to notice that the blanks occur in the original M.S.

NOTE BENE

Although for the mute woman Esther Russell it was not relevant, there was at the time express legal procedure preventing women from testifying in court. Ref, 'The admissibility of women witnesses: A debate anent Receaving women to be witness' in ane exculpa(tio)n. Misc The Priorsfield Club Vol V. pp.259–260.

Cold, starvation and other inconveniences of prison often caused death before the meeting of the assizes to consider judgement took place. In rare cases, a member of the community would offer assurances for the accused.

G.B.

Acknowledgements

As time passes I realise that the final production of a book is team effort rather than an solo achievement. Writing is a solitary process, occasionally heady with time passing swiftly and long hours of patience and graft. There are also periods of time when the encouragement, critical advice and skills of others are essential to bring an idea to full fruition. I wish to thank all the team at Sparsile particularly Lesley Affrossman, Wendy Ross, Alex and Madeleine.

I am fortunate to have a circle of creatives to share my ideas with and I am grateful to all those who have shared their responses with me. Feedback sessions at The Royal Hotel in Stromness with Babette Stevenson, Shaun Gardiner and Lynn Johnson gave helpful impressions on the idea of a narrative centred around a character that does not speak. Fiona Flemming, also part of this group, gave additional comments and support in the form of friendship, strong coffee and good wholesome book talk.

Part of the inspiration behind a 'voiceless' central character came from my knowledge of the Orkney Witchcraft Trials and their recent commemoration. I am indebted to the patient and knowledgable staff at the Orkney Archive for providing reference material that informed the epilogue and in particular Lucy Gibbon, Andrea Massey, Sarah Maclean, Yvonne Nicoll and Colin Rendall.

'Join a writing group' is the excellent advice for any aspiring writer. It's not just about getting feedback, it's about being connected to a likeminded group of people who enjoy spending time with words. I am grateful to all the members of the Stromness Writing Group. Within the group I am fortunate to have a perceptive and forthright friend in L Coward who supports my continuing writing endeavours.

My understanding of the connection between breath, mind and body has grown thanks to time spent at the Linklater Voice Centre. The weeks spent learning techniques that release the natural depth and range of voice have been key in the development of Esther's character. I am indebted to the late Kristin Linklater, Rena Johnston and Yvonne Harcus and all the team who made these experiences so life-affirming and life-changing.

I must also mention Lucy Alsop, who has been generous with her friendship and her skills in helping deliver this manuscript. I am thankful for her professionalism, enthusiasm and laughter, all of which have been invaluable.

Although I have been living in Orkney for over a decade I remain sensitive to the limits of my dialect usage and local knowledge. I am very grateful to Tracy Leslie and Nathalie Clitheroe for their honest feedback on an early draft of this manuscript. It seems an age since I excitedly printed and delivered its pages and we sat over cups of tea and discussed dialect differences between areas of Orkney. Thank you.

I am grateful for the patience of my husband and my children. I am blessed with lively encouragement from my daughter and the glimmers of pride from my sons all keeps me creating and curious.

This book is dedicated to my sisters, brilliant in so many ways. I must also thank my parents who remain steadfast in their support, and unafraid to express their pleasure in having a daughter who creates with and loves words.